BOOKS FOR YOUNG PERSONS,

PUBLISHED BY

JAMES MILLER,

522 BROADWAY.

English History. By Mrs. HYDE.
Facts and Fancies. By Miss SEDGWICK.
Favorite Fairy Tales for Little Folks. With 70 illustrations by Thwaites and others.
Favorite Scholar. By MARY HOWITT. Illustrated.
Gulliver's Travels. A new edition. Illustrated.
Impulse and Principle. By Miss ABBOTT.
Lilies from Lebanon; or, Scripture Stories. By Miss GRAHAM.
Mother Goose's Melodies. A new and beautiful edition, with original illustrations.
The Same, colored.
Magic Ring, and other Oriental Fairy Tales. From the German of Herder, Liebeskind, and Krummacher. Illustrated.
Magnet Stories. By the author of "Trap to Catch a Sunbeam."
New Fortune-Teller.
Original Poems for Infant Minds. By JANE TAYLOR.
Parent's Assistant. By Miss EDGEWORTH.
Private Purse. By Mrs. S. C. HALL.
Philip Grey. By S. G. GOODRICH.
Parlor Magic.
Pebbles from Jordan; or, Bible Examples of Every Day Truth. By Miss GRAHAM. Illustrated.
Popular Fairy Tales for Little Folks. Beautifully illustrated.
Right and Wrong, and The Gold Cross. Illustrated.
Robinson Crusoe. Printed on tinted paper, and beautifully illustrated.
Stories by a Mother. By the author of "Always Happy."
Undine and Sintram. Translated from the German of Fouque. New edition.
Well (The) in the Rock, and other Stories. By VIRGINIA F. TOWNSEND. Illustrated.
Shoes of Fortune. By HANS ANDERSEN.
Picture Book without Pictures. "
A Christmas Greeting. "
The Story-Teller. "
The Ugly Duck. "
Little Ellie. "
The Mud-King's Daughter. "
Little Rudy. "

UNDINE,

OR,

THE WATER-SPIRIT.

ALSO,

SINTRAM,

AND HIS COMPANIONS.

FROM THE GERMAN OF

FRIEDRICH DE LA MOTTE FOUQUÉ.

NEW YORK:
PUBLISHED BY JAMES MILLER,
(SUCCESSOR TO C. S. FRANCIS & CO.,)
522 BROADWAY.

UNDINE,

FROM THE GERMAN OF THE

BARON DE LA MOTTE FOUQUÉ,

BY

REV. THOMAS TRACY.

BIOGRAPHICAL NOTICE.

THE peculiar genius of FOUQUÉ is so fully developed in the two stories of Undine and Sintram, and that genius is so strictly individual, the reflection of the personal sympathy and culture of the man, that the author's life might be almost said to be written in those tales. Critics complain of the want of comprehensiveness in Fouqué's writings. He had an eye, they say, simply for one thing, a pure Christian Chivalry, and of this he was a dreamer. Surely, without detracting from the laws of Art, there is room for one such dreamer in the world, in this low thinking age. The young, the fair, the good, will be ever content to dream with him. Fouqué practised the chivalry which he taught. He was twice in arms in defence of his country in early youth, and again, "with the Lyre and the Sword," in the war against Napoleon. He was wounded at Culm, and present at Leipzig. His grandfather was the intimate of the great Frederic, attained the rank of General, and fought in the Seven Years' War. The grandson, as may be seen in the Preface to Sintram, delighted to go further back into antiquity for the honour of the family name.

Friedrich Baron de la Motte Fouqué was born on the 12th February, 1777, and died 23d October, 1842. Before his death he published a corrected edition of his Select Works, in 12 volumes. They include his great dramatic poem, The Hero of the North, a version of the old Nibelungen-Lied; The Magic Ring and Sintram, kindred tales of Chivalry; "the faultless completeness of Undine;" Aslauga's Knight, and various dramatic and poetical productions.

CONTENTS.

UNDINE.

PREFACE.

The following translation of Undine, one of the minor romances of Frederic, Baron de la Motte Fouqué, is from the fourth impression of the original, that of Berlin, 1826. It was made in the winter of 1835, and has since received such revision and improvement, as the kindness of literary friends, in connection with my own wish to do as little injustice to the genius of the author as I could, has enabled me to give it.

This is no place for discussing the characteristics of Fouqué, but he has one excellence of composition so rich and rare, that I may be permitted to allude to it here:—I mean his harmonious union of fiction and fact, his exquisite blending of the natural and supernatural. So perfect do we find this union to be, such a melting indeed of both into one, that we hardly know in which of the two we feel ourselves most at home. We have the true feeling of real life, embellished by the magic of imagination,—just as the frost-work, which at times we see almost spiritualizing our groves and shrubberies in winter, constitutes so much of their peculiar charm;—and this double excellence it was, that led me to select and translate a few specimens of this writer's Natural and Supernatural.

Undine is a beautifully imaginative tale, a master-piece in this department of German literature. With a simplicity of the antique cast it combines the most picturesque wildness, unbroken interest, excellent principles, a peculiar vein of pleasantry, and even what we seldom look for in works of this kind, touches of genuine pathos. We are esteemed, and I presume justly, a less imaginative race than the people of Germany. Our traditions, local superstitions, early influences, education, habits of thought, and other circumstances of life, are of a more common-place order than theirs. We are not, it may be, less fond of legendary lore, since love of the marvellous seems to be a universal impulse in our nature; but we seek its enjoyment with the mere calm approval of fancy, while they welcome it with much of the warmth of good faith. Still, if "the World of Reality, not the Fairyland of Romance," *be* our maxim, the spirit of truth and tenderness is nowhere wholly extinct: long as it may lie slumbering in the soul, it is too inseparable a part of our being ever to die. Is not imagination a germ of immortality?

I am gratified to perceive that many writers allude to this fiction in terms of warm commendation. Menzel, in his development of German Literature, of which we have lately been favored with an able translation, speaks of this and the "Vial-Genie," or "Mandrake," another miniature romance by the same author, in these words: "Fouqué's 'Undine' will always continue one of the most delightful creations of German poetry. Also the little story of the "Mandrake" belongs to the best elaborations of the old national sagas," or tales of the supernatural, derived from the voice of traditional superstition. But the most accurate appreciation that I have seen of Undine, I find among those golden fragments of the richest of minds, the Specimens of the Table Talk of S. T. Coleridge. This is the passage to which I refer: "Undine is a most exquisite work. It shows the general want of any sense for the fine and the subtle in the public taste, that this romance made no deep impression. Undine's character, before she receives a soul, is marvellously beautiful."

The author, to whom we are so much indebted for these Specimens and other Literary Remains, and to whom we had hoped, alas! to be more and more indebted, as well for these labours of love as for those of his own classical genius, observes in a note: "Mr. Coleridge's admiration of this little romance was unbounded. He said there was something in Undine even beyond Scott,—that Scott's best characters and conceptions were *composed;* by which I understood him to mean, that Baillie Nicol Jarvie, for example, was made up of old particulars, and received its individuality from the author's power of fusion, being in the result an admirable product, as Corinthian brass was said to be the conflux of the spoils of a city. But Undine, he said, was one and single in projection, and had presented to his imagination, what Scott had never done, an absolutely new idea."

This character being formed according to the principles of the Rosicrucian philosophy, it has been suggested to me, that to enable the reader to understand and appreciate her story, I ought to prefix a sketch of that system to my translation, and I once thought of profiting by the suggestion. On reflection, however, I cannot but view the work as complete in itself. Whatever seems requisite, even for readers least conversant with such lore, Fouqué has contrived to incorporate, and I think very happily too, with the texture of his fable. See the developments of the eighth chapter. Everybody enjoys the delightful marvels of the ARABIAN NIGHTS, marvels that have almost become numbered among the common-places of our experience; even children understand the machinery of genii, magicians, talismans, rings, lamps, and enchanted horses.

The reader will allow me to observe, in closing these brief notices, that, supported as well by my own feeling as by the judgment of Menzel, Coleridge, and, I may add, by the general voice of criticism, I view UNDINE not only as a work of art, but as something far superior, an exquisite creation of genius. If I have failed to do justice to her peculiar traits, in thus introducing her to him in the costume of our language, it is not owing to want of admiration, or of studiously endeavoring to be faithful to my trust; and, aware of the difficulty of presenting her the "vision of beauty" that Fouqué "found" her, he will forgive the fond impulse of my ambition. What welcome she may receive among us, it remains for the noble knights and lovely ladies of our country to show. She does not come as a stranger,—she has already been more than once greeted with favour; still, wide as may be her fame in the world of letters, she seems, as yet, to be more talked of in the world of common readers, than, if I may so speak, known in person. TO ALL lovers of the imaginative, therefore,—to every "simple, affectionate, and wonder-loving heart,"—her fortunes are again committed.

THIS translation of UNDINE was first published in 1839, as the third volume of the New York "LIBRARY OF ROMANCE," of which "PHANTASMION" formed the first and second. It was republished also, the same year, in the London "STANDARD LIBRARY." Encouraged by its favourable reception, and feeling that every thing of value, in a picture so closely allied to poetry as this, depends on skilfully disposing the colours of thought, the lights and shades of expression, I have since that edition again and again compared it with the German, and spared no pains to render it less unworthy of the welcome with which it has been honoured.

What I proposed to myself, as a general if not an invariable rule in translating and revising, was this, to adhere to the verbal import of the original, whenever a freer rendering did not give promise of more clearness, beauty, or force of expression, in English. Freedom and fidelity, indeed, have been my continual aim; but, notwithstanding the imperfections which I have from time to time detected and removed, when I perceive how faint a shadow my version is of the vivid original, I am able to make no higher boast than of having *tried* to copy the author's fineness and subtlety of conception, as well as the ease and simplicity of his execution. Still, however inadequate the translation may be, and however perfect a copy some more expert translator may produce, few or none will ever submit to a like process of revision and improvement to make it such; and though "a labour of love," as one of my reviewers has been pleased to call my work,—a striving after accuracy of thought and expression, as if it were a case of conscience,—it is a labour that I would fain hope I shall seldom find it necessary to repeat.

The preceding remarks formed the "Advertisement" to the "Miniature Romances from the German," published in Boston, 1841. Since that time, the translation of UNDINE has passed through more editions in London, than it is necessary or I am able to mention. In all of them, omissions have been made, and other unauthorized liberties have been taken; but that of Mr. James Burns, in his recent volumes o' Fouqué, I consider by far the best I have seen. I thank the editor for the labor he has bestowed upon my version. I should have been more pleased, indeed, if he had not removed the author's headings from the chapters, if he had not chosen to unite two chapters in one, and if he had not injured several passages by the changes he has made: still he has revised my work with so much care and good taste, that, in preparing it for Messrs. Wiley & Putnam's publication, I have derived many verbal improvements from his copy. While I am glad to welcome this English fellow-worker to the same delightful field, I cannot but cherish the assurance, that his translations of German romance, both original and selected, will be as warmly welcomed by all lovers of the Natural and Supernatural as by myself.

T. TRACY.

DEDICATION.

VISION of beauty, dear Undine,
  Since led by storied light,
  I found you, mystic sprite,
How soothing to my heart your voice has been.

You press beside me, angel mild,
  Soft breathing all your woes,
  And winning brief repose,—
A wayward, tender, timid child.

Still my guitar has caught the tone,
  And from its gate of gold
  Your whispered sorrows rolled,
Till through the world their sound is flown.

And many hearts your sweetness love,
  Though strange your freaks and state,
  And while I sing your fate,
The wild and wondrous tale approve.

Now would they warmly, one and all,
  Your fortunes trace anew:
  Then, sweet, your way pursue,
And, fearless, enter bower and hall.

Greet noble knights with homage due;
  But greet, all trusting there,
  The lovely German fair:
"Welcome," they cry, "the maiden true!"

And if toward ME one dart a glance,
  Say, "*He's* a loyal knight,
  Who serves you, ladies bright,—
Guitar and sword,—at tourney, feast, and dance."

FOUQUÉ.

UNDINE.

CHAPTER I.

How a Knight came to a Fisherman's Cottage.

ONCE on a beautiful evening, it may now be many hundred years ago, there was a worthy old fisherman who sat before his door mending his nets.

Now the corner of the world where he dwelt, was exceedingly picturesque. The green turf on which he had built his cottage, ran far out into a great lake; and this slip of verdure appeared to stretch into it as much through love of its clear waters, blue and bright, as the lake, moved by a like impulse, strove to fold the meadow, with its waving grass and flowers, and the cooling shade of the trees, in its fond embrace. Such were the freshness and beauty of both, that they seemed to be drawn toward each other, and the one to be visiting the other as a guest.

With respect to human beings, indeed, in this pleasant spot, excepting the fisherman and his family, there were few or rather none to be met with. For in the back-ground of the scene, toward the west and north-west, lay a forest of extraordinary wildness, which, owing to its gloom and its being almost impassable, as well as to fear of the strange creatures and visionary forms to be encountered there, most people avoided entering, unless in cases of extreme necessity. The pious old fisherman, however, many times passed through it without harm, when he carried the fine fish, which he caught by his beautiful strip of land, to a great city lying only a short distance beyond the extensive forest.

Now the reason he was able to go through this wood with so much ease, may have been chiefly this, because he entertained scarcely any thoughts but such as were of a religious nature; and besides, every time he crossed the evil-reported shades, he used to sing some holy song with a clear voice and from a sincere heart.

Well, while he sat by his nets this evening, neither fearing nor devising evil, a sudden terror seized him, as he heard a rushing in the darkness of the wood, that resembled the trampling of a mounted steed, and the noise continued every instant drawing nearer and nearer to his little territory.

What he had dreamed in his reveries, when abroad in many a stormy night, respecting the mysteries of the forest, now flashed through his mind in a moment; especially the figure of a man of gigantic stature and snow-white appearance, who kept nodding his head in a portentous manner. Yet, when he raised his eyes toward the wood, the form came before him in perfect distinctness, as he saw the nodding man burst forth from the mazy web-work of leaves and branches. But he immediately felt emboldened, when he reflected that nothing to give him alarm had ever befallen him even in the forest; and moreover, that on this open neck of land the evil spirit, it was likely, would be still less daring in the exercise of its power. At the same time, he prayed aloud with the most earnest sincerity of devotion, repeating a passage of the Bible. This inspired him with fresh courage; and soon perceiving the illusion, the strange mistake into which his imagination had betrayed him, he could with difficulty refrain from laughing. The white, nodding figure he had seen, became transformed in the twinkling of an eye, to what in reality it was, a small brook, long and familiarly known to him, which ran foaming from the forest, and discharged itself into the lake.

But what had caused the startling sound, was a knight, arrayed in sumptuous apparel, who beneath the shadows of the trees come riding toward the cottage. His doublet was of dark violet, embroidered with gold, and his scarlet cloak hung gracefully over it; on his cap of burnished gold waved red and violet plumes, and in his golden shoulder-belt flashed a sword, richly ornamented and extremely beautiful. The white barb that bore the knight, was more slenderly built than war-horses usually are; and he touched the turf with a step so light and elastic, that the green and flower-woven carpet seemed hardly to receive the slightest break from his tread. The old fisherman, notwithstanding, did not feel perfectly secure in his mind, although he was forced to believe, that no evil could be feared from an appearance so prepossessing; and therefore, as good manners dictated, he took off his hat on the knight's coming near, and quietly remained by the side of his nets.

When the stranger stopped, and asked whether he with his horse could have shelter and entertainment there for the night, the fisherman returned answer: "As to your horse, fair Sir, I have no better stable for him than this shady meadow, and no better provender than the grass that is growing here. But with respect to yourself, you shall be welcome to our humble cottage, and to the best supper and lodging we are able to give you."

The knight was well contented with this reception; and alighting from his horse, which his host assisted him to relieve from saddle and bridle, he let him hasten away to the fresh pasture, and thus spoke: "Even had I found you less hospitable and kindly disposed, my worthy old friend, you would still, I suspect, hardly have got rid of me to-day; for here, I perceive, a broad lake lies before us, and as to riding back into that wood of wonders, with the shades of evening deepening around me, may Heaven in its grace preserve me from the thought!"

"Pray, not a word of the wood, or of returning into it!" said the fisherman, and took his guest into the cottage.

There, beside the hearth, from which a frugal fire was diffusing its light through the clean dusky room, sat the fisherman's aged wife in a great chair. At the entrance of their noble guest, she rose and gave him a courteous welcome, but sat down again in her seat of honour, not making the slightest offer of it to the stranger. Upon this the fisherman said with a smile:

"You must not be offended with her, young gentleman, because she has not given up to you the best chair in the house; it is a custom among poor people to look upon this as the privilege of the aged."

"Why, husband!" cried the old lady with a quiet smile, "where can your wits be wandering? Our guest, to say the least of him, must belong to a Christian country, and how is it possible then, that so well-bred a young man, as he appears to be, could dream of driving old people from their chairs? Take a seat, my young master," continued she, turning to the knight; "there is still quite a snug little chair across the room there, only be careful not to shove it about too roughly, for one of its legs, I fear, is none of the firmest."

The knight brought up the seat as carefully as she could desire, and good-humouredly sat down upon it; while it seemed to him for a moment, that he must be somehow related to this little household, and have just returned home from abroad.

These three worthy people now began to converse in the most friendly and familiar manner. In relation to the forest, indeed, concerning which the knight occasionally made some inquiries, the old man chose to know but little; at any rate he was of opinion, that slightly touching upon it, at this hour of twilight, was most suitable and safe; but of the cares and comforts of their home and their business abroad, the aged couple spoke more freely, and listened also with eager curiosity, as the knight recounted to them his travels, and how he had a castle near one of the sources of the Danube, and that his name was Sir Huldbrand of Ringstetten.

Already had the stranger, while they were in the midst of their talk, been aware at times of a splash against the little low window, as if some one were dashing water against it. The old man, every time he heard the noise, knit his brows with vexation; but at last, when the whole sweep of a shower came pouring like a torrent against the panes, and bubbling through the decayed frame into the room, he started up indignant, rushed to the window, and cried with a threatening voice:

"Undine! will you never leave off these fooleries? not even to-day, when we have a stranger-knight with us in the cottage?"

All without now became still, only a low titter was just perceptible, and the fisherman said, as he came back to his seat: "You will have the goodness, my honored guest, to pardon this freak, and it may be a multitude more, but she has no thought of evil or any thing improper. This mischievous Undine, to confess the truth, is our adopted daughter, and she stoutly refuses to give over this frolicksome childishness of hers, although she has already entered her eighteenth year. But in spite of this, as I said before, she is at heart one of the very best children in the world."

"*You* may say so," broke in the old lady, shaking her head, —"you can give a better account of her than I can. When you return home from fishing, or from selling your fish in the city, you may think her frolics very delightful. But to have her figuring about you the whole day long, and never, from morning to night, to hear her speak one word of sense; and then, as she grows older, instead of having any help from her in the family, to find her a continual cause of anxiety, lest her wild humours should completely ruin us,—that is quite a different affair, and enough at last to weary out the patience even of a saint."

"Well, well," replied the master of the house, with a smile, "you have your trials with Undine, and I have mine with the lake. The lake often beats down my dams, and breaks the meshes of my nets, but for all that I have a strong affection for it; and so have you, in spite of your mighty crosses and vexations, for our nice pretty little child. Is it not true?"

"One cannot be very angry with her," answered the old lady, as she gave her husband an approving smile.

That instant the door flew open, and a girl of slender form, almost a very miniature of woman, her hair flaxen and her complexion fair, in one word, a blonde-like miracle of beauty, slipped laughing in, and said: "You have only been making a mock of me, father; for where now is the guest you mentioned?"

The same moment, however, she perceived the knight also, and continued standing before the comely young man in fixed astonishment. Huldbrand was charmed with her graceful figure, and viewed her lovely features with the more intense interest, as he imagined it was only her surprise that permitted him to have the opportunity, and that she would soon turn away from his gaze with increased bashfulness. But the event was the very reverse of what he expected. For after now regarding him quite a long while, she felt more confidence, moved nearer, knelt down before him, and, while she played with a gold medal, which he wore attached to a rich chain on his breast, exclaimed:

"Why, you beautiful, you friendly guest! how have you reached our poor cottage at last? Have you been obliged, for years and years, to wander about the world, before you could catch one glimpe of our nook? Do you come out of that wild forest, my lovely friend?"

The old woman was so prompt in her reproof, as to allow him no time to answer. She commanded the maiden to rise, show better manners, and go to her work. But Undine, without making any reply, drew a little footstool near Huldbrand's chair, sat down upon it with her netting, and said in a gentle tone: "I will work here."

The old man did as parents are apt to do with children, to whom they have been over-indulgent. He affected to observe nothing of Undine's strange behaviour, and was beginning to talk about something else. But this was what the little girl would not suffer him to do. She broke in upon him: "I have asked our kind guest, from whence he has come among us, and he has not yet answered me."

"I come out of the forest, you lovely little vision," Huldbrand returned, and she spoke again:

"You must also tell me how you came to enter that forest, so feared and shunned, and the marvellous adventures you met with there; for there is no escaping, I guess, without something of this kind."

Huldbrand felt a slight shudder, on remembering what he had witnessed, and looked involuntarily toward the window; for it seemed to him, that one of the strange shapes, which had come upon him in the forest, must be there grinning in through the glass; but he discerned nothing except the deep darkness of night, which had now enveloped the whole prospect. Upon this, he became more collected, and was just on the point of beginning his account, when the old man thus interrupted him:

"Not so, Sir knight; this is by no means a fit hour for such relations."

But Undine, in a state of high excitement, sprang up from her little cricket, braced her beautiful arms against her sides, and cried, placing herself directly before the fisherman: "He shall *not* tell his story, father? he shall not? But it is my will:—he shall!—he shall, stop him who may!"

Thus speaking, she stamped her neat little foot vehemently on the floor, but all with an air of such comic and good-humoured simplicity, that Huldbrand now found it quite as hard to withdraw his gaze from her wild emotion, as he had before from her gentleness and beauty. The old man, on the contrary, burst out in unrestrained displeasure. He severely reproved Undine for her disobedience and her unbecoming carriage toward the stranger, and his good old wife joined him in harping on the same string.

By these rebukes Undine was only excited the more. "If you want to quarrel with me," she cried, "and will not let me hear what I so much desire, then sleep alone in your smoky old hut!"—And swift as an arrow she shot from the door, and vanished amid the darkness of the night.

CHAPTER II.

In what manner Undine had come to the Fisherman.

HULDBRAND and the fisherman sprang from their seats, and were rushing to stop the angry girl; but before they could reach the cottage door, she had disappeared in the cloud-like obscurity without, and no sound, not so much even as that of her light foot-step, betrayed the course she had taken. Huldbrand threw a glance of inquiry toward his host: it almost seemed to him, as if his whole interview with a sweet apparition, which had so suddenly plunged again amid the night, were no other than a continuation of the wonderful forms, that had just played their mad pranks with him in the forest; but the old man muttered between his teeth:

"This is not the first time she has treated us in this manner. Now must our hearts be filled with anxiety, and our eyes find no sleep, the livelong night; for who can assure us, in spite of her past escapes, that she will not some time or other come to harm, if she thus continue out in the dark and alone until daylight?"

"Then pray, for God's sake, father, let us follow her," cried Huldbrand anxiously.

"Wherefore should we?" replied the old man; "it would be a sin, were I to suffer you, all alone, to search after the foolish girl amid the lonesomeness of night; and my old limbs would fail to carry me to this wild rover, even if I knew to what place she has hurried off."

"Still we ought at least to call after her, and beg her to return," said Huldbrand; and he began to call in tones of earnest entreaty: "Undine! Undine! come back, pray come back!"

The old man shook his head, and said: "All your shouting,

however loud and long, will be of no avail; you know not as yet, Sir knight, what a self-willed thing the little wilding is." But still, even hoping against hope, he could not himself cease calling out every minute, amid the gloom of night: "Undine! ah, dear Undine! I beseech you, pray come back,—only this once."

It turned out, however, exactly as the fisherman had said. No Undine could they hear or see; and as the old man would on no account consent that Huldbrand should go in quest of the fugitive, they were both obliged at last to return into the cottage. There they found the fire on the hearth almost gone out, and the mistress of the house, who took Undine's flight and danger far less to heart than her husband, had already gone to rest. The old man blew up the coals, put on dry wood, and by means of the renewed flame hunted for a jug of wine, which he brought and set between himself and his guest.

"You, Sir knight, as well as I," said he, "are anxious on the silly girl's account, and it would be better, I think, to spend part of the night in chatting and drinking, than keep turning and turning on our rush-mats, and trying in vain to sleep. What is your opinion?"

Huldbrand was well pleased with the plan; the fisherman pressed him to take the vacant seat of honor, its worthy occupant having now left it for her couch; and they relished their beverage and enjoyed their chat, as two such good men and true ever ought to do. To be sure, whenever the slightest thing moved before the windows, or at times when just nothing at all was moving, one of them would look up and exclaim, "There she comes!"—Then would they continue silent a few moments, and afterward, when nothing appeared, would shake their heads, brea he out a sigh, and go on with their talk.

But as they could neither of them think of any thing except Undine, the best plan they could devise was, that the old fisherman should relate, and the knight should hear, in what manner Undine had come to the cottage. So the fisherman began as follows:

"It is now about fifteen years, since I one day crossed the wild forest with fish for the city market. My wife had remained at home, as she was wont to do; and at this time for a reason of more than common interest; for although we were beginning to feel the advances of age, God had bestowed upon us an infant of wonderful beauty. It was a little girl, and we already began to ask ourselves the question, whether we ought not, for the advantage of the new-comer, to quit our solitude, and, the better to bring up this precious gift of Heaven, to remove to some more inhabited place. Poor people, to be sure, cannot in these cases do all you may think they ought, Sir knight; but still, gracious God! we must all do as much for our children as we possibly can.

"Well, I went on my way, and this affair would keep running in my head. This tongue of land was most dear to me, and I shrunk from the thought of leaving it, when, amidst the bustle and brawls of the city, I was obliged to reflect in this manner by myself: 'In a scene of tumult like this, or at least in one not much more quiet, I too must soon take up my abode.' But in spite of these feelings, I was far from murmuring against the kind providence of God; on the contrary, when I received this new blessing, my heart breathed a prayer of thankfulness too deep for words to express. I should also speak an untruth, were I to say, that any thing befell me, either on my passage through the forest to the city, or on my returning homeward, that gave me more alarm than usual, as at that time I had never seen any appearance there, which could terrify or annoy me. The Lord was ever with me in those awful shades."

Thus speaking, he took his cap reverently from his bald head, and continued to sit, for a considerable time, in devout thought. He then covered himself again, and went on with his relation:

"On this side the forest, alas! it was on this side, that woe burst upon me. My wife came wildly to meet me, clad in mourning apparel, and her eyes streaming with tears. 'Gracious God!' I cried with a groan; 'where's our child? Speak!'

"'With the Being on whom you have called, dear husband,' she answered; and we now entered the cottage together, weeping in silence. I looked for the little corse, almost fearing to find what I was seeking; and then it was I first learnt how all had happened.

"My wife had taken the little one in her arms, and walked out to the shore of the lake. She there sat down by its very brink; and while she was playing with the infant, as free from all fear as she was full of delight, it bent forward on a sudden, as if seeing something very beautiful in the water. My wife saw her laugh, the dear angel, and try to catch the image in her little hands; but in a moment,—with a motion swifter than sight,—she sprung from her mother's arms, and sunk in the lake, the watery glass into which she had been gazing. I searched for our lost darling again and again; but it was all in vain; I could nowhere find the least trace of her.

"Well, we were again childless parents, and were now, on the same evening, sitting together by our cottage hearth. We had no desire to talk, even if our tears would have permitted us. As we thus sat in mournful stillness, gazing into the fire, all at once we heard something without,—a slight rustling at the door. The door flew open, and we saw a little girl, three or four years old, and more beautiful than I am able to tell you, standing on the threshold, richly dressed and smiling upon us. We were struck dumb with astonishment, and I knew not for a time, whether the tiny form were a real human being, or a mere mockery of enchantment. But I soon perceived water dripping from her golden hair and rich garments, and that the pretty child had been lying in the water, and stood in immediate need of our help.

"'Wife,' said I, 'no one has been able to save our child for us; still we doubtless ought to do for others, what would make ourselves the happiest parents on earth, could any one do us the same kindness.'

"We undressed the little thing, put her to bed, and gave her something warming to drink: at all this she spoke not a word, but only turned her eyes upon us,—eyes blue and bright as sea or sky,—and continued looking at us with a smile.

"Next morning, we had no reason to fear, that she had received any other harm than her wetting, and I now asked her about her parents, and how she could have come to us. But the account she gave, was both confused and incredible. She must surely have been born far from here, not only because I have been unable, for these fifteen years, to learn any thing of her birth, but because she then said, and at times continues to say, many things of so very singular a nature, that we neither of us know, after all, whether she may not have dropped among us from the moon. Then her talk runs upon golden castles, crystal domes, and Heaven knows what extravagances beside. What of her story, however, she related with most distinctness, was this, that while she was once taking a sail with her mother on the great lake, she fell out of the boat into the water; and that when she first recovered her senses, she was here under our trees, where the gay scenes of the shore filled her with delight.

"We now had another care weighing upon our minds, and one that caused us no small perplexity and uneasiness. We of course very soon determined to keep and bring up the child we had found, in place of our own darling that had been drowned; but who could tell us whether she had been baptized or not? She herself could give us no light on the subject. When we asked her the question, she commonly made answer, that she well knew she was created for God's praise and glory, and that as to what might promote the praise and glory of God, she was willing to let us determine.

"My wife and I reasoned in this way: 'If she has not been baptized, there can be no use in putting off the ceremony; and if she has been, it is more dangerous to have too little of a good thing than too much.'

"Taking this view of our difficulty, we now endeavored to hit upon a good name for the child, since while she remained without one, we were often at a loss, in our familiar talk, to know what to call her. We at length decided, that Dorothea would be most suitable for her, as I had somewhere heard it said, that this name signified *a Gift of God;* and surely she had been sent to us by Providence as a gift, to comfort us in our misery. She, on the contrary, would not so much as hear Dorothea mentioned: she insisted, that as she had been named Undine by her parents, Undine she ought still to be called.

It now occurred to me, that this was a heathenish name, to be found in no calendar, and I resolved to ask the advice of a priest in the city. He too would hear nothing of the name, Undine; and yielding to my urgent request, he came with me through the enchanted forest, in order to perform the rite of baptism here in my cottage.

"The little maid stood before us so smart in her finery, and with so winning an air of gracefulness, that the heart of the priest softened at once in her presence; and she had a way of coaxing him so adroitly, and even of braving him at times with so merry a queerness, that he at last remembered nothing of his many objections to the name of Undine.

"Thus then was she baptized Undine; and during the holy ceremony, she behaved with great propriety and gentleness, wild and wayward as at other times she invariably was. For in this my wife was quite right, when she mentioned what care and anxiety the child has occasioned us. If I should relate to you"——

At this moment the knight interrupted the fisherman, with a view to direct his attention to a deep sound, as of a rushing flood, which had caught his ear, within a few minutes, between the words of the old man. And now the waters came pouring on with redoubled fury before the cottage windows. Both sprang to the door. There they saw, by the light of the now risen moon, the brook which issued from the wood, rushing wildly over its banks, and whirling onward with it both stones and branches of trees in its rapid course. The storm, as if awakened by the uproar, burst forth from the clouds, whose immense masses of vapour coursed over the moon with the swiftness of thought; the lake roared beneath the wind, that swept the foam from its waves; while the trees of this narrow peninsula groaned from root to top-most branch, as they bowed and swung above the torrent.

"Undine! in God's name, Undine!" cried the two men in an agony. No answer was returned; and now, regardless of every thing else, they hurried from the cottage, one in this direction, the other in that, searching and calling.

CHAPTER III.

How they found Undine again.

THE longer Huldbrand sought Undine beneath the shades of night, and failed to find her, the more anxious and confused he became. The impression that she was a mere phantom of the forest, gained a new ascendency over him; indeed, amid the howling of the waves and the tempest, the crashing of the trees, and so entire a change of the scene, that it bore no resemblance to its former calm beauty, he was tempted to view the whole peninsula, together with the cottage and its inhabitants, as little more than some mockery of his senses; but still he heard, afar off, the fisherman's anxious and incessant shouting, "UNDINE! UNDINE!" and also his aged wife, who, with a loud voice and a strong feeling of awe, was praying and chanting hymns amid the commotion.

At length, when he drew near to the brook which had overflowed its banks, he perceived by the moonlight, that it had taken its wild course directly in front of the haunted forest, so as to change the peninsula into an island.

"Merciful God!" he breathed to himself "if Undine has ventured one step within that fearful wood, what will become of her? Perhaps it was all owing to her sportive and wayward spirit, because I could give her no account of my adventures there. And now the stream is rolling between us, she may be weeping alone on the other side in the midst of spectral horrors!"

A shuddering groan escaped him, and clambering over some stones and trunks of overthrown pines, in order to step into the impetuous current, he resolved, either by wading or swimming, to seek the wanderer on the further shore. He felt, it is true, all the dread and shrinking awe creeping over him, which he had already suffered by daylight among the now tossing and roaring branches of the forest. More than all, a tall man in white, whom he knew but too well, met his view, as he stood grinning and nodding on the grass beyond the water; but even monstrous forms, like this, only impelled him to cross over toward them, when the thought rushed upon him, that Undine might be there alone, and in the agony of death.

He had already grasped a stout branch of a pine, and stood supporting himself upon it in the whirling current, against which he could with difficulty keep himself erect; but he advanced deeper in, with a courageous spirit. That instant, a gentle voice of warning cried near him: "Do not venture, do not venture!—that OLD MAN, the STREAM, is too full of tricks to be trusted!"—He knew the soft tones of the voice; and while he stood as it were entranced, beneath the shadows which now duskily veiled the moon, his head swum with the swell and rolling of the waves, as he every moment saw them foaming and dashing above his knee. Still he disdained the thought of giving up his purpose.

"If you are not really there, if you are merely gambolling round me like a mist, may I too bid farewell to life, and become a shadow like you, dear, dear Undine!"* Thus calling aloud, he again moved deeper into the stream. "Look round you,—ah pray look round you, beautiful young stranger! why rush on death so madly!" cried the voice a second time close by him; and looking on one side, as the moon by glimpses un-

* This intensive form of expression is almost as familiar in English as in German, and I have not scrupled occasionally to employ it. The following example from THALABA, is one of the most impressive in the language:

"No sound but the wild, wild wind,
And the snow crunching under his feet."

These lines from the Ancient Mariner afford another example, and one still more remarkable:

"Alone, alone, all, all alone,
Alone on a wide, wide sea."

veiled its light, he perceived a little island formed by the flood, and, reclined upon its flowery turf beneath the high branches of embowering trees, he saw the smiling and lovely Undine.

O with what a thrill of delight, compared with the suspense and pause of a moment before, the young man now plied his sturdy staff! A few steps freed him from the flood, that was rushing between himself and the maiden, and he stood near her on the little spot of green-sward, in secret security, covered by the primeval trees that rustled above them. Undine had partially risen, within her tent of verdure, and she now threw her arms around his neck, so that she gently drew him down upon the soft seat by her side.

"Here you shall tell me your story, my handsome friend," she breathed in a low whisper; "here the cross old people cannot disturb us. And, besides, our roof of leaves here will make quite as good a shelter, it may be, as their poor cottage."

"It is heaven itself," cried Huldbrand; and folding her in his arms, he kissed the lovely and affectionate girl with fervour.

The old fisherman, meantime, had come to the margin of the stream, and he shouted across to the young lovers: "Why how is this, Sir knight! I received you with the welcome which one true-hearted man gives to another, and now you sit there caressing my foster-child in secret, while you suffer me in my anxiety to go roaming through the night in quest of her."

"Not till this moment did I find her myself, old father," cried the knight across the water.

"So much the better," said the fisherman; "but now make haste, and bring her over to me upon firm ground."

To this, however, Undine would by no means consent. She declared, that she would rather enter the wild forest itself with the beautiful stranger, than return to the cottage, where she was so thwarted in her wishes, and from which the handsome knight would soon or late go away. Then closely embracing

Huldbrand, she sung the following verse with the warbling sweetness of a bird:

"A Rill would leave its misty vale,
And fortunes wild explore;
Weary at length it reached the main,
And sought its vale no more."

The old fisherman wept bitterly at her song, but his emotion seemed to awaken little or no sympathy in her. She kissed and caressed her new friend, whom she called her darling, and who at last said to her: "Undine, if the distress of the old man does not touch your heart, it cannot but move mine. We ought to return to him."

She opened her large blue eyes upon him in perfect amazement, and spoke at last with a slow and lingering accent: "If you think so,—it is well; all is right to me, which you think right. But the old man over there must first give me his promise, that he will allow you, without objection, to relate what you saw in the wood, and——well, other things will settle themselves."*

"Come, do only come!" cried the fisherman to her, unable to utter another word. At the same time, he stretched his arms wide over the current toward her, and, to give her assurance that he would do what she required, nodded his head; this motion caused his white hair to fall strangely over his face, and Huldbrand could not but remember the nodding white man of the forest. Without allowing anything, however, to produce in him the least confusion, the young knight took the beautiful girl in his arms, and bore her across the narrow channel, which the stream had torn away between her little island and the solid shore. The old man fell upon Undine's neck, and found it impossible either to express his joy, or to kiss her enough; even the ancient dame came up, and embraced the

* "Undine evidently meant to have added another condition, but then thinking it superfluous, only remarks,—'well, other things will settle themselves.'"

recovered girl most cordially. Every word of censure was carefully avoided; the more so indeed, as even Undine, forgetting her waywardness, almost overwhelmed her foster-parents with caresses and the prattle of tenderness.

When at length the excess of their joy at recovering their child had subsided, and they seemed to have come to themselves, morning had already dawned, opening to view and brightening the waters of the lake. The tempest had become hushed, and small birds sung merrily on the moist branches.

As Undine now insisted upon hearing the recital of the knight's promised adventures, the aged couple, smiling with good-humour, yielded to her wish. Breakfast was brought out beneath the trees, which stood behind the cottage toward the lake on the north, and they sat down to it with delighted hearts,—Undine lower than the rest (since she would by no means allow it to be otherwise) at the knight's feet on the grass. These arrangements being made, Huldbrand began his story in the following manner.

CHAPTER IV.

Of what had happened to the Knight in the forest.

"It is now about eight days since I rode into the free imperial city, which lies yonder on the further side of the forest. Soon after my arrival, a splendid tournament and running at the ring took place there, and I spared neither my horse nor my lance in the encounters.

"Once, while I was pausing at the lists, to rest from the brisk exercise, and was handing back my helmet to one of my attendants, a female figure of extraordinary beauty caught my attention, as, most magnificently attired, she stood looking on at one of the balconies. I learnt, on making inquiry of a person near me, that the name of the gay young lady was Bertalda, and that she was a foster-daughter of one of the powerful dukes of this country. She too, I observed, was gazing at me, and the consequences were such, as we young knights are wont to experience: whatever success in riding I might have had before, I was now favoured with still better fortune. That evening I was Bertalda's partner in the dance, and I enjoyed the same distinction during the remainder of the festival."

A sharp pain in his left hand, as it hung carelessly beside him, here interrupted Huldbrand's relation, and drew his eye to the part affected. Undine had fastened her pearly teeth, and not without some keenness too, upon one of his fingers, appearing at the same time very gloomy and displeased. On a sudden, however, she looked up in his eyes with an expression of tender melancholy, and whispered almost inaudibly: "You blame me, but it was all your own fault."*

* "That is, you act or speak in such a manner, as to make me treat you rudely. Why do you say such provoking things?—It is a kind of tender reproof, in self defence." C. F.

She then covered her face, and the knight, strangely embarrassed and thoughtful, went on with his story:

"This lady Bertalda of whom I spoke, is of a proud and wayward spirit. The second day I saw her she pleased me by no means so much as she had the first, and the third day still less. But I continued about her, because she showed me more favour than she did any other knight; and it so happened, that I playfully asked her to give me one of her gloves.

"'When you have entered the haunted forest all alone,' said she; 'when you have explored its wonders, and brought me a full account of them, the glove is yours.'

"As to getting her glove, it was of no importance to me whatever, but the word had been spoken, and no honourable knight would permit himself to be urged to such a proof of valour a second time."

"I thought," said Undine, interrupting him, "that she loved you."

"It did appear so," replied Huldbrand.

"Well!" exclaimed the maiden laughing, "this is beyond belief; she must be very stupid and heartless. To drive from her one who was dear to her! And, worse than all, into that ill-omened wood! The wood and its mysteries, for all I should have cared, might have waited a long while."

"Yesterday morning, then," pursued the knight, smiling brightly upon Undine, "I set out from the city, my enterprise before me. The early light lay rich upon the verdant turf. It shone so rosy on the slender boles of the trees, and there was so merry a whispering among the leaves, that in my heart I could not but laugh at people, who feared meeting any thing to terrify them in a spot so delicious. 'I shall soon trot through the forest, and as speedily return,' I said to myself in the overflow of joyous feeling; and ere I was well aware, I had entered deep among the green shades, while of the plain that lay behind me, I was no more able to catch a glimpse.

"Then the conviction for the first time impressed me, that in a forest of so great extent I might very easily become bewildered, and that this perhaps might be the only danger, which was likely to threaten those who explored its recesses. So I made a halt, and turned myself in the direction of the sun, which had meantime risen somewhat higher; and while I was looking up to observe it, I saw something black among the boughs of a lofty oak. My first thought was,—'It is a bear!' and I grasped my weapon of defence; the object then accosted me from above in a human voice, but in a tone most harsh and hideous: 'If I overhead here do not gnaw off these dry branches, Sir Wiseacre, what shall we have to roast you with, when midnight comes?' And with that it grinned, and made such a rattling with the branches, that my courser became mad with affright, and rushed furiously forward with me, before I had time to see distinctly what sort of a devil's beast it was."

"You must not name it," said the old fisherman, crossing himself; his wife did the same without speaking a word; and Undine, while her eye sparkled with glee, looked at her beloved knight and said: "The best of the story is, however, that as yet they have not actually roasted you. But pray make haste, my handsome young friend. I long to hear more."

The knight then went on with his adventures: "My horse was so wild, that he well-nigh rushed with me against limbs and trunks of trees. He was dripping with sweat, through terror, heat, and the violent straining of his muscles. Still he refused to slacken his career. At last, altogether beyond my control, he took his course directly up a stony steep; when suddenly a tall white man flashed before me, and threw himself athwart the way my mad steed was taking. At this apparition he shuddered with new affright, and stopt, trembling. I took this chance of recovering my command of him, and now for the first time perceived, that my deliverer, so far from being a white MAN, was only a brook of silver brightness, foaming near me in its descent from the hill, while it crossed and arrested my horse's course with its rush of waters."

"Thanks, thanks, dear BROOK," cried Undine, clapping her

little hands. But the old man shook his head, and, deeply musing, looked vacantly down before him.

"Hardly had I well settled myself in my saddle, and got the reins in my grasp again," Huldbrand pursued, "when a wizard-like dwarf of a man was already standing at my side, diminutive and ugly beyond conception, his complexion of a brownish yellow, and his nose scarcely of less magnitude than all the rest of him. The fellow's mouth was slit almost from ear to ear, and he showed his teeth with a simpering smile of idiot courtesy, while he overwhelmed me with bows and scrapes innumerable. The farce now becoming excessively irksome, I thanked him in the fewest words I could well use, turned about my still trembling charger, and purposed either to seek another adventure, or, should I meet with none, to pick my way back to the city; for the sun, during my wild chase, had passed the meridian, and was now hastening toward the west. But this villain of a manikin sprung at the same instant, and, with a turn as rapid as lightning, stood before my horse again. 'Clear the way there!' I fiercely shouted; 'the beast is wild, and will make nothing of running over you.'

"'He will, will he!' cried the imp with a snarl, and snorting out a laugh still more frightfully idiotic; 'pay me, first pay what you owe me,—I stopt your fine little nag for you; without my help, both you and he would be now sprawling below there in that stony ravine. Hu! from what a horrible plunge I've saved you.'

"'Well, pray don't stretch your mouth any wider,' said I, 'but take your drink-money and be off, though every word you say is false. See, it was the kind brook there, you miserable thing, and not you, that saved me.' And at the same time I dropt a piece of gold into his wizard cap which he had taken from his head while he was begging before me.

"I then trotted off and left him; but, to make bad worse, he screamed after me, and on a sudden, with inconceivable quickness, he was close by my side. I started my horse into a gallop; he galloped on with me, impossible for him as it appeared; and with this strange movement, half-ludicrous and half horrible, forcing at the same time every limb and feature into distortion, he kept raising the gold piece as high as he could stretch his arm, and screaming at every leap: 'Counterfeit! false! false coin! counterfeit!' and such were the croaking sounds that issued from his hollow breast, you would have supposed, that every time he made them, he must have tumbled upon the ground dead. All this while, his disgusting red tongue hung lolling far out of his mouth.

"Discomposed at the sight, I stopped and asked him: 'What do you mean by your screaming? Take another piece of gold, take two more,—but leave me.'

"He then began to make his hideous salutations of courtesy again, and snarled out as before: 'Not gold, it shall not be gold, my smart young gentleman; I have too much of that trash already, as I will show you in no-time.'

"At that moment, and thought itself could not have been more instantaneous, I seemed to have acquired new powers of sight. I could see through the solid green plain, as if it were green glass, and the smooth surface of the earth were round as a globe; and within it I saw crowds of goblins, who were pursuing their pastime, and making themselves merry with silver and gold. They were tumbling and rolling about, heads up and heads down: they pelted one another in sport with the precious metals, and with irritating malice blew gold dust in one another's eyes. My odious companion stood half within and half without; he ordered the others to reach him up a vast quantity of gold; this he showed to me with a laugh, and then flung it again ringing and chinking down the measureless abyss.

"After this contemptuous disregard of gold, he held up the piece I had given him, showing it to his brother gnomes below, and they laughed themselves half dead at a bit so worthless, and hissed me. At last, raising their fingers all smutched with ore, they pointed them at me in scorn, and wilder and wilder, and thicker and thicker, and madder and madder, the crowd were clambering up to where I sat gazing at these wonders Then terror seized me, as it had before seized my horse. I drove my spurs into his sides; and how far he rushed headlong with me through the forest, during this second of my wild heats, it is impossible to say.

"At last, when I had now come to a dead halt again, the cool of evening was around me. I caught the gleam of a white foot-path through the branches of the trees; and presuming it would lead me out of the forest toward the city, I was desirous of working my way into it; but a face perfectly white and indistinct, with features forever changing, kept thrusting itself out and peering at me between the leaves. I tried to avoid it; but wherever I went, there too appeared the unearthly face. I was maddened with rage at this interruption, and drove my steed at the appearance full-tilt; when such a cloud of white foam came rushing upon me and my horse, that we were almost blinded and glad to turn about and escape. Thus from step to step it forced us on, and ever aside from the foot-path, leaving us, for the most part, only one direction open. But when we advanced in this, although it kept following close behind us, it did not occasion the smallest harm or inconvenience.

"At times, when I looked about me at the form, I perceived that the white face, which had splashed upon us its shower of foam, was resting on a body equally white and of more than gigantic size. Many a time, too I received the impression. that the whole appearance was nothing more than a wandering stream or torrent, but respecting this I could never attain to any certainty. We both of us, horse and rider, became weary, as we shaped our course according to the movements of the white man, who continued nodding his head at us, as if he would say, 'Perfectly right! perfectly right!'—And thus, at length, we came out here at the edge of the wood, where I saw the fresh turf, the waters of the lake, and your little cottage, and where the tall white man disappeared."

"Well, Heaven be praised that he is gone!" cried the old fisherman; and he now fell to considering how his guest could most conveniently return to his friends in the city. Upon this, Undine began tittering to herself, but so very low that the sound was hardly perceivable. Huldbrand, observing it, said: "I had hoped you would see me remain here with pleasure; why then do you now appear so happy, when our talk turns upon my going away?"

"Because you cannot go away," answered Undine. "Pray make a single attempt; try with a wherry, with your horse or alone, as you please, to cross that forest-stream which has burst its bounds. Or rather, make no trial at all, for you would be dashed to pieces by the stones and trunks of trees, which you see driven on with such violence. And as to the lake, I am well acquainted with that; even my father dares not venture out with his wherry far enough to help you."

Huldbrand rose, smiling, in order to look about, and observe whether the state of things were such, as Undine had represented it to be; the old man accompanied him, and the maiden, in mockery, went gamboling and playing her antics beside them. They found all, in fact, just as Undine had said, and that the knight, whether willing or not willing, must submit to remain on the island, so lately a peninsula, until the flood should subside.

When the three were now returning to the cottage, after their ramble, the knight whispered in the ear of the little girl: "Well, dear Undine, how is it with you? Are you angry on account of my remaining?"

"Ah," she pettishly made answer, "not a word of that. If I had not bitten you, who knows what fine things you would have put into your story about Bertalda!"

CHAPTER V.

How the Knight lived on the point of land, now encircled by the lake.

At some period of your life, my dear reader, after being much driven to and fro in the world, you may have reached a situation where all was well with you; that love for the calm security of our own fireside, which we all feel as an affection born with us, again rose within you; you imagined that your home would again bloom forth, as from a cherished grave, with all the flowers of childhood, the purest and most impassioned love; and that, in such a spot, it must be delightful to take up your abode, and build your tabernacle for life. Whether you were mistaken in this, and afterward made a severe expiation for your error, it suits not my purpose to inquire, and you would be unwilling yourself, it may be, to be saddened by a recollection so ungrateful. But again awake within you that foretaste of bliss, so inexpressibly sweet, that angelic salutation of peace, and you will be able, perchance, to understand something of the knight Huldbrand's happiness, while he remained on the point of land, now surrounded by the lake.

He frequently observed, and no doubt with heartfelt satisfaction, that the forest-stream continued every day to swell and roll on with a more impetuous sweep; that, by tearing away the earth, it scooped out a broader and broader channel; and that the time of his seclusion on the island became, in consequence, more and more extended. Part of the day he wandered about with an old cross-bow, which he found in a corner of the cottage, and had repaired, in order to shoot the water-fowl that flew over; and all that he was lucky enough to hit, he brought home for a good roast in the kitchen. When he came in with his booty, Undine seldom failed to greet him with a scolding, because he had cruelly deprived her dear merry friends of life, as they were sporting above in the blue ocean of the air; nay more, she often wept bitterly, when she viewed the water-fowl dead in his hand. But at other times, when he returned without having shot any, she gave him a scolding equally serious, since, owing to his indolent strolling and awkward handling of the bow, they must now put up with a dinner of pickerel and crawfish. Her playful taunts ever touched his heart with delight; the more so, as she afterwards strove to make up for her pretended ill-humour with the most endearing of caresses.

In this familiarity of the young people, their aged friends saw a resemblance to the feelings of their own youth: they appeared to look upon them as betrothed, or even as a young married pair, that lived with them in their age, to afford them assistance on their island, now torn off from the mainland. The loneliness of his situation strongly impressed also young Huldbrand with the feeling, that he was already Undine's bridegroom. It seemed to him, as if, beyond those encompassing floods, there were no other world in existence, or at any rate as if he could never cross them, and again associate with the world of other men; and when at times his grazing steed raised his head and neighed to him, seemingly inquiring after his nightly achievements and reminding him of them, or when his coat of arms sternly shone upon him from the embroidery of his saddle, and the caparisons of his horse, or when his sword happened to fall from the nail on which it was hanging in the cottage, and flashed on his eye as it slipped from the scabbard in its fall,—he quieted the doubts of his mind by saying to himself: "Undine cannot be a fisherman's daughter; she is, in all probability, a native of some remote region, and a member of some illustrious family."

There was one thing, indeed, to which he had a strong aversion: this was to hear the old dame reproving Undine. The wild girl, it is true, commonly laughed at the reproof, making no attempt to conceal the extravagance of her mirth; but it appeared to him like touching his own honour; and still he found it impossible to blame the aged wife of the fisherman, since Undine always deserved at least ten times as many reproofs as she received: so he continued to feel in his heart an affectionate tenderness for them all, even for the ancient mistress of the house, and his whole life flowed on in the calm stream of contentment.

There came, however, an interruption at last. The fisherman and the knight had been accustomed at dinner, and also in the evening, when the wind roared without, as it rarely failed to do toward night, to enjoy together a flask of wine. But now their whole stock, which the fisherman had from time to time brought with him from the city, was at last exhausted, and they were both quite out of humour at the circumstance. That day Undine laughed at them excessively, but they were not disposed to join in her jests with the same gaiety as usual. Toward evening she went out of the cottage, to escape, as she said, the sight of two such long and tiresome faces.

While it was yet twilight, some appearances of a tempest seemed to be again mustering in the sky, and the waves already rushed and roared around them: the knight and the fisherman sprung to the door in terror, to bring home the maiden, remembering the anguish of that night, when Huldbrand had first entered the cottage. But Undine met them at the same moment, clapping her little hands in high glee.

"What will you give me," she cried, "to provide you with wine? or rather, you need not give me any thing," she continued; "for I am already satisfied, if you look more cheerful, and are in better spirits, than throughout this last most wearisome day. Do only come with me one minute; the forest-stream has driven ashore a cask; and I will be condemned to sleep a whole week, if it is not a wine-cask."

The men followed her, and actually found, in a bushy cove of the shore, a cask, which inspired them with as much joy, as if they were sure it contained the generous old wine, for which they were thirsting. They first of all, and with as much expedition as possible rolled it toward the cottage; for heavy clouds were again rising in the west, and they could discern the waves of the lake, in the fading light, lifting their white foaming heads, as if looking out for the rain, which threatened every instant to pour upon them. Undine helped the men, as much as she was able; and as the shower, with a roar of wind, came suddenly sweeping on in rapid pursuit, she raised her finger with a merry menace toward the dark mass of clouds, and cried: "You cloud, you cloud, have a care!—beware how you wet us; we are some way from shelter yet."

The old man reproved her for this sally, as a sinful presumption; but she laughed to herself with a low tittering, and no mischief came from her wild behaviour. Nay more, what was beyond their expectation, they all three reached their comfortable hearth unwet, with their prize secured; but the moment the cask had been broached, and proved to contain wine of a remarkably fine flavour, then the rain first poured unrestrained from the black cloud, the tempest raved through the tops of the trees, and swept far over the billows of the deep.

Having immediately filled several bottles from the large cask, which promised them a supply for a long time, they drew round the glowing hearth; and comfortably secured from the violence of the storm, they sat tasting the flavour of their wine, and bandying their quips and pleasantries.

As reflection returned upon him, the old fisherman all at once became very grave, and said: "Ah, great God! here we sit, rejoicing over this rich gift, while he to whom it first belonged, and from whom it was wrested by the fury of the stream, must there also, it is more than probable, have lost his life."

"His fate, I trust, was not quite so melancholy as that," said Undine, while, smiling, she filled the knight's cup to the brim.

But he exclaimed: "By my unsullied honour, old father, if I knew where to find and rescue him, no fear of exposure to the night, nor any peril, should deter me from making the attempt. But I give you all the assurance I am able to give, that if I ever reach an inhabited country again, I will find out the owner of this wine or his heirs, and make double and triple reimbursement."

The old man was gratified with this assurance; he gave the knight a nod of approbation, and now drained his cup with an easier conscience and more relish.

Undine, however, said to Huldbrand: "As to the repayment and your gold, you may do whatever you like. But what you said about your venturing out, and searching, and exposing yourself to danger, appears to me far from wise. I should cry my very eyes out, should you perish there on such a wild jaunt; and is it not true, that you would prefer staying here with me and the good wine?"

"Most assuredly," answered Huldbrand, smiling.

"Well, then," replied Undine, "you see you spoke unwisely. For charity begins at home; our neighbour ought not to be our first thought; and whatever is a calamity to him, would be one in our own case also."

The mistress of the house turned away from her, sighing and shaking her head, while the fisherman forgot his wonted indulgence toward the graceful little girl, and thus reproved her:

"That sounds exactly as if you had been brought up by heathens and Turks;" and he finished his reproof by adding: "May God forgive both me and you,—unfeeling child!"

"Well, say what you will, this is what *I* think and feel," replied Undine, "whoever brought me up,—and how can a thousand of your words help it?"

"Silence!" exclaimed the fisherman in a voice of stern rebuke; and she, who with all her wild spirit was at the same time extremely alive to fear, shrunk from him, moved close up to Huldbrand, trembling, and said very softly:

"Are you also angry, dear friend?"

The knight pressed her soft hand, and tenderly stroked her locks. He was unable to utter a word; for his vexation, arising from the old man's severity toward Undine, closed his lips; and thus the two couple sat opposite to each other at once heated with anger and in embarrassed silence.

CHAPTER VI.

A Wedding.

In the midst of this painful stillness, a low knocking was heard at the door, which struck all in the cottage with dismay; for there are times when a slight circumstance, coming unexpectedly upon us, startles us like something supernatural. But here it was a further source of alarm, that the enchanted forest lay so near them, and that their place of abode seemed at present inaccessible to the visit of any human being. While they were looking upon one another in doubt, the knocking was again heard, accompanied with a deep groan. The knight sprang to seize his sword. But the old man said in a low whisper:

"If it be what I fear it is, no weapon of yours can protect us."

Undine, in the mean while, went to the door, and cried with the firm voice of fearless displeasure: "Spirits of the earth! if mischief be your aim, Kühleborn shall teach you better manners."

The terror of the rest was increased by this wild speech; they looked fearfully upon the girl, and Huldbrand was just recovering presence of mind enough to ask what she meant, when a voice reached them from without:

"I am no spirit of the earth, though a spirit still in its earthly body. You that are within the cottage there, if you fear God and would afford me assistance, open your door to me."

By the time these words were spoken, Undine had already opened it; and the lamp throwing a strong light upon the stormy night, they perceived an aged priest without, who stepped back in terror, when his eye fell on the unexpected sight of a little damsel of such exquisite beauty. Well might he think there must be magic in the wind, and witchcraft at work, where a form of such surpassing loveliness appeared at the door of so humble a dwelling. So he lifted up his voice in prayer:

"Let all good spirits praise the Lord God!"

"I am no spectre," said Undine with a smile. "Do you think, indeed, I look so very frightful? And more,—you cannot but bear me witness yourself, that I am far from shrinking terrified at your holy words. I too have knowledge of God, and understand the duty of praising him; every one, to be sure, has his own way of doing this, and this privilege he meant we should enjoy, when he gave us being. Walk in, father; you will find none but worthy people here."

The holy man came bowing in, and cast round a glance of scrutiny, wearing at the same time a very placid and venerable air. But water was dropping from every fold of his dark garments, from his long white beard, and the white locks of his hair. The fisherman and the knight took him to another apartment, and furnished him with a change of raiment, while they handed his own clothes into the room they had left, for the females to dry. The aged stranger thanked them in a manner the most humble and courteous, but on the knight's offering him his splendid cloak to wrap round him, he could not be persuaded to take it, but chose instead an old gray overcoat that belonged to the fisherman.

They then returned to the common apartment. The mistress of the house immediately offered her great chair to the priest, and continued urging it upon him, till she saw him fairly in possession of it. "You are old and exhausted," said she, "and are moreover a man of God."

Undine shoved under the stranger's feet her little cricket, on which at other times she used to sit near to Huldbrand, and showed herself, in thus promoting the comfort of the worthy old man, in the highest degree gentle and amiable. On her paying him these little attentions, Huldbrand whispered some raillery in her ear, but she replied gravely:

"He is a minister of that Being, who created us all, and holy things are not to be treated with lightness."

The knight and the fisherman now refreshed the priest with food and wine; and when he had somewhat recovered his strength and spirits, he began to relate how he had the day before set out from his cloister, which was situated afar off beyond the great lake, in order to visit the bishop, and acquaint him with the distress, into which the cloister and its tributary villages had fallen, owing to the extraordinary floods. After a long and wearisome wandering, on account of the same rise of the waters, he had been this day compelled toward evening to procure the aid of a couple of stout boatmen, and cross over an arm of the lake which had burst its usual boundary.

"But hardly," continued he, "had our small ferry-boat touched the waves, when that furious tempest burst forth, which is still raging over our heads. It seemed as if the billows had been waiting our approach, only to rush upon us with a madness the more wild. The oars were wrested from the grasp of my men in an instant; and shivered by the resistless force, they drove further and further out before us upon the waves. Unable to direct our course, we yielded to the blind power of nature, and seemed to fly over the surges toward your remote shore, which we already saw looming through the mist and foam of the deep. Then it was at last, that our boat turned short from its course, and rocked with a motion that became more and more wild and dizzy: I know not whether it was overset, or the violence of the motion threw me overboard. In my agony and struggle at the thought of a near and terrible death, the waves bore me onward, till one of them cast me ashore here beneath the trees of your island."

"Yes, an island!" cried the fisherman. "A short time ago it was only a point of land. But now, since the forest-stream and lake have become all but mad, it appears to be entirely changed."

"I observed something of it," replied the priest, "as I stole along the shore in the obscurity; and hearing nothing around me but a sort of wild uproar, I perceived at last, that the noise came from a point, exactly where a beaten foot-path disappeared. I now caught the light in your cottage, and ventured hither, where I cannot sufficiently thank my Father in heaven, that, after preserving me from the waters, he has also conducted me to such pious people as you are; and the more so, as it is difficult to say, whether I shall ever behold any other persons in this world except you four."

"What mean you by those words?" asked the fisherman.

"Can you tell me, then, how long this commotion of the elements will last?" returned the holy man. "And the years of my pilgrimage are many. The stream of my life may easily sink into the ground and vanish, before the overflowing of that forest-stream shall subside. Indeed, taking a general view of things, it is not impossible, that more and more of the foaming waters may rush in between you and yonder forest, until you are so far removed from the rest of the world, that your small fishing-canoe may be incapable of passing over, and the inhabitants of the continent entirely forget you in your old age amid the dissipation and diversions of life."

At this melancholy foreboding, the old lady shrunk back with a feeling of alarm, crossed herself, and cried: "May God forbid!"

But the fisherman looked upon her with a smile, and said: "What a strange being is man! Suppose the worst to happen: our state would not be different, at any rate your own would not, dear wife, from what it is at present. For have you, these many years, been further from home than the border of the forest? And have you seen a single human being besides Undine and myself?—It is now only a short time since the coming of the knight and the priest. They will remain with us, even if we do become a forgotten island; so after all you will derive the best advantage from the disaster."

"I know not," replied the ancient dame, "it is a dismal

thought, when brought fairly home to the mind, that we are forever separated from mankind, even though, in fact, we never do know nor see them."

"Then *you* will remain with us, then you will remain with us!" whispered Undine in a voice scarcely audible and half singing, while with the intense fervour of the heart she nestled more and more closely to Huldbrand's side. But he was absorbed in the deep and strange musings of his own mind. The region, on the other side of the forest-river, seemed, since the last words of the priest, to have been withdrawing further and further, in dim perspective, from his view; and the blooming island on which he lived, grew green and smiled more freshly before the eye of his mind. His bride glowed like the fairest rose,—not of this obscure nook only, but even of the whole wide world, and the priest was now present.

Beside these hopes and reveries of love, another circumstance influenced him: the mistress of the family was directing an angry glance at the fair girl, because, even in the presence of the priest, she was leaning so fondly on her darling knight; and it seemed as if she was on the point of breaking out in harsh reproof. Then was the resolution of Huldbrand taken; his heart and mouth were opened; and turning toward the priest, he said, "Father, you here see before you an affianced pair, and if this maiden and these worthy people of the island have no objection, you shall unite us this very evening."

The aged couple were both exceedingly surprised. They had often, it is true, thought of this, but as yet they had never mentioned it; and now when the knight made the attachment known, it came upon them like something wholly new and unexpected. Undine became suddenly grave, and cast her eyes upon the floor in a deep reverie, while the priest made inquiries respecting the circumstances of their acquaintance, and asked the old people whether they gave their consent to the union. After a great number of questions and answers, the affair was arranged to the satisfaction of all; and the mistress of the house went to prepare the bridal apartment for the young couple, and also, with a view to grace the nuptial solemnity to seek for two consecrated tapers, which she had for a long time kept by her for this occasion.

The knight in the mean while busied himself about his gold chain, for the purpose of disengaging two of its links, that he might make an exchange of rings with his bride. But when she saw his object, she started from her trance of musing, and exclaimed:

"Not so! my parents were far from sending me into the world so perfectly destitute; on the contrary, they must have foreseen, even at so early a period, that such a night as this would come."

Thus speaking, she was out of the room in a moment, and a moment after returned with two costly rings, of which she gave one to her bridegroom, and kept the other for herself. The old fisherman was beyond measure astonished at this; and his wife, who was just re-entering the room, was even more surprised than he, that neither of them had ever seen these jewels in the child's possession.

"My parents," said Undine, "made me sew these trinkets to that beautiful raiment, which I wore the very day I came to you. They also charged me on no account whatever, to mention them to any one before the evening I should be married. At the time of my coming, therefore, I took them off in secret, and have kept them concealed to the present hour."

The priest now cut short all further questioning and wondering, while he lighted the consecrated tapers, placed them on a table, and ordered the bridal pair to stand directly before him. He then pronounced the few solemn words of the ceremony, and made them one; the elder couple gave the younger their blessing; and the bride, slightly trembling and thoughtful, leaned upon the knight.

The priest then spoke plainly and at once: "You are strange people after all; for why did you tell me you were the only inhabitants of the island? So far is this from being true, I have seen, the whole time I have been performing the ceremony, a tall, stately man, in a white mantle, stand opposite to me, looking in at the window. He must be still waiting before the door, if peradventure you would invite him to come in."

"God forbid!" cried the old lady, shrinking back; the fisherman shook his head without opening his lips, and Huldbrand sprang to the window. It appeared to *him*, that he could still discern some vestige of a form, white and indistinct as a vapour, but it soon wholly disappeared in the gloom. He convinced the priest that he must have been quite mistaken in his impression; and now, inspired with the freedom and familiarity of perfect confidence, they all sat down together round a bright and comfortable hearth.

CHAPTER VII.

What further happened on the evening of the wedding.

BEFORE the nuptial ceremony, and during its performance, Undine had shown a modest gentleness and maidenly reserve; but it now seemed as if all the wayward freaks that effervesced within her, were foaming and bursting forth with an extravagance only the more bold and unrestrained. She teased her bridegroom, her foster-parents, and even the priest, whom she had just now revered so highly, with all sorts of childish tricks and vagaries; and when the ancient dame was about to reprove her too frolicksome spirit, the knight, by a few serious and expressive words, imposed silence upon *her* by calling Undine his wife.

The knight was himself, indeed, just as little pleased with Undine's childish behaviour as the rest; but still, all his winking, hemming, and expressions of censure were to no purpose. It is true, whenever the bride observed the dissatisfaction of her husband,—and this occasionally happened,—she became more quiet, placed herself beside him, stroked his face with caressing fondness, whispered something smilingly in his ear, and in this manner smoothed the wrinkles that were gathering on his brow. But the moment after, some wild whim would make her resume her antic movements, and all went worse than before.

The priest then spoke in a kind, although serious tone: "My pleasant young friend, surely no one can witness your playful spirit without being diverted; but remember betimes so to attune your soul, that it may produce a harmony ever in accordance with the soul of your wedded bridegroom."

"SOUL!" cried Undine, with a laugh, nearly allied to one of derision; "what you say has a remarkably pretty sound, and for most people, too, it may be a very instructive rule and profitable caution. But when a person has no soul at all, how, I pray you, can such attuning be possible? And this in truth is just my condition."

The priest was much hurt, but continued silent in holy displeasure, and turned away his face from the maiden in sorrow. She, however, went up to him with the most winning sweetness, and said:

"Nay, I entreat you, first listen to some particulars, before you frown upon me in anger; for your frown of anger is painful to me, and you ought not to give pain to a creature, that has itself done nothing injurious to you. Only have patience with me, and I will explain to you every word of what I meant."

She had come to the resolution, it was evident, to give a full account of herself, when she suddenly faltered, as if seized with an inward shuddering, and burst into a passion of tears. They were none of them able to understand the intenseness of her feelings, and with mingled emotions of fear and anxiety, they gazed on her in silence. Then wiping away her tears, and looking earnestly at the priest, she at last said:

"There must be something lovely, but at the same time something most awful, about a SOUL. In the name of God, holy man, were it not better that we never shared a gift so mysterious?"

Again she paused and restrained her tears, as if waiting for an answer. All in the cottage had risen from their seats, and stept back from her with horror. She, however, seemed to have eyes for no one but the holy man; a fearful curiosity was painted on her features, and this made her emotion appear terrible to the others.

"Heavily must the soul weigh down its possessor," she pursued, when no one returned her any answer, "very heavily! for already its approaching image overshadows me with anguish and mourning. And, alas! I have till now been so merry and light-hearted!"—And she burst into another flood of tears, and covered her face with her veil.

The priest, going up to her with a solemn look, now addressed himself to her, and conjured her in the name of God most holy, if any evil or spirit of evil possessed her, to remove the light covering from her face. But she sunk before him on her knees, and repeated after him every sacred expression he uttered, giving praise to God, and protesting that she wished well to the whole world.

The priest then spoke to the knight: "Sir bridegroom, I leave you alone with her, whom I have united to you in marriage. So far as I can discover, there is nothing of evil in her, but of a truth much that is wonderful. What I recommend to you in domestic life, is prudence, love, and fidelity."

Thus speaking, he left the apartment, and the fisherman with his wife followed him, crossing themselves.

Undine had sunk upon her knees; she uncovered her face and exclaimed, while she looked fearfully round upon Huldbrand: "Alas, you will now refuse to look upon me as your own; and still I have done nothing evil, poor unhappy child that I am!" She spoke these words with a look so infinitely sweet and touching, that her bridegroom forgot both the confession that had shocked, and the mystery that had perplexed him; and hastening to her, he raised her in his arms. She smiled through her tears, and that smile was like the rosy morning-light playing upon a small stream. "You cannot desert me!" she whispered with a confiding assurance, and stroked the knight's cheeks with her little soft hands. He was thus in some degree withdrawn from those terrible apprehensions, that still lay lurking in the recesses of his soul, and were persuading him that he had been married to a fairy, or some spiteful and mischievous being of the spirit-world; but, after all, only this single question, and that almost unawares, escaped from his lips:

"Dearest Undine, pray tell me this one thing; what was it you meant by 'spirits of the earth' and 'Kühleborn,' when the priest stood knocking at the door?"

"Mere fictions! mere tales of children!" answered Undine,

laughing, now quite restored to her wonted gaiety. "I first awoke your anxiety with them, and you finally awoke mine. This is the end of the story and of our nuptial evening."

"Nay, not exactly that," replied the enamoured knight, extinguishing the tapers, and a thousand times kissing his beautiful and beloved bride, while, lighted by the moon that shone brightly through the windows, he bore her into their bridal apartment.

CHAPTER VIII.

The Day after the Wedding.

THE fresh light of morning awoke the young married pair. Undine bashfully hid her face beneath their covering, and Huldbrand lay lost in silent reflection. Whenever during the night he had fallen asleep, strange and horrible dreams of spectres had disturbed him ; and these shapes, grinning at him by stealth, strove to disguise themselves as beautiful females ; and from beautiful females they all at once assumed the appearance of dragons. And when he started up, aroused by the intrusion of these hideous forms, the moonlight shone pale and cold before the windows without ; he looked affrighted at Undine, in whose arms he had fallen asleep, and she was reposing in unaltered beauty and sweetness beside him. Then pressing her rosy lips with a light kiss, he again fell into a slumber, only to be awakened by new terrors.

When he had now perfectly awoke, and well considered all the circumstances of this connection, he reproached himself for any doubt, that could lead him into error in regard to his lovely wife. He also earnestly begged her to pardon the in justice he had done her, but she only gave him her fair hand, heaved a sigh from the depth of her heart, and remained silent. Yet a glance of fervent tenderness, an expression of the soul beaming in her eyes, such as he had never witnessed there before, left him in undoubting assurance, that Undine was innocent of any evil against him whatever.

He then rose with a serene mind, and leaving her, went to the common apartment, where the inmates of the house had already met. The three were sitting round the hearth with an air of anxiety about them, as if they feared trusting themselves to raise their voice above a low apprehensive undertone. The priest appeared to be praying in his inmost spirit, with a view to avert some fatal calamity. But when they observed the young husband come forth so cheerful, a brighter hope rose within them, and dispelled the cloudy traces that remained upon their brows; yes, the old fisherman began to be facetious with the knight, but in a manner so perfectly becoming, that his aged wife herself could not help smiling with great good humour.

Undine had in the mean time got ready, and now entered the door, when they were all on the point of rushing to meet her, and yet all remained fixed in perfect admiration, so changed and at the same time so familiar was the young woman's appearance. The priest, with paternal affection beaming from his countenance, first went up to her, and as he raised his hand to pronounce a blessing, the beautiful bride, trembling with religious awe, sunk on her knees before him; she begged his pardon, in terms both respectful and submissive, for any foolish things she might have uttered the evening before, and entreated him, in a very pathetic tone, to pray for the welfare of her soul. She then rose, kissed her foster-parents, and, after thanking them for all the kindness they had shown her, said: "O, I now feel in my inmost heart, how great, how infinitely great, is what you have done for me, you dear, dear friends of my childhood!"

At first she was wholly unable to tear herself away from their affectionate caresses; but the moment she saw the good old mother busy in getting breakfast, she went to the hearth, applied herself to cooking the food and putting it on the table, and would not suffer her to take the least share in the work.

She continued in this frame of spirit the whole day; calm, kind, attentive;—at the same time a little mistress of a family, and a tender, modest young woman. The three, who had been longest acquainted with her, expected every instant to see her capricious spirit break out in some whimsical change or sportive vagary. But their fears were quite unnecessary. Undine continued as mild and gentle as an angel. The priest found it all but impossible to remove his eyes from her, and he often said to the bridegroom

"The bounty of Heaven, Sir, through me its unworthy instrument, entrusted to you last evening an invaluable treasure; regard and cherish it as you ought to do, and it will promote your temporal and eternal welfare."

Toward evening, Undine was hanging upon the knight's arm with lowly tenderness, while she drew him gently out before the door, where the setting sun shone richly over the fresh grass, and upon the high, slender boles of the trees. Her emotion was visible: the dew of sadness and love swam in her eyes, while a tender and fearful secret seemed to hover upon her lips; but sighs, and those scarcely perceptible, were all that made known the wish of her heart. She led her husband further and further onward without speaking. When he asked her questions she replied only with looks, in which, it is true, there appeared to be no immediate answer to his inquiries, but yet a whole heaven of love and timid attachment. Thus they reached the margin of the swollen forest-stream, and the knight was astonished to see it gliding away with so gentle a murmuring of its waves, that no vestige of its former swell and wildness was now discernible.

"By morning it will be wholly drained off," said the beautiful woman, almost weeping, "and you will then be able to travel, without any thing to hinder you, whithersoever you will."

"Not without you, dear Undine," replied the knight, laughing; "for pray remember, even were I disposed to leave you, both the church and the spiritual powers, the emperor and the laws of the realm, would require the fugitive to be seized and restored to you."

"All this depends on you,—all depends on you;" whispered his little companion, half weeping and half smiling. "But I still feel sure, that you will not leave me; I love you too deeply to fear that misery. Now bear me over to that little island, which lies before us. There shall the decision be made. I could easily, indeed, glide through that mere rippling of the water without your aid, but it is so grateful to rest in your arms; and should you determine to put me away, I shall have sweetly rested in them once more, . . . for the last time."

Huldbrand was so full of strange anxiety and emotion, that he knew not what answer to make her. He took her in his arms and carried her over, now first realizing the fact, that this was the same little island, from which he had borne her back to the old fisherman, the first night of his arrival. On the further side, he placed her upon the soft grass, and was throwing himself lovingly near his beautiful burden; but she said to him, "Not here, but there, opposite to me. I shall read my doom in your eyes, even before your lips pronounce it; now listen very attentively to what I shall relate to you." And she began:

"You must know, my own love, that there are beings in the elements, which bear the strongest resemblance to the human race, and which, at the same time, but seldom become visible to you. The wonderful salamanders sparkle and sport amid the flames; deep in the earth the meagre and malicious gnomes pursue their revels; the forest-spirits belong to the air, and wander in the woods; while in the seas, rivers, and streams live the wide-spread race of water-spirits. These last, beneath resounding domes of crystal, through which the sky appears with sun and stars, inhabit a region of light and beauty; lofty coral trees glow with blue and crimson fruits in their gardens; they walk over the pure sand of the sea, among infinitely variegated shells, and amid whatever of beauty the old world possessed, such as the present is no more worthy to enjoy;—creations, which the floods covered with their secret veils of silver; and now these noble monuments glimmer below* stately and solemn, and bedewed by the water which loves them, and calls

* No reader of English poetry need be reminded of Southey's admirable description of the submarine City of Baly in his Curse of Kehama:

"In sunlight and sea-green,
The thousand palaces were seen
Of that proud city, whose superb abodes
Seemed reared by giants for the immortal gods.
How silent and how beautiful they stand,
Like things of nature."

forth from their crevices exquisite moss-flowers and enwreathing tufts of sedge.

"Now the nation that dwell there, are very fair and lovely to behold, for the most part more beautiful than human beings. Many a fisherman has been so fortunate, as to catch a view of a delicate maiden of the waters, while she was floating and singing upon the deep. He then spread to remotest shores the fame of her beauty; and to such wonderful females men are wont to give the name of Undines. But what need of saying more? You, my dear husband, now actually behold an Undine before you."

The knight would have persuaded himself, that his lovely wife was under the influence of one of her odd whims, and that she was only amusing herself and him with her extravagant inventions. He wished it might be so. But with whatever power of words he *said* this to himself, he still could not credit the hope for a moment; a strange shivering shot through his soul; unable to utter a word, he gazed upon the sweet speaker with a fixed eye. She shook her head in distress, heaved a sigh from her full heart, and then proceeded in the following manner:

"In respect to the circumstances of our life, we should be far superior to yourselves, who are another race of the human family,—for we also call ourselves human beings, as we resemble them in form and features,—had we not one great evil peculiar to ourselves. Both we, and the beings I have mentioned as inhabiting the other elements, vanish into air at death, and go out of existence, spirit and body, so that no vestige of us remains; and when you hereafter awake to a purer state of being, we shall remain where sand, and sparks, and wind, and waves remain. We of course have no souls; the element moves us, and, again, is obedient to our will, while we live, though it scatters us like dust, when we die; and as we have nothing to trouble us, we are as merry as nightingales, little goldfishes, and other pretty children of nature.

"But all beings aspire to rise in the scale of existence higher than they are. It was therefore the wish of my father, who is a powerful water-prince in the Mediterranean Sea, that his only daughter should become possessed of a soul, although she should have to endure many of the sufferings of those who share that gift.

"Now the race to which I belong, have no other means of obtaining a soul, than by forming with an individual of your own the most intimate union of love. I am now possessed of a soul, and I, the very soul itself, thank you, dear Huldbrand, with a warmth of heart beyond expression, and never shall I cease to thank you, unless you render my whole future life miserable. For what will become of me, if you avoid and reject me? Still I would not keep you as my own by artifice. And should you decide to cast me off, then do it now, . . . leave me here, and return to the shore alone. I will plunge into this brook, where my uncle will receive me; my uncle, who here in the forest, far removed from his other friends, passes his strange and solitary existence. But he is powerful, as well as revered and beloved by many great rivers; and as he brought me hither to our friends of the lake, a light-hearted and laughing child, he will also restore me to the home of my parents, a woman, gifted with a soul, full of affection, and heir to suffering."

She was about to add something more, when Huldbrand, with the most heartfelt tenderness and love, clasped her in his arms, and again bore her back to the shore. There, amid tears and kisses, he first swore never to forsake his affectionate wife, and esteemed himself even more happy than the Grecian sculptor, Pygmalion, for whom Venus gave life to his beautiful statue, and thus changed it into a beloved wife. Supported by his arm, and in the sweet confidence of affection, Undine returned to the cottage; and now she first realized with her whole heart, how little cause she had for regretting what she had left, the crystal palaces of her mysterious father.

CHAPTER IX.

How the Knight took his young wife with him.

NEXT morning, when Huldbrand awoke from slumber, and perceived that his beautiful wife was not by his side, he began to give way again to his wild imaginations: these represented to him his marriage, and even the charming Undine herself, as only a shadow without substance, a mere illusion of enchantment. But she entered the door at the same moment, kissed him, seated herself on the bed by his side, and said:

"I have been out somewhat early this morning, to see whether my uncle keeps his word. He has already restored the waters of the flood to his own calm channel, and he now flows through the forest, a rivulet as before, in a lonely and dreamlike current. His friends too, both of the water and the air, have resumed their usual peaceful tenor; all in this region will again proceed with order and tranquillity; and you can travel homeward without fear of the flood, whenever you choose."

It seemed to the mind of Huldbrand, that he must be wrapt in some reverie or waking dream, so little was he able to understand the nature of his wife's strange relative. Notwithstanding this, he made no remark upon what she had told him, and the infinite charm of her beauty, gentleness, and affection soon lulled every misgiving to rest.

Some time afterward, while he was standing with her before the door, and surveying the verdant point of land with its boundary of bright waters, such a feeling of bliss came over him in this cradle of his love, that he exclaimed:

"Shall we then, so early as to-day, begin our journey?

Why should we? It is probable, that abroad in the world we shall find no days more delightful, than those we have spent in this little green isle, so secret and so secure. Let us remain here, and see the sun go down two or three times more."

"Just as my lord shall command," replied Undine meekly. "Only we must remember, that our aged friends will, at all events, see me depart with pain; and should they now, for the first time, discover the true soul in me, and how fervently I can now love and honour them, their feeble eyes would surely become blind with weeping. As yet, they consider my present calm and exemplary conduct as of no better promise than my former occasional quietness,—merely the calm of the lake—just while the air remains tranquil,—and they will soon learn to cherish a little tree or flower, as they have cherished me. Let me not, then, make known to them this newly bestowed, this love-inspired heart, at the very moment they must lose it for this world; and how could I conceal what I have gained, if we continued longer together?"

Huldbrand yielded to her representation, and went to the aged couple to confer with them respecting his journey, on which he proposed to set out that very hour. The priest offered himself as a companion of the young married pair; and, after their taking a short farewell, he held the bridle, while the knight lifted his beautiful wife upon his horse; and with rapid step they crossed the dry channel with her toward the forest. Undine wept in silent but intense emotion; the old people, as she moved away, were more clamorous in the expression of their grief. They appeared to feel, at the moment of separation, all that they were losing in their affectionate foster-daughter.

The three travellers reached the thickest shades of the forest without interchanging a word. It must have been a picturesque sight, in that hall of leafy verdure, to see this lovely woman's form sitting on the noble and richly ornamented steed, on her right hand the venerable priest in the white garb of his order, on her left the blooming young knight, clad in splendid raiment of scarlet, gold, and violet, girt with a sword that flashed in the sun, and attentively walking beside her. Huldbrand had no eyes but for his fair wife; Undine, who had dried her tears of tenderness, had no eyes but for him; and they soon entered into the still and voiceless converse of looks and gestures, from which after some time they were awakened by the low discourse, which the priest was holding with a fourth traveller, who had meanwhile joined them unobserved.

He wore a white gown, resembling in form the dress of the priest's order, except that his hood hung very low over his face, and that the whole drapery floated in such wide folds around him, as obliged him every moment to gather it up and throw it over his arm, or by some management of this sort to get it out of his way, and still it did not seem in the least to impede his movement. When the young couple became aware of his presence, he was saying:

"And so, venerable Sir, many as have been the years I have dwelt here in this forest, I have never received the name of hermit in your sense of the word. For, as I said before, I know nothing of penance, and I think too, that I have no particular need of it. Do you ask me why I am so attached to the forest? It is because its scenery is so peculiarly picturesque, and affords me so much pastime, when, in my floating white garments, I pass through its world of leaves and dusky shadows;—and then a sweet sunbeam glances down upon me, at times, before I think of it."

"You are a very singular man," replied the priest, "and I should like to have a more intimate acquaintance with you."

"And who then may you be yourself, to pass from one thing to another?" inquired the stranger.

"I am called father Heilmann," answered the holy man, "and I am from the cloister of our Lady of the Salutation, beyond the lake."

"Well, well," replied the stranger, "my name is Kühleborn, and were I a stickler for the nice distinctions of rank, I might with equal propriety require you to give me the title of noble lord of Kühleborn, or free lord of Kühleborn,* for I am as free as a bird in the forest, and, it may be, a trifle more so. For example, I now have something to tell that young lady there.' And before they were aware of his purpose, he was on the other side of the priest, close to Undine, and stretching himself high into the air, in order to whisper something in her ear. But she shrunk from him in terror, and exclaimed:

"I have nothing more to do with you."

"Ho, ho," cried the stranger, with a laugh, "you have made a grand marriage indeed, since you no longer know your own relations! Have you no recollection of your uncle Kühleborn, who so faithfully bore you on his back to this region?"

"However that may be," replied Undine, "I entreat you never to appear in my presence again. I am now afraid of you; and will not my husband fear and forsake me, if he sees me associate with such strange company and kindred?"

"You must not forget, my little niece," said Kühleborn, "that I am with you here as a guide; otherwise those madcap spirits of the earth, the gnomes that haunt this forest, would play you some of their mischievous pranks. Let me therefore still accompany you in peace; even the old priest there had a better recollection of me, than you appear to have; for he just now assured me, that I seemed to be very familiar to him, and that I must have been with him in the ferry-boat, out of which he tumbled into the waves. He certainly did see me there, for I was no other than the water-spout that tore him out of it, and kept him from sinking, while I safely wafted him ashore to your wedding."

Undine and the knight turned their eyes upon father Heilmann; but he appeared to be moving forward, just as if he were dreaming or walking in his sleep, and no longer to be conscious of a word that was spoken. Undine then said to Kühleborn: "I already see yonder the end of the forest. We

* "Freiherr," baron. There is something peculiarly whimsical in this quiet humour of 'lord or baron Kühleborn.'

have no further need of your assistance, and nothing now gives us alarm but yourself. I therefore beseech you by our mutual love and good will, to vanish and allow us to proceed in peace."

Kühleborn seemed to be transported with fury at this: he darted a frightful look at Undine, and grinned fiercely upon her. She shrieked aloud, and called her husband to protect her. The knight sprung round the horse as quick as lightning, and, brandishing his sword, struck at Kühleborn's head. But, instead of severing it from his body, the sword merely flashed through a torrent, which rushed foaming near them from a lofty cliff; and with a splash, which much resembled in sound a burst of laughter, the stream all at once poured upon them, and gave them a thorough wetting. The priest, as if suddenly awaking from a trance, coolly observed: "This is what I nave been some time expecting, because the brook has descended from the steep so close beside us,—though at first sight, indeed, it appeared to look just like a man, and to possess the power of speech."

As the waterfall came rushing from its crag, it distinctly uttered these words in Huldbrand's ear: "Rash knight! valiant knight! I am not angry with you; I have no quarrel with you; only continue to defend your charming little wife with the same spirit, you bold knight! you rash blade!"

After advancing a few steps further, the travellers came out upon open ground. The imperial city lay bright before them; and the evening sun, which gilded its towers with gold, kindly dried their garments that had been so completely drenched.

CHAPTER X.

How they lived in the city.

The sudden disappearance of the young knight, Huldbrand of Ringstetten, had occasioned much remark in the imperial city, and no small concern among those of the people, who, as well on account of his expertness in tourney and dance as of his mild and amiable manners, had become greatly attached to him. His attendants were unwilling to quit the place without their master, although not a soul of them had been courageous enough to follow him into the fearful recesses of the forest. They remained therefore at their public house, idly hoping, as men are wont to do, and, by the expression of their fears, keeping the fate of their lost lord fresh in remembrance.

Now when the violent storms and floods had been observed, immediately after his departure, the destruction of the handsome stranger became all but certain: even Bertalda had quite openly discovered her sorrow, and detested herself for having induced him to take that fatal excursion into the forest. Her foster-parents, the duke and dutchess, had meanwhile come to take her away, but Bertalda persuaded them to remain with her until some certain news of Huldbrand should be obtained, whether he were living or dead. She endeavored also to prevail upon several young knights, who were assiduous in courting her favour, to go in quest of the noble adventurer in the forest But she refused to pledge her hand as the reward of the enterprise, because she still cherished, it might be, a hope of being claimed by the returning knight; and no one would consent, for a glove, a ribband, or even a kiss, to expose his life to bring back so very dangerous a rival.

When Huldbrand now made his sudden and unexpected appearance, his attendants, the inhabitants of the city, and almost every one rejoiced: we must acknowledge, indeed, that this was not the case with Bertalda; for although it might be quite a welcome event to others, that he brought with him a wife of such exquisite loveliness, and father Heilmann as a witness of their marriage, Bertalda could not but view the affair with grief and vexation. She had in truth become attached to the young knight with her whole soul, and then her mourning for his absence, or supposed death, had shown this more than she could now have wished.

But notwithstanding all this, she conducted herself like a prudent woman in circumstances of such delicacy, and lived on the most friendly terms with Undine, whom the whole city looked upon as a princess, that Huldbrand had rescued in the forest from some evil enchantment. Whenever any one questioned either herself or her husband relative to surmises of this nature, they had wisdom enough to remain silent, or wit enough to evade the inquiries. The lips of father Heilmann had been sealed in regard to idle gossip of every kind; and besides, on Huldbrand's arrival, he had immediately returned to his cloister: so that people were obliged to rest contented with their own wild conjectures, and even Bertalda herself ascertained nothing more of the truth than others.

For the rest, Undine daily regarded this fair girl with increasing fondness. "We must have been heretofore acquainted with each other," she often used to say to her, "or else there must be some mysterious connection between us; for it is incredible that any one so perfectly without cause,—I mean without some deep and secret cause,—should be so fondly attached to another, as I have been to you from the first moment of our meeting."

Even Bertalda could not deny, that she felt a confiding impulse, an attraction of tenderness, toward Undine, much as she deemed this fortunate rival the cause of her bitterest disappointment. Under the influence of this mutual regard, they found means to persuade, the one her foster-parents, and the other her husband, to defer the day of separation to a period more and more remote; nay more, they had already begun to talk of a plan for Bertalda's sometime accompanying Undine to Castle Ringstetten, near one of the sources of the Danube.

Once on a fine evening, while they were promenading the city by starlight, they happened to be talking over their scheme just as they passed the high trees, that bordered the public walk. The young married pair, though it was somewhat late, had called upon Bertalda to invite her to share their enjoyment; and all three now proceeded familiarly up and down beneath the dark-blue heaven, not seldom interrupted in their converse by the admiration, which they could not but bestow upon the magnificent fountain in the middle of the square, and upon the wonderful rush and shooting upward of its water. All was sweet and soothing to their minds; among the shadows of the trees stole in glimmerings of light from the adjacent houses; a low murmur as of children at play, and of other persons who were enjoying their walk, floated around them; they were so alone, and yet sharing so much of social happiness in the bright and stirring world, that whatever had appeared difficult by day, now became smooth and easy of its own accord, and the three friends could no longer see the slightest cause for hesitation in regard to Bertalda's taking the journey.

At that instant, just as they were fixing the day of their departure, a tall man approached them from the middle of the square, bowed respectfully to the company, and spoke something in the young bride's ear. Though displeased with the interruption and its cause, she walked aside a few steps with the stranger, and both began to whisper, as it seemed, in a foreign tongue. Huldbrand thought he recognized the strange man of the forest; and he gazed upon him so fixedly, that he neither heard nor answered the astonished inquiries of Bertalda. All at once Undine clapped her hands with delight, and turned back from the stranger, laughing: he, frequently shaking his head, retired with a hasty step and discontented air, and descended into the fountain. Huldbrand now felt perfectly certain, that his conjecture was correct. But Bertalda asked: "And what, my dear Undine, did the master of the fountain wish to say to you?"

The young wife laughed within herself, and made answer: "The day after to-morrow, my dear child, when the anniversary of your name-day* returns, you shall be informed." And this was all she could be prevailed upon to disclose. She merely asked Bertalda to dinner on the appointed day, and requested her to invite her foster-parents; and soon afterward they separated.

"Kühleborn?" said Huldbrand to his lovely wife with an inward shudder, when they had taken leave of Bertalda, and were now going home through the darkening streets.

"Yes, it was he," answered Undine, "and he would have wearied me with foolish warnings without end. But in the midst of them, quite contrary to his intention, he delighted me with a most welcome piece of news. If you, my dear lord and husband, wish me to acquaint you with it now, you need only command me, and I will freely, and from my heart, tell you all without reserve. But would you confer upon your Undine a very, very great pleasure, only wait till the day after to-morrow, and then you too shall have your share of the surprise."

The knight was quite willing to gratify his wife, in regard to what she had asked with so beautiful a spirit; and this spirit she discovered yet more, for while she was that night falling asleep, she murmured to herself with a smile: "How she will rejoice and be astonished at what her master of the fountain has told me,—the dear, happy Bertalda!"

* Or saint's day. A literary friend, from whose kindness I have derived the best aid in revising and correcting my version, informs me, that this term "refers to a German custom of celebrating, not only the birth-day, but also the name-day, that is, the day which in the almanac bears the person's Christian name. The old almanacs contained a name for each day in the year, being either the name of a saint, or some other remarkable personage in history."

CHAPTER XI.

Festival of Bertalda's name-day.

The company were sitting at dinner; Bertalda, adorned with jewels and flowers without number, the presents of her foster-parents and friends, and looking like some goddess of Spring, sat beside Undine and Huldbrand at the head of the table. When the sumptuous repast was ended, and the dessert was placed before them, permission was given that the doors should be left open: this was in accordance with the good old custom in Germany, that the common people might see and rejoice in the festivity of their superiors. Among these spectators the servants carried round cake and wine.

Huldbrand and Bertalda waited with secret impatience for the promised explanation, and never, except when they could not well help it, moved their eyes from Undine. But she still continued silent, and merely smiled to herself with secret and heartfelt satisfaction. All who were made acquainted with the promise she had given, could perceive that she was every moment on the point of revealing a happy secret; and yet, as children sometimes delay tasting their choicest dainties, she still withheld the communication, with a denial that made it the more desired. Bertalda and Huldbrand shared the same delightful feeling, while in anxious hope they were expecting the unknown disclosure, which they were to receive from the lips of their friend.

At this moment, several of the company pressed Undine to give them a song. This appeared to her to be quite a well-timed request, and, immediately ordering her lute to be brought, she sung the following words:

"Morning so bright,*
Wild-flowers so gay,
Where high grass so dewy
Crowns the wavy lake's border.

"On the meadow's verdant bosom,
What glimmers there so white?
Have wreaths of snowy blossoms,
Soft-floating, fallen from heaven?

"Ah, see! a tender infant!—
It plays with flowers, unwitting;
It strives to grasp morn's golden beams.—
O where, sweet stranger, where's your home?
Afar from unknown shores,
The waves have wafted hither
This helpless little one.

'Nay, clasp not, tender darling,
With tiny hand the flowers;
No hand returns the pressure,
The flowers are strange and mute.
They clothe themselves in beauty,
They breathe a rich perfume,

* In reading some of the verses of Fouqué, we cannot but remember the question of Hamlet to the player,—'Is this a prologue, or the posy of a ring?' As one example, among many, we may take the original of his miniature picture here:

"Morgen so hell,
Blumen so bunt,
Gräser so duftig und hoch
An wallenden See's Gestade."

These four little lines, descriptive of the scene of Undine's song, simple as they are, cost me more trouble in trying to mould them into a fit English form, than I well like to acknowledge. I made several attempts, without much success, to translate them to my mind. Among these versions, the following had the merit of not being the worst:

'The morning beams in glory,
Where wild-flowers gaily bloom
Where dewy grass is waving
The lake's fresh marge along;'

but after all, the more verbal rendering, as it now stands, seemed to be preferable.

But cannot fold around you
A mother's loving arms ;—
Far, far away that mother's fond embrace.

" Life's early dawn just opening faint,
Your eye yet beaming Heaven's own smile,
So soon your first, best guardians gone ;—
Severe, poor child, your fate,—
All, all to you unknown.

" A noble duke has cross'd the mead,
And near you check'd his steed's career:
Wonder and pity touch his heart ;
With knowledge high and manners pure
He rears you,—makes his castle home your own.

" How great, how infinite, your gain !
Of all the land you bloom the loveliest,
Yet, ah ! that first, best blessing,
The bliss of parents' fondness,
You left on strands unknown."

Undine let fall her lute and paused with a melancholy smile; the eyes of Bertalda's noble foster-parents were filled with tears.

" Ah yes, it was so,—such *was* the morning on which I found you, poor orphan," cried the duke with deep emotion; " the beautiful singer is certainly right; still

' That first, best blessing,
The bliss of parents' fondness,'

it was beyond our power to give you."—

" But we must hear also, what happened to the poor parents," said Undine, as she struck the chords, and sung:

" Through her chambers roams the mother,
Searching, searching everywhere ;
Seeks, and knows not what, with yearning,
Childless home still finding there.

" Childless home !—O sound of anguish
She alone the anguish knows,
There by day who led her dear one,
There who rock'd its night repose.

"Beechen buds again are swelling.*
Sunshine warms again the shore,
Ah, fond mother, cease your searching,
Comes the loved and lost no more.

"Then when airs of eve are fresh'ning,
Home the father wends his way,
While with smiles his woe he's veiling,
Gushing tears his heart betray.

"Well he knows, within his dwelling,
Still as death he'll find the gloom,
Only hear the mother moaning,—
No sweet babe to *smile* him home."

"O tell me, in the name of Heaven tell me, Undine, where are my parents?" cried the weeping Bertalda. "You certainly know; you must have discovered them, all wonderful as you are, for otherwise you would never have thus torn my heart. Can they be already here? May I believe it possible?" Her eye glanced rapidly over the brilliant company, and rested upon a lady of high rank, who was sitting next to her foster-father.

Then, inclining her head, Undine beckoned toward the door, while her eyes overflowed with the sweetest emotion. "Where are the poor parents waiting?" she asked; and the old fisherman, diffident and hesitating, advanced with his wife from the crowd of spectators. Swift as the rush of hope within them they threw a look of inquiry, now at Undine, and now at the beautiful lady, who was said to be their daughter.

"It is she! it is she there before you!" exclaimed the restorer of their child, her voice half choked with rapture; and both the aged parents embraced their recovered daughter, weeping aloud and praising God.

But, shocked and indignant, Bertalda tore herself from their arms. Such a discovery was too much for her proud spirit to

* For the epithet 'swelling,' I should prefer to read 'greening,' as 'grünen' is the more picturesque expression of the original, had I found any authority to justify me in its use.

bear,—especially at the moment when she had doubtless expected to see her former splendour increased, and when hope was picturing to her nothing less brilliant than a royal canopy and a crown. It seemed to her as if her rival had contrived all this, and with the special view to humble her before Huldbrand and the whole world. She reproached Undine; she reviled the old people; and even such offensive words as "deceiver, bribed and perjured imposters," burst from her lips.

The aged wife of the fisherman then said to herself, but in a very low voice: "Ah, my God! what a wicked vixen of a woman she has grown! and yet I feel in my heart, that she is my child."

The old fisherman, however, had meanwhile folded his hands, and offered up a silent prayer, that she might *not* be his daughter.

Undine, faint and pale as death, turned from the parents to Bertalda, from Bertalda to the parents; she was suddenly cast down from all that heaven of happiness, of which she had been dreaming, and plunged into an agony of terror and disappointment, which she had never known even in dreams.

"Have you a soul? Can you really have a soul, Bertalda?" she cried again and again to her angry friend, as if with vehement effort she would rouse her from a sudden delirium or some distracting dream, and restore her to recollection.

But when Bertalda became every moment only more and more enraged, as the disappointed parents began to weep aloud, and the company with much warmth of dispute, were espousing opposite sides, she begged with such earnestness and dignity, for the liberty of speaking in this her husband's dining-hall, that all around her were in an instant hushed to silence. She then advanced to the upper end of the table, where, both humbled and haughty, Bertalda had seated herself, and, while every eye was fastened upon her, spoke in the following manner:

"My friends, you appear dissatisfied and disturbed; and you are interrupting with your strife a festivity, that I had hoped would bring joy both to you and myself. Ah, my God! I knew nothing of these your heartless maxims, these your unnatural ways of thinking, and never so long as I live, I fear, shall I become reconciled to them. The disclosure I have made, it seems, is unwelcome to you; but I am not to blame for such a result. Believe me, little as you may imagine this to be the case, it is wholly owing to yourselves. One word more, therefore, is all I have to add, but this is one that must be spoken:—I have uttered nothing but truth. Of the certainty of the fact I give you the strongest assurance; no other proof can I or will I produce; but this I will affirm in the presence of God. The person who gave me this information, was the very same who decoyed the infant Bertalda into the water, and who, after thus taking her from her parents, placed her on the green grass of the meadow, where he knew the duke was to pass."

"She is an enchantress," cried Bertalda, "a witch, that has intercourse with evil spirits. This she acknowledges herself."

"Never! I deny it," replied Undine, while a whole heaven of innocence and truth beamed from her eyes. "I am no witch; look upon me, and say if I am."

"Then she utters both falsehood and folly," cried Bertalda, "and she is unable to prove that I am the child of these low people. My noble parents, I entreat you to take me from this company, and out of this city, where they do nothing but expose me to shame."

But the aged duke, a man of honourable feeling, remained unmoved, and his lady remarked: "We must thoroughly examine into this matter. God forbid, that we should move a step from this hall, before we do so."

Encouraged by this kind word, the aged wife of the fisherman drew near, made a low obeisance to the dutchess, and said: "Exalted and pious lady, you have opened my heart. Permit me to tell you, that if this evil-disposed maiden is my daughter, she has a mark, like a violet, between her shoulders, and another of the same kind on the instep of her left foot. If she will only consent to go out of the hall with me——"

"I will not consent to uncover myself before the peasant woman," interrupted Bertalda, haughtily turning her back upon her.

"But before me you certainly will," replied the dutchess, gravely. "You will follow me into that room, young woman, and the worthy old lady shall go with us."

The three disappeared, and the rest continued where they were, in the hush of breathless expectation. In a few minutes the females returned, Bertalda pale as death, and the dutchess said: "Justice must be done; I therefore declare, that our lady hostess has spoken the exact truth. Bertalda is the fisherman's daughter; no further proof is required; and this is all, of which on the present occasion you need to be informed."

The princely pair went out with their adopted daughter; the fisherman, at a sign from the duke, followed them with his wife. The other guests retired in silence, or but half suppressing their murmurs, while Undine, weeping as if her heart would break, sunk into the arms of Huldbrand.

CHAPTER XII.

How they departed from the city.

THE lord of Ringstetten would certainly have been more gratified, had the events of this day been different; but even such as they now were, he could by no means look upon them as unwelcome, since his fair wife had discovered so much natural feeling, kindness of spirit, and cordial affection.

"If I have given her a soul," he could not help saying to himself, "I have assuredly given her a better one than my own;" and now what chiefly occupied his mind, was to soothe and comfort his weeping wife, and even so early as the morrow to remove her from a place, which, after this cross accident, could not fail to be distasteful to her. Yet it is certain, that the opinion of the public concerning her was not changed. As something extraordinary had long before been expected of her, the mysterious discovery of Bertalda's parentage had occasioned little or no surprise; and every one who became acquainted with Bertalda's story, and with the violence of her behaviour on that occasion, was only disgusted and set against her. Of this state of things, however, the knight and his lady were as yet ignorant; besides, whether the public condemned Bertalda or herself, the one view of the affair would have been as distressing to Undine as the other; and thus they came to the conclusion, that the wisest course they could take, was to leave behind them the walls of the old city with all the speed in their power.

With the earliest beams of morning, a brilliant carriage, for Undine, drove up to the door of the inn; the horses of Huldbrand and his attendants stood near stamping the pavement, impatient to proceed. The knight was leading his beautiful wife from the door, when a fisher-girl came up and met them in the way.

"We have no occasion for your fish," said Huldbrand, accosting her, "we are this moment setting out on a journey."

Upon this the fisher-girl began to weep bitterly, and then it was that the young couple first knew her to be Bertalda. They immediately returned with her to their apartment, where she informed them, that, owing to her unfeeling and violent conduct of the preceding day, the duke and dutchess had been so displeased with her, as entirely to withdraw from her their protection, though not before giving her a generous portion. The fisherman, too, had received a handsome gift, and had, the evening before, set out with his wife for their peninsula.

"I would have gone with them," she pursued, "but the old fisherman, who is said to be my father,"— — —

"He certainly is your father, Bertalda," said Undine, interrupting her. "Pray consider what I tell you: the stranger, whom you took for the master of the water-works, gave me all the particulars. He wished to dissuade me from taking you with me to Castle Ringstetten, and therefore disclosed to me the whole mystery."

"Well then," continued Bertalda, "my father,—if it must needs be so,—my father said: 'I will not take you with me until you are changed. If you will leave your home here in the city, and venture to come to us alone through the ill-omened forest, that shall be a proof of your having some regard for us. But come not to me as a lady; come merely as a fisher-girl.' —I will do, therefore, just what he commanded me; for since I am abandoned by all the word, I will live and die in solitude, a poor fisher-girl with parents equally poor. The forest, indeed, appears very terrible to me. Horrible spectres make it their haunt, and I am so timorous. But how can I help it?— I have only come here at this early hour, to beg the noble lady of Ringstetten to pardon my unbecoming behaviour of yesterday. Dear madam, I have the fullest persuasion, that you meant to do me a kindness, but you were not aware, how severely you would wound and injure me; and this was the reason, that, in my agony and surprise, so many rash and frantic expressions burst from my lips.—Forgive me, ah forgive me! I am in truth so unhappy already. Do but consider what I was only yesterday morning, what I was even at the beginning of your yesterday's festival, and what I am at the present moment!"—

Her words now became inarticulate, lost in a passionate flow of tears, while Undine, bitterly weeping with her, fell upon her neck. So powerful was her emotion, that it was a long time before she could utter a word. But at length she said:

"You shall still go with us to Ringstetten; all shall remain just as we lately arranged it; only, in speaking to me, pray continue to use the familiar and affectionate terms,* that we have been wont to use, and do not pain me with the sound of 'madam' and 'noble lady,' any more. Consider, we were changed for each other, when we were children; even then we were united by a like fate, and we will strengthen this union with such close affection, as no human power shall dissolve. Only first of all you must go with us to Ringstetten. In what manner we shall share our sisterly enjoyments there, we will leave to be talked over after we arrive."

Bertalda looked up to Huldbrand with timid inquiry. He pitied the fair girl in her affliction, took her hand, and begged her, tenderly, to entrust herself to him and his wife.

"We will send a message to your parents," continued he, "giving them the reason why you have not come;—and he would have added much more about his worthy friends of the peninsula, when, perceiving that Bertalda shrunk in distress at

* The words of the original are, "nur nenne mich wieder Du," "*only do call me* THOU *again.*" The use of the personal pronouns, *thou* and *thee*, so familiar and endearing in the German idiom, gives an entirely different impression in English. In the conversations of this tale, examples of this peculiarity occur on almost every page. The translator has of course avoided a mode of expression, which most of his readers would feel to be stiff, strange, and unsuitable.

the mention of them, he refrained. Then taking her under the arm, as they left the room, he lifted her first into the carriage, after her Undine, and was soon riding blithely beside them; so persevering was he, too, in urging forward their driver, that in a short time they had left behind them the limits of the city, and with these a crowd of painful recollections; and now the ladies experienced a satisfaction, more and more exquisite, as their carriage rolled on through the picturesque scenes, which their progress was continually presenting.

After a journey of some days, they arrived, on a fine evening, at Castle Ringstetten. The young knight being much engaged with the overseers and menials of his establishment, Undine and Bertalda were left alone. Eager for novelty, they took a walk upon the high rampart of the fortress, and were charmed with the delightful landscape, which fertile Suabia spread around them. While they were viewing the scene, a tall man drew near, who greeted them with respectful civility, and who seemed to Bertalda much to resemble the director of the city fountain. Still less was the resemblance to be mistaken, when Undine, indignant at his intrusion, waved him off with an air of menace; while he, shaking his head, retreated with rapid strides, as he had formerly done, then glided among the trees of a neighbouring grove, and disappeared.

"Do not be terrified, dear Bertalda," said Undine; "the hateful master of the fountain shall do you no harm this time." And then she related to her the particulars of her history, and who she was herself,—how Bertalda had been taken away from the people of the peninsula, and Undine left in her place. This relation, at first, filled the young maiden with amazement and alarm; she imagined her friend must be seized with a sudden madness. But, from the consistency of her story, she became more and more convinced that all was true, it so well agreed with former occurrences, and still more convinced from that inward feeling, with which truth never fails to make itself known to us. She could not but view it as an extraordinary circumstance, that she was herself now living, as it were, in the midst of one of those wild fictions of romance, which she had formerly heard related for mere amusement. She gazed upon Undine with awe, but could not avoid feeling a shudder, which seemed to separate her from her friend; and she could not but wonder when the knight, at their evening repast, showed himself so kind and full of love toward a being, who appeared, after the discoveries just made, more like a phantom of the spirit-world than one of the human race.

CHAPTER XIII.

How they lived at Castle Ringstetten.

The writer of this history, because it moves his own heart, and he wishes it may equally move the hearts of others, begs you, dear reader, to grant him a single favour. Excuse him, if he now passes over a considerable period of time, and gives you only a general account of its events. He is well aware, that, perfectly conforming to the rules of art and step by step, he might delineate the process by which Huldbrand's warmth of attachment for Undine began to decline, and to be transferred to Bertalda; how Bertalda gradually became more and more attached, and met the young man's glance with the glow of love; how they both seemed rather to fear the poor wife, as a being of another species, than to sympathize with her; how Undine wept, and her tears produced remorse in the knight's heart, yet without awakening his former tenderness, so that his treatment of her would discover occasional impulses of kindness, but a cold shuddering would soon drive him from her side, and he would hasten to the society of Bertalda, as a more congenial being of his own race;—all this, the writer is aware, he could describe with the minute touches of truth, and perhaps this is the course that he ought to pursue. But his heart would feel the task to be too melancholy; for, having suffered calamities of this nature, he is impressed with terror even at the remembrance of their shadows.

You have probably experienced a similar feeling yourself, my dear reader, for such is the inevitable allotment of mortal man. Happy are you, if you have rather endured than inflicted this misery, since, in matters of this kind, more blessed is he that receives than he that gives. For when *you* have been the suffering party, and such remembrances come over the mind, only a soft pensiveness steals into the soul, and perhaps a tender tear trickles down your cheek, while you regret the fading of the flowers, in which you once took a delight so exquisite. But of this no more; we would not linger over the evil, and pierce our hearts with pangs a thousand-fold repeated, but just briefly hint the course of events, as I said before.

Poor Undine was extremely distressed, and the other two were far from being happy; Bertalda in particular, whenever she was in the slightest degree opposed in her wishes, attributed the cause to the jealousy and oppression of the injured wife. In consequence of this suspicious temper, she was daily in the habit of discovering a haughty and imperious demeanour, to which Undine submitted in sad and painful self-denial; and, such was the blind delusion of Huldbrand, he usually supported the impropriety in the most decisive terms.

What disturbed the inmates of the castle still more, was the endless variety of wonderful apparitions, which assailed Huldbrand and Bertalda in the vaulted passages of the building, and of which nothing had ever been heard before within the memory of man. The tall white man, in whom Huldbrand but too well recognized Undine's uncle Kühleborn, and Bertalda the spectral master of the water-works, often passed before them with threatening aspect and gestures; more especially, however, before Bertalda, so that she had already several times fainted or fallen ill through terror, and had in consequence frequently thought of quitting the castle. But partly owing to her excessive fondness for Huldbrand, as well as to a reliance on what she termed her innocence, since no declaration of mutual attachment had ever been distinctly made, and partly also because she knew not whither to direct her steps, she lingered where she was.

The old fisherman, on receiving the message from the lord of Ringstetten, that Bertalda was his guest, returned answer in some lines almost too illegible to be deciphered, but still the best his advanced life and long disuse of writing permitted him to form.

"I have now become," he wrote, "a poor old widower, for my beloved and faithful wife is dead. But lonely as I now sit in my cottage, I prefer Bertalda's remaining where she is, to her living with me. Only let her do nothing to hurt my dear Undine,—otherwise she will have my curse."

The last words of this letter Bertalda flung to the winds; but the permission to remain from home, which her father had granted her, she remembered and clung to, just as we are all of us wont to do in like circumstances.

One day, a few moments after Huldbrand had ridden out, Undine called together the domestics of the family, and ordered them to bring a large stone, and carefully to cover with it a magnificent fountain, that was situated in the middle of the castle court. The servants ventured to hint as an objection, that it would oblige them to bring their water from the valley below, which was at an inconvenient distance. Undine smiled with an expression of melancholy.

"I am sorry, dear children," replied she, "to increase your labour; I would rather bring up the water-vessels myself; but this fountain must indeed be closed. Believe me when I say, that it must be done, and that only by doing it can we avoid a greater evil."

The domestics were all rejoiced to gratify their gentle mistress; and making no further inquiry, they seized the enormous stone. While they were raising it in their hands, and were now on the point of adjusting it over the fountain, Bertalda came running to the place, and cried with an air of command, that they must stop; that the water she used, so improving to her complexion, she was wont to have brought from this fountain, and that she would by no means allow it to be closed.

This time, however, while Undine showed her usual gentleness, she showed more than her usual resolution, and remained firm to her purpose: she said it belonged to her, as mistress of the castle, to direct the regulations of the household according to her own best judgment, and that she was accountable in this to no one but her lord and husband.

"See, O pray, see!" exclaimed the dissatisfied and indignant Bertalda, "how the beautiful water is curling and curving, winding and waving there, as if disturbed at being shut out from the bright sunshine, and from the cheerful view of the human countenance, for whose mirror it was created."

In truth, the water of the fountain was agitated, and foaming, and hissing in a surprising manner; it seemed as if there were something within, possessing life and will, that was struggling to free itself from confinement. But Undine only the more earnestly urged on the accomplishment of her commands. This earnestness was scarcely required. The servants of the castle were as happy in obeying their sweet-tempered lady, as in opposing the haughty spirit of Bertalda; and with whatever rudeness the latter might scold and threaten, still the stone was in a few minutes lying firm over the opening of the fountain. Undine leaned thoughtfully over it, and wrote with her beautiful fingers on the flat surface. She must, however, have had something very acrid and corrosive in her hand; for when she retired, and the domestics went up to examine the stone, they discovered various strange characters upon it, which none of them had seen there before.

When the knight returned home toward evening, Bertalda received him with tears and complaints of Undine's conduct. He threw a severe look at his poor wife, and she cast down her eyes in distress. Still she spoke with great firmness: "My lord and husband, you never reprove even a bond-slave, before you hear his defence,—how much less then your wedded wife!"

"Speak, what moved you to this singular conduct?" said the knight, with a gloomy countenance.

"I could wish to tell you, when we are entirely alone," said Undine, with a sigh.

"You can tell me equally well in the presence of Bertalda," he replied.

"Yes, if you command me," said Undine, "but do not command me. Pray, pray, do not!"

She looked so humble, affectionate, and obedient, that the heart of the knight was touched and softened, as if he felt the influence of a ray from better times. He kindly took her arm within his, and led her to his apartment, where she spoke as follows:

"You already know something, my beloved lord, of Kühleborn, my evil-disposed uncle, and have often felt displeasure at meeting him in the passages of this castle. Several times has he terrified Bertalda even to swooning. He does this, because he possesses no soul, being a mere elementary mirror of the outward world, while of the world within he can give no reflection. Then, too, he sometimes observes, that you are displeased with me, that in my childish weakness I weep at this, and that Bertalda, it may be, is laughing at the same moment. Hence it is, that he conceives every sort of wrong and unkindness to exist, and in various ways mixes with our circle unbidden. What do I gain by reproving him? by showing displeasure, and sending him away? He does not believe a word I say. His poor imperfect nature affords him no conception, that the pains and pleasures of love have so mysterious a resemblance and are so intimately connected, that no power on earth is able to separate them. Even in the midst of tears, a smile is dawning on the cheek, and smiles call forth tears from their secret recesses."

She looked up at Huldbrand, smiling and weeping; and he again felt within his heart all the magic of his former love. She perceived it, and pressed him more tenderly to her, while with tears of joy she went on thus:

"When the disturber of our peace would not be dismissed with words, I was obliged to shut the door upon him; and the only entrance by which he has access to us, is that fountain. His connexion with the other water-spirits, here in this region, is cut off by the valleys that border upon us, and his kingdom first commences further off on the Danube, in whose tributary streams some of his good friends have their abode. For this reason I caused the stone to be placed over the opening of the fountain, and inscribed characters upon it, which baffle all the efforts of my suspicious and passionate uncle, so that he now has no power of intruding either upon you, or me, or Bertalda. Human beings, it is true, notwithstanding the characters I have inscribed there, are able to raise the stone without any extraordinary trouble; there is nothing to prevent them. If you choose, therefore, remove it according to Bertalda's desire, but she assuredly knows not what she asks. The rude Kühleborn looks with peculiar ill-will upon her; and should much come to pass that he has imperfectly predicted to me, and which may well happen without your meaning any evil,—I fear, I fear, my dear husband, that you yourself would be exposed to peril."

Huldbrand felt the generosity of his amiable wife in the depth of his heart, since she had been so active in confining her formidable defender, and even at the very moment she was reproached for it by Bertalda. Influenced by this feeling, he pressed her in his arms with the tenderest affection, and said with emotion: "The stone shall remain unmoved; all remains and ever shall remain, just as you choose to have it, my dear, very dear Undine!"

At these long withheld expressions of tenderness, she returned his caresses with lowly delight, and at length said: "My dearest husband, since you are so very kind and indulgent to-day, may I venture to ask a favour of you? Pray observe, it is with you as with Summer. Even amid its highest splendour, Summer puts on the flaming and thundering crown of glorious tempests, in which it strongly resembles a king and god on earth. You too are sometimes terrible in your rebukes; your eyes flash lightning, while thunder resounds in your voice; and although this may be quite becoming to you, I in my folly cannot but sometimes weep at it. But never, I entreat you, behave thus toward me on a river, or even when we are near a piece of water. For if you should, pray consider what the consequences will be: my relations would acquire a right to exercise authority over me. They would tear me from you in their fury with inexorable force, because they would conceive that one of their race was injured; and I should be compelled, as long as I lived, to dwell below in the crystal palaces, and never dare ascend to you again; or should *they send* me up to you,—O God! that would be infinitely more deplorable still. No, no, my beloved husband, let it not come to that, if your poor Undine is dear to you."

He solemnly promised to do as she desired, and, inexpressibly happy and full of affection, the married pair returned from the apartment. At this very moment, Bertalda came with some work-people, whom she had meanwhile ordered to attend her, and said with a fretful air, which she had assumed of late:—

"Well, now the secret consultation is at an end, it is to be hoped the stone may come down. Go out, workmen, and execute your business."

The knight, however, highly resenting her impertinence, said in brief and very decisive terms: "The stone remains where it is." He reproved Bertalda also for the vehemence that she had shown toward his wife. Whereupon the workmen, smiling with secret satisfaction, withdrew; while Bertalda, pale with rage, hurried away to her room.

When the hour of supper came, Bertalda was waited for in vain. They sent for her; but the domestic found her apartments empty, and brought back with him only a sealed billet, addressed to the knight. Trembling with alarm, he tore it open, and read:

"I feel with shame, that I am only the daughter of a poor fisherman. That I for one moment forgot this, I will make expiation in the miserable hut of my parents. Farewell to you and your beautiful wife!"

Undine was troubled at heart. Most earnestly she entreated Huldbrand to hasten after their friend, who had flown, and bring her back with him. Alas! she had no occasion to urge him. His passion for Bertalda again burst forth with vehemence. He hurried round the castle, inquiring whether any one had seen which way the fair fugitive had gone. He could gain no information, and was already in the court on his horse, determining to take at a venture the road by which he had conducted Bertalda to the castle; when there appeared a shield-boy, who assured him, that he had met the lady on the path to the Black Valley. Swift as an arrow, the knight sprung through the gate in the direction pointed out, without hearing Undine's voice of agony, as she cried after him from the window:

"To the Black Valley? O not there! Huldbrand, not there! or if you will go, for Heaven's sake take me with you!"

But when she perceived that all her calling was of no avail she ordered her white palfrey to be instantly saddled, and followed the knight without permitting a single servant to accompany her.

CHAPTER XIV.

How Bertalda returned with the Knight.

THE Black Valley lies secluded far among the mountains. What its present name may be, I am unable to say. At the time of which I am speaking, the country-people gave it this appellation from the deep obscurity produced by the shadows of lofty trees, more especially by a crowded growth of firs, that covered this region of moor-land. Even the brook, which gushed out among the crags, and wound its way down a ravine into the valley, assumed there the same dark hue, and showed nothing of that cheerful aspect which streams are wont to wear, that have the blue sky immediately over them.

It was now the dusk of evening, and the view between the heights had become extremely wild and gloomy. The knight, in great anxiety, skirted the border of the brook; he was at one time fearful, that by delay he should allow the fugitive to advance too far before him; and then again, in his too eager rapidity, he was afraid he might somewhere overlook and pass by her, should she be desirous of concealing herself from his search. He had in the mean time penetrated pretty far into the valley, and might hope soon to overtake the maiden, provided he were pursuing the right track. The fear, indeed, that he might not as yet have gained this track, made his heart beat with more and more of anxiety. In the stormy night, which was now impending, and which always hovered more fearfully over this valley, where would the delicate Bertalda shelter herself, should he fail to find her? At last, while these thoughts were darting across his mind, he saw something white glimmer through the branches on the ascent of the mountain. He felt quite certain, that the object he discerned was Bertalda's robe, and he directed his course toward it. But his horse refused to go forward; he reared with a fury so uncontrollable, and his master was so unwilling to lose a moment, that (especially as he saw the thickets were altogether impassable on horseback) he dismounted, and, having fastened his snorting steed to an elm, worked his way with caution through the matted underwood. The branches, moistened by the cold drops of the evening dew, keenly smote his forehead and cheeks; thunder muttered remotely from the further side of the mountains; and every thing put on so strange and mystic an appearance, that he began to feel a dread of the white figure, which now lay only a short distance from him upon the ground. Still he could see with perfect clearness, that it was a female, either asleep or in a swoon, and dressed in long white garments, such as Bertalda had worn the past day. Approaching quite near to her, he made a rustling with the branches and a ringing with his sword, —but she did not move.

"Bertalda!" he cried; at first low, then louder and louder; still she heard him not. At last, when he uttered the dear name with an energy yet more powerful, a hollow echo, from the mountain-summits around the valley, returned the deadened sound, "BERTALDA!" Still the sleeper continued insensible. He stooped low, with a view to examine her countenance, but the duskiness of the valley and the obscurity of twilight would not allow him to distinguish her features. While with painful uncertainty he was bending over her, a flash of lightning suddenly shot across the valley. By this stream of light, he saw a frightfully distorted visage close to his own, and a hoarse voice struck him with startling abruptness: "You enamoured shepherd, give me a kiss!"

Huldbrand sprang upon his feet with a cry of horror, and the hideous figure rose with him.

"Home!" it cried with a deep murmur; "the fiends are abroad. Home! or I have you!" And it stretched toward him its long white arms.

"Malicious Kühleborn," exclaimed the knight with restored

energy, "if Kühleborn you are, what business have you here! —what's your will, you goblin!—There, take your kiss!"—And in fury he flashed his sword at the form. But the form vanished like vapour; and a rush of water, giving the knight as good a drenching as wetting him to the skin could make it, left him in no doubt with what foe he had been engaged.

"He wishes to frighten me back from my pursuit of Bertalda," said he to himself; "he imagines, that I shall be terrified at his senseless enchantments, and resign the poor distressed girl to his power, so that he can wreak his vengeance upon her at will. But, impotent spirit of the flood! he shall find himself mistaken. What the heart of man can do, when it exerts the full force of its will, the strong energy of its noblest powers, of this the feeble enchanter has no comprehension."

He felt the truth of his words, and that, in thus giving utterance to his thoughts, he had inspired his heart with fresh courage. Fortune too appeared to favour him; for, before reaching his fastened steed, he distinctly heard the voice of Bertalda, where she was now weeping and now moaning not far before him, amid the roar of the thunder and the tempest, which every moment increased. He flew swiftly toward the sound, and found the trembling maiden, just as she was attempting to climb the steep, and striving, to the extent of her power, to escape from the dreadful darkness of this valley. He stepped before her, while he spoke in tones of the most soothing tenderness; and bold and proud as her resolution had so lately been, she now felt nothing but the liveliest joy, that the man, whom she so passionately loved, would rescue her from this frightful solitude, and extending to her his arms of welcome would still cast a brightness over her existence in their reunion at the castle. She followed almost unresisting, but so spent with fatigue, that the knight was glad to support her to his horse, which he now hastily unfastened from the elm: his intention was to lift the fair wanderer upon him, and then to lead him carefully by the reins through the uncertain shades of this lowland tract.

But, owing to the mad appearance of Kühleborn, the horse had become altogether unmanageable. Rearing and wildly snorting as he was, the knight must have used uncommon effort to mount the beast himself; to place the trembling Bertalda upon him was impossible. They were compelled, therefore, to return home on foot. While with one hand the knight drew the steed after him by the bridle, he supported the tottering Bertalda with the other. She exerted all the strength she had remaining, in order to escape from this vale of terrors as speedily as possible; but weariness weighed her down like lead, and a universal trembling seized her limbs, partly in consequence of what she had suffered from the extreme harassment with which Kühleborn had pursued her, and in part from her continual fear, arising from the roar of the tempest and thunder amid the mountain forest.

At last she slid from the arm of her conductor; and, sinking upon the moss, she said: "I can no more; let me lie here, my noble lord. I suffer the punishment due to my folly, and nothing can save me now; I must perish here through faintness and dismay."

"Never, my sweet friend, will I leave you," cried Huldbrand, vainly trying to restrain the furious animal he was leading; for the horse was all in a foam, and began to chafe more ungovernably than before, till the knight was glad merely to keep him at such a distance from the exhausted maiden, as would secure her from still greater fear and alarm. But hardly had he withdrawn five steps with the frantic steed, when she began to call after him in the most sorrowful accents, fearful that he would actually leave her in this horrible wilderness. He was wholly at a loss what course to take. Gladly would he have given the enraged beast his liberty,—he would have let him rush away amid the night, and exhaust his fury,—had he not shuddered at the thought, that in this narrow defile his iron-shod hoofs might come trampling and thundering over the very spot where Bertalda lay.

While he was in this extreme peril and embarrassment, a feeling of delight, not to be expressed, shot through him, when he heard the rumbling wheels of a wagon, as it came slowly descending the stony slope behind them. He called out for help: answer was returned in the deep voice of a man, bidding them have patience, but promising assistance; and two horses of grayish white soon after shone through the bushes, and near them their driver in the white frock of a carter; and next appeared a great sheet of white linen, with which the goods he seemed to be conveying, were covered. The whitish grays, in obedience to a shout from their master, stood still. He came up to the knight, and aided him in checking the fury of the foaming charger.

"I know well enough," said he, "what is the matter with the brute. The first time I travelled this way, my horses were just as wilful and headstrong as yours. The reason is, there is a water-spirit haunts this valley, and a wicked wight they say he is, who takes delight in mischief and witcheries of this sort. But I have learned a charm; and if you will let me whisper it in your horse's ear, he will stand just as quiet as my silver grays there."

"Try your luck, then, and help us as quick as possible!" said the impatient knight.

Upon this the wagoner drew down the head of the rearing courser close to his own, and spoke some half-dozen words in his ear. The animal instantly stood still and subdued; only his quick panting and smoking sweat showed his recent violence.

Huldbrand had little time to inquire, by what means this had been effected. He agreed with the man, that he should take Bertalda in his wagon, where, as he said, a quantity of soft cotton was stowed, and he might in this way convey her to Castle Ringstetten; the knight could accompany them on horseback. But the horse appeared to be too much exhausted to carry his master so far. Seeing this, the man advised him to mount the wagon with Bertalda. The horse could be tied to it behind.

"It is down hill," said he, "and the load for my grays will therefore be light."

The knight accepted his offer, and entered the wagon with Bertalda; the horse followed quietly after, while the wagoner, sturdy and attentive, walked beside them.

Amid the silence and deepening obscurity of the night, the tempest became more and more remote and hushed; in the comfortable feeling of their security and their commodious passage, a confidential conversation arose between Huldbrand and Bertalda. He reproved her in the most gentle and affectionate terms for her resentful flight; she excused herself with humility and feeling; and from every tone of her voice it was evident,—just as a lamp guides a lover amid the secrecy of night to his waiting mistress,—that she still cherished her former affection for him. The knight felt the *sense* of what she said far more than the *words* themselves, and he answered simply to this sense,—to the feeling and not the confession of love.

In the midst of this interchange of murmured feelings, the wagoner suddenly shouted with a startling voice: "Up, my grays, up with your feet! Hey, my hearts, now together, show your spirit! Do it handsomely! remember who you are!"

The knight bent over the side of the wagon, and saw that the horses had dashed into the midst of a foaming stream, and were, indeed, almost swimming, while the wheels of the wagon were rushing round and flashing like mill-wheels, and the teamster had got on before to avoid the swell of the flood.

"What sort of a road is this? It leads into the middle of the stream!" cried Huldbrand to his guide.

"Not at all, Sir," returned he with a laugh, "it is just the contrary. The stream is running in the middle of our road. Only look about you, and see how all is overflowed."

The whole valley, in fact, was covered and in commotion, as the waters, suddenly raised and visibly rising, swept over it.

"It is Kühleborn, that devil of a water-spirit, who wishes to drown us!" exclaimed the knight. "Have you no charm of protection against him, companion?"

"Charm! to be sure I have one," answered the wagoner "but I cannot and must not make use of it, before you know who I am."

"Is this a time for riddles?" cried the knight. "The flood is every moment rising higher and higher, and what does it concern *me* to know who *you* are?"

"But mayhap it does concern you though," said the guide, "for I AM KÜHLEBORN."

Thus speaking, he thrust his face into the wagon, and laughed with every feature distorted; but the wagon remained a wagon no longer, the grayish white horses were horses no longer; all was transformed to foam,—all sunk into the waves that rushed and hissed around them,—while the wagoner himself, rising in the form of a gigantic surge, dragged the vainly struggling courser under the waters, then rose again huge as a liquid tower, burst over the heads of the floating pair, and was on the point of burying them irrecoverably beneath it.

At that instant, the soft voice of Undine was heard through the uproar; the moon emerged through the clouds, and by its light Undine became visible on the heights above the valley. She rebuked, she threatened the flood below her: the menacing and tower-like billow vanished muttering and murmuring; the waters gently flowed away under the beams of the moon; while Undine, like a hovering white dove, came sweeping down from the hill, raised the knight and Bertalda, and supported them to a green spot of turf, where, by her earnest efforts, she soon restored them, and dispelled their terrors. She then assisted Bertalda to mount the white palfrey, on which she had herself been borne to the valley, and thus all three returned homeward to Castle Ringstetten.

CHAPTER XV.

Passage down the Danube to Vienna.

After this last adventure, they lived at the castle undisturbed and in peaceful enjoyment. The knight was more and more impressed with the heavenly goodness of his wife, which she had so nobly shown by her instant pursuit, and by the rescue she had effected in the Black Valley, where the power of Kühleborn again commenced. Undine herself felt that peace and security which the mind never fails to experience, so long as it has the consciousness of being in the path of rectitude; and she had this additional comfort, that, in the newly awakened love and regard of her husband, Hope and Joy were rising upon her with their myriad beams of promise.

Bertalda, on the other hand, showed herself grateful, humble, and timid, without taking to herself any merit for so-doing. Whenever Hulbrand or Undine began to explain to her their reason for covering the fountain, or their adventures in the Black Valley, she would earnestly entreat them to spare her the recital, since the fountain had occasioned her too much shame, and the Black Valley too much terror, to be made topics of conversation. With respect to these, therefore, she learnt nothing further from either of them; and why was it necessary that she should be informed? Peace and Happiness had visibly taken up their abode at Castle Ringstetten. They enjoyed their present blessings in perfect security; and in relation to the future, they now imagined it impossible, that life could produce any thing but pleasant flowers and fruits.

In this grateful union of friendship and affection, winter came and passed away; and spring, with its foliage of tender green and its heaven of softest blue, succeeded to gladden the hearts of the inmates of the castle. The season was in harmony with their minds, and their minds imparted their own hue and tone to the season. What wonder, then, that its storks and swallows inspired them also with a disposition to travel! On a bright morning, while they were taking a walk down to one of the sources of the Danube, Huldbrand spoke of the magnificence of this noble stream, how it continued swelling as it flowed through countries enriched by its waters, with what splendour Vienna rose and sparkled on its banks, and how it grew lovelier and more imposing almost the whole of its progress.

"It must be glorious to trace its course down to Vienna!" Bertalda exclaimed with warmth; but, immediately resuming the humble and modest demeanour she had recently shown, she paused and blushed in silence.

This slight circumstance was extremely touching to Undine; and with the liveliest wish to gratify her friend, she said: "And who or what shall prevent our taking this little voyage?"

Bertalda leapt up with delight, and the two females the same moment began painting this enchanting trip on the Danube in the most brilliant colours. Huldbrand, too, agreed to the project with pleasure; only he once whispered with something of alarm in Undine's ear: "But, at that distance, Kühleborn becomes possessed of his power again?"

"Let him come, let him come," she answered with a laugh; "I shall be there, and he dares do none of his mischief in my presence."

Thus was the last impediment removed; they prepared for the expedition, and soon set out upon it with lively spirits and the brightest hopes.

But be not surprised, O man, if events almost always happen very differently from what you expect. That malign power, which lies in ambush for our destruction, delights to lull its chosen victim asleep with sweet songs and golden delusions: while, on the other hand, the messenger of Heaven, sent to rescue us from peril, often thunders at our door with the violence of alarm and terror

During the first days of their passage down the Danube, they were unusually gratified. The further they advanced upon the waters of this proud river, the views became more and more picturesque and attractive. But here, amid scenes otherwise most delicious, and from which they had promised themselves the purest delight, here again the stubborn Kühleborn, dropping all disguise, began to show his power of annoying them. He had no other means of doing this, indeed, than mere tricks and illusions, for Undine often rebuked the swelling waves or the contrary winds, and then the insolence of the enemy was instantly humbled and subdued; but his attacks were renewed, and Undine's reproofs again became necessary; so that the pleasure of this little water-party was completely destroyed. The boatmen, too, were continually whispering to one another in dismay, and eyeing their three superiors with distrust; while even the servants began more and more to form dismal surmises, and to watch their master and mistress with looks of suspicion.

Huldbrand often said to himself, in the silence of his soul: "This comes to pass, when like marries not like,—when a man forms an unnatural union with a female of the sea." Still, excusing himself, as we are most of us so fond of doing, he frequently pursued a train of thought like this: "I did not in fact know that she *was* a maid of the sea. It is my misfortune, that all my steps are haunted and disturbed by the wild humours of her kindred, but it is not my crime."

Making reflections like these, he felt himself in some measure strengthened; but, on the other hand, he only the more entertained a feeling of ill-humour against Undine, almost amounting to malevolence. He cast upon her glances of fretfulness and ill-nature, and the unhappy wife but too well understood their meaning.

One day, grieved by this unkindness, as well as exhausted by her continual exertions to foil the artifices of Kühleborn, while rocked and soothed by the gentle motion of the bark, she toward evening fell into a deep slumber. But hardly had she closed her eyes, when every person in the boat, in whatever direction he might look upon the water, saw the head of a man, beyond imagination frightful: each head rose out of the waves, not like that of a person swimming, but quite perpendicular, as if firmly fastened to the watery mirror, and yet moving on with the bark. Every one wished to show to his companion what terrified himself, and each perceived the same expression of horror on the face of the other, only his hand and eye were directed to a different quarter, as if to a point where the monster, half laughing and half threatening, rose opposite to himself.

When, however, they wished to make one another understand the sight, and all cried out, "Look there!" "No, there!" the frightful heads all became visible to each, and the whole river around the boat swarmed with the most horrible faces. All raised a scream of terror at the sight, and Undine started from sleep. The moment she opened her eyes upon the mad group, the deformed visages disappeared. But Huldbrand was made furious by so many hideous visions. He would have burst out in wild imprecations, had not Undine, with the most submissive air, and in the gentlest tone of supplication, thus entreated him:

"For God's sake, my husband, do not express displeasure against me here,—we are on the water."

The knight was silent and sat down, absorbed in deep thought. Undine whispered in his ear: "Would it not be better, my love, to give up this foolish voyage, and return to Castle Ringstetten in peace?"

But Huldbrand murmured wrathfully: "So I must become a prisoner in my own castle? and not be allowed to breathe a moment but while the fountain is covered? Would to Heaven that your cursed kindred"——

At these fatal words, Undine pressed her fair hand on his lips with the most touching tenderness. He said no more, but, assuming an air of composure, pondered on all that Undine had lately warned him to avoid.

Bertalda, meanwhile, had given herself up to a crowd of wild and wandering thoughts. Of Undine's origin she knew a good deal, but not the whole; and the terrible Kühleborn especially remained to her an awful, an impenetrable mystery; never, indeed, had she once heard his name. Musing upon this series of wonders, she unclasped, without being fully conscious of what she was doing, a gold necklace, which Huldbrand, on one of the preceding days of their passage, had bought for her of a travelling trader; and she was now letting it swing in sport just over the surface of the stream, while, in her dreamy mood, she enjoyed the bright reflection it threw on the water, so clear beneath the glow of evening. That instant, a huge hand flashed suddenly up from the Danube, seized the necklace in its grasp, and vanished with it beneath the flood. Bertalda shrieked aloud, and a laugh of mockery and contempt came pealing up from the depth of the river.*

The knight could now restrain his wrath no longer. He started up, gazed fiercely upon the deep, poured forth a torrent of reproaches, heaped curses upon all who interfered with his

* This fine passage of Fouqué bears a strong resemblance to a finer one in Southey's THALABA, Book V.

"And he drew off Abdaldar's ring,
And cast it in the gulf.
A skinny hand came up,
And caught it as it fell,
And peals of devilish laughter shook the cave."

The reader, if he take any interest in the coincidences of genius, may like to compare with these passages, the following verse from king Arthur's death in PERCY'S RELIQUES:

"A hande and an arme did meet the sworde,
And flourish'd three times in the air;
Then sunke beneathe the renninge streme,
And of the duke was seene noe mair."

See also this same incident of the HAND very strongly pictured in Tennyson's MORTE D'ARTHUR. The whole poem, indeed, is so full of power, beauty, and tenderness, that we hope the author will take a hint from it, as a suggestion of his good genius, relative to his talent in this style of composition.

friends or troubled his life, and dared them all, water-spirits or mermaids, to come within the sweep of his sword.

Bertalda, meantime, wept for the loss of the ornament so very dear to her heart, and her tears were to Huldbrand as oil poured upon the flame of his fury; while Undine held her hand over the side of the boat, dipping it in the waves, softly murmuring to herself, and only at times interrupting her strange mysterious whisper, when she addressed her husband in a voice of entreaty "Do not reprove me here, beloved; blame all others, as you will, but here, do not reprove me *here.* Surely you know the reason!" And, in truth, though he was trembling with excess of passion, he with strong effort kept himself from uttering a single word against her.

She then brought up in her wet hand, which she had been holding under the waves, a coral necklace of such exquisite beauty, such sparkling brilliancy, as dazzled the eyes of all who beheld it. "Take this," said she, holding it out kindly to Bertalda; "I have ordered it to be brought, to make some amends for your loss, and do not, dear heart, be troubled any more."

But the knight rushed between them, and, snatching the beautiful ornament out of Undine's hand, hurled it back into the flood, and in a flame of rage exclaimed: "So then, you have a connexion with them forever? In the name of all witches and enchanters, go and remain among them with your presents, you sorceress, and leave us human beings in peace!"

But poor Undine, with a look of mute amazement and eyes streaming with tears, gazed on him, her hand still stretched out, just as it was when she had so lovingly offered her brilliant gift to Bertalda. She then began to weep more and more, as if her heart would break, like a tender, innocent child, very bitterly grieved. At last, all wearied out, she said:

"Alas, dearest, all is over now,—farewell! They shall do you no harm; only remain true, that I may have power to keep them from you. But I, alas, must go away, I must go away, even in this early dawn of youth and bliss. O woe, woe, what have you done! O woe, woe!"

And she vanished over the side of the boat.—Whether she plunged into the stream, or whether, like water melting into water, she flowed away with it, they knew not, her disappearance so much resembled both united, and neither by itself. But she was gone, gliding on with the Danube, instantly and completely; only little waves were yet whispering and sobbing around the boat,* and they seemed almost distinctly to say "O woe, woe! Ah, remain true! O woe!"

But Huldbrand, in a passion of burning tears, threw himself upon the deck of the bark, and a deep swoon soon wrapped the wretched man in a blessed forgetfulness of misery.

* The original of this clause is, "nur flüsterten noch kleine Wellchen schluchzend um den Kahn." If the translator may be allowed to express his admiration, without being considered intrusive, he would say that nothing could have been more exquisitely conceived than this circumstance.

CHAPTER XVI.

What further happened to Huldbrand.

The brief period of our mourning,—ought we to view it as a misfortune, or as a blessing? I mean that deep mourning of the heart, which gushes up from the very well-springs of our being; that mourning, which becomes so perfectly one with the lost object of our affection, that this even ceases to be a lost thing to the sorrowing heart; and which desires to make the whole life a holy office dedicated to the image of the departed, until we too pass that bourne which separates it from our view.

Some men there are, indeed, who have this profound tenderness of spirit, and who thus consecrate their affections to the memory of the departed; but still their mourning softens into an emotion of gentle melancholy, having none of the intenseness of the first agony of separation. Other and foreign images intervene, and impress themselves upon the mind; we learn at last the transitory nature of every thing earthly, even from that of our affliction; and I cannot therefore but view it as a misfortune, that the period of our mourning is so brief.

The lord of Ringstetten learnt the truth of this by experience; but whether he derived any advantage from the knowledge, we shall discover in the sequel of this history. At first he could do nothing but weep, weep as bitterly as the poor amiable Undine had wept, when he snatched out of her hand that brilliant ornament, with which she so beautifully wished to make amends for Bertalda's loss. And then he stretched his hand out as she had done, and wept again like her with renewed violence. He cherished a secret hope, that even the springs of life would at last become exhausted by weeping; and when we have been severely afflicted, has not a similar thought passed through the minds of many of us with a painful pleasure? Bertalda wept with him; and they lived together a long while at Castle Ringstetten in undisturbed quiet, honouring the memory of Undine, and having almost wholly forgotten their former attachment.

Owing to this tender remembrance of Huldbrand, and to encourage him in conduct so exemplary, the good Undine, about this time, often visited his dreams; she soothed him with soft and affectionate caresses, and then went away again, weeping in silence; so that when he awoke, he sometimes knew not how his cheeks came to be so wet,—whether it was caused by *her* tears, or only by his own.

But as time advanced, these visions became less frequent, and the severity of the knight's sorrow was softened; still he might never while he lived, it may be, have entertained any other wish than thus to think of Undine in silence, and to speak of her in conversation, had not the old fisherman arrived unexpectedly at the castle, and earnestly insisted on Bertalda's returning with him, as his child. He had received information of Undine's disappearance, and he was not willing to allow Bertalda to continue longer at the castle with the now unmarried knight. "For," said he, "whether my daughter loves me or not, is at present what I care not to know; but her good name is at stake, and where that commands or forbids, not a word more need be said."

This resolution of the old fisherman, and the fearful solitude, that, on Bertalda's departure, threatened to oppress the knight in every hall and passage of the deserted castle, brought a circumstance into distinct consciousness, which, owing to his sorrow for Undine, had of late been slumbering and completely forgotten,—I mean his attachment to the fair Bertalda; and this he made known to her father.

The fisherman had many objections to make to the proposed marriage. The old man had loved Undine with exceeding tenderness, and it was doubtful to his mind, whether the mere disappearance of his beloved child could be properly viewed as her death. But were it even granted, that her corse were lying stiff and cold at the bottom of the Danube, or swept away by the current to the ocean, still Bertalda would not be guiltless in her death; and it was unfitting for her to step into the place of the poor banished wife. The fisherman, however, had felt a strong regard also for the knight: this, and the entreaties of his daughter, who had become much more gentle and respectful, as well as her tears for Undine, all exerted their influence; and he must at last have been forced to give up his opposition, for he remained at the castle without objection, and a courier was sent off express to father Heilmann, who in former and happier days had united Undine and Huldbrand, requesting him to come and perform the ceremony at the knight's second marriage.

But hardly had the holy man read through the letter from the lord of Ringstetten, ere he set out upon the journey, and made much greater dispatch on his way to the castle, than the messenger from there had made in reaching him. Whenever his breath failed him in his rapid progress, or his old limbs ached with fatigue, he would say to himself: "Perhaps I may still be in season to prevent a sin; then sink not, weak and withered body, before I arrive at the end of my journey!" And with renewed vigour he pressed forward, hurrying on without rest or repose, until, late one evening, he entered the embowered court-yard of Castle Ringstetten.

The betrothed pair were sitting arm-in-arm under the trees, and the aged fisherman in a thoughtful mood sat near them. The moment they saw father Heilmann, they rose with a spring of joy, and pressed round him with eager welcome. But he, in few words, urged the bridegroom* to accompany him into the castle; and when Huldbrand stood mute with surprise, and delayed complying with his earnest request, the pious priest said to him:

* The *betrothed*, are called *bride* and *bridegroom* in Germany.

"Why do I then defer speaking, my lord of Ringstetten, until I can address you in private? There is no occasion for the delay of a moment. What I have to say, as much concerns Bertalda and the fisherman as yourself; and what we cannot avoid hearing at some time, it is best to hear as soon as possible. Are you then so very *certain*, knight Huldbrand, that your first wife is actually dead? It hardly appears so to me. I will say nothing, indeed, of the mysterious state in which she may be now existing; in truth, I know nothing of it with certainty. But that she was a most devoted and faithful wife, so much is beyond all dispute. And for fourteen nights past, she has appeared to me in a dream, standing at my bed-side, wringing her tender hands in anguish, and imploring me with deep sighs: 'Ah, prevent him, dear father! I am still living! Ah! save his life! ah! save his soul!'

"What this vision of the night could mean, I was at first unable to divine; then came your messenger, and I have now hastened hither, not to unite, but, as I hope, to separate, what ought not to be joined together. Leave her, Huldbrand! Leave him, Bertalda! He still belongs to another; and do you not see on his pale cheek the traces of that grief, which the disappearance of his wife has produced there? That is not the look of a bridegroom, and the spirit breathes the presage on my soul: 'If you do not leave him, you will never, never be happy.'"

The three felt in their inmost hearts, that father Heilmann spoke the truth; but still they affected not to believe him, or they strove rather to resist their conviction. Even the old fisherman had become so infatuated, that he conceived the marriage to be now indispensable, as they had so often, during the time he had been with them, mutually agreed to the arrangement. They all, therefore, with a determined and gloomy eagerness, struggled against the representations and warnings of the holy man, until, shaking his head and oppressed with sorrow, he finally quitted the castle, not choosing to accept their offered shelter even for a single night, or indeed so much as to taste a morsel of the refreshment they brought him. Huldbrand persuaded himself, however, that the priest was a mere visionary, and sent at day-break to a monk of the nearest monastery, who, without scruple, promised to perform the ceremony in a few days.

CHAPTER XVII.

The Knight's Dream.

It was at the earliest moment of dawn, when night begins faintly to brighten into morning twilight, that Huldbrand was lying on his couch, half waking and half sleeping. Whenever he attempted to compose himself to sleep, he was seized with an undefined terror, that made him shrink back from the enjoyment, as if his slumber were crowded with spectres. But whenever he made an effort to rouse himself, the wings of a swan seemed to be waving around him, and soothing him with the music of their motion, and thus in a soft delusion of the senses he sunk back into his state of imperfect repose.

At last, however, he must have fallen perfectly asleep; for, while the sound of the swan-wings was murmuring around him, he seemed to be lifted by their regular strokes, and to be wafted far away over land and sea, and still their music swelled on his ear most sweetly. "The music of the swan! the song of the swan!" he could not but repeat to himself every moment; "is it not a sure foreboding of death?" Probably, however, it had yet another meaning. All at once he seemed to be hovering over the Mediterranean Sea. A swan with her loud melody sung in his ear, that this *was* the Mediterranean Sea; and while he was looking down upon the waves, they became transparent as crystal, so that he could see through them to the very bottom.

At this a thrill of delight shot through him, for he could see Undine, where she was sitting beneath the clear domes of crystal. It is true, she was weeping very bitterly, and such was the excess of her grief, that she bore only a faint resemblance to the bright and joyous being she had been, during those happy days they had lived together at Castle Ringstetten, both on their arrival there and afterward, a short time before they set out upon their fatal passage down the Danube. The knight could not avoid dwelling upon all this with deep emotion, but it did not appear that Undine was aware of his presence.

Kühleborn had meanwhile approached her, and was about to reprove her for weeping, when she assumed the boldness of superiority, and looked upon him with an air so majestic and commanding, that he was well-nigh terrified and confounded by it.

"Although I too now dwell here beneath the waters," said she, "yet I have brought my soul with me; and therefore I may well be allowed to weep, little as you may conceive the meaning of such tears. They are even a blessed privilege, as every thing is such a privilege, to one gifted with the true soul."

He shook his head with disbelief of what she said, and, after musing a moment or two, replied: "And yet, niece, you are subject to our laws of the element, as a being of the same nature with ourselves; and, should HE prove unfaithful to you and marry again, you are obliged to take away his life."

"He remains a widower to this very hour," replied Undine, "and he still loves me with the passion of a sorrowful heart."

"He is, however, a bridegroom withal," said Kühleborn, with a chuckle of scorn; "and let only a few days wear away, and anon comes the priest with his nuptial blessing, and then you must go up and execute your share of the business, the death of the husband with two wives."

"I have not the power," returned Undine, with a smile. "Do you not remember? I have sealed up the fountain securely, not only against myself but all of the same race."

"Still, should he leave his castle," said Kühleborn, "or should he once allow the fountain to be uncovered, what then? for doubtless he thinks there is no great murder in such trifles."*

"For that very reason," said Undine, still smiling amid her

* "Denn er denkt gewiss *blutwenig* an alle diese Dinge." 'For he surely thinks *very little* of all these things.' The temptation to render this odd idiom, *blutwenig*, by some equivalent phrase in English, was a whim too strong to be resisted.

tears, "for that very reason he is this moment hovering in spirit here over the Mediterranean Sea, and dreaming of this voice of warning which our conversation affords him. With a view to give him this warning, I have studiously disposed the whole vision."

That instant Kühleborn, inflamed with rage, looked up at the knight, wrathfully threatened him, stamped upon the ground, and then, swift as the passion that possessed him, sprang up from beneath the waves. He seemed to swell in his fury to the size of a whale. Again the swans began to sing, to wave their wings, to fly; the knight seemed to be soaring away over mountains and streams, and at last to alight at Castle Ringstetten, where he awoke upon his couch.

Upon his couch he actually did awake, and his attendant, entering at the same moment, informed him, that father Heilmann was still lingering in the neighbourhood; that he had, the evening before, met with him in the forest, where he was sheltering himself under a booth, which he had formed by interweaving the branches of trees, and covering them with moss and fine brush-wood; and that to the question, 'What he was doing there, since he had so firmly refused to perform the nuptial ceremony?' his answer was:

"There are yet other ceremonies to perform, beside those at the altar of marriage; and though I did not come to officiate at the wedding, I can still officiate at a very different solemnity. All things have their season, and we must be ready for them all. Besides, marrying and mourning are by no means very far from each other, as every one, not wilfully blinded, must know full well."

In consequence of these words and of his dream, the knight made a variety of reflections, some wild and some not unmixed with alarm. But a man is apt to consider it very disagreeable to give over an affair, which he has once settled in his mind as certain, and therefore all went on just according to the old arrangement.

CHAPTER XVIII.

How the Knight Huldbrand solemnized his marriage.

SHOULD I relate to you the events of the marriage festival at Castle Ringstetten, it would seem as if you were viewing a crowded assemblage of bright and joyous things, but all overspread with a black mourning crape, through whose darkening veil the whole splendour appeared less to resemble pleasure, than a mockery of the nothingness of all earthly joys.

It was not that any spectral visitation disturbed the scene of festivity; for the castle, as we well know, had been secured against the mischief and menaces of water-spirits. But the knight, the fisherman, and all the guests, were unable to banish the feeling, that the chief personage of the feast was still wanting, and that this chief personage could be no other than the amiable Undine, so dear to them all.

Whenever a door was heard to open, all eyes were involuntarily turned in that direction; and if it was nothing but the steward with new dishes, or the cup-bearer with a supply of wine of higher flavour than the last, they again looked down in sadness and disappointment; while the flashes of wit and merriment that had been passing at times from one to another, ceased, and were succeeded by tears of mournful remembrance.

The bride was the least thoughtful of the company, and therefore the most happy; but even she, occasionally, found it difficult to realize the fact, that she was sitting at the head of the table, wearing a green garland and gold-embroidered garments, while Undine was lying a corse, stiff and cold, at the bottom of the Danube, or carried out by the current into the ocean. For, ever since her father had suggested something of this sort, his words were continually sounding in her ear; and this day, in particular, they would neither fade from her memory nor yield to other thoughts.

Evening had scarcely arrived, when the company returned to their homes; not dismissed by the impatience of the bridegroom, as wedding parties are sometimes broken up, but constrained solely by painful associations, joyless melancholy, and forebodings of evil. Bertalda retired with her maidens, and the knight with his attendants, to undress; but these young bridemaids and bridemen, such was the gloomy tenor of this festival, made no attempt to amuse bride or bridegroom with the usual pleasantry and frolicksome good-humour of the occasion.

Bertalda wished to awake a livelier spirit; she ordered them to spread before her a brilliant set of jewels, a present from Huldbrand, together with rich apparel and veils, that she might select from among them the brightest and most beautiful for her dress in the morning. The attendants rejoiced at this opportunity of pouring forth good wishes and promises of happiness to their young mistress, and failed not to extol the beauty of the pride with their liveliest eloquence. They became more and more absorbed in this admiration and flattery, until Bertalda at last, looking in a mirror, said with a sigh:

"Ah, but do you not see plainly how freckled I am growing? Look here on the side of my neck."

They looked at the place, and found the freckles, indeed, as their fair mistress had said; but they called them mere beauty-spots, the faintest touches of the sun, such as would only heighten the whiteness of her delicate complexion. Bertalda shook her head, and still viewed them as a blemish.

"And I could remove them," she said at last, sighing. "But the castle-fountain is covered, from which I formerly used to have that precious water, so purifying to the skin. O, had I this evening only a single flagon of it!"

"Is that all?" cried an alert waiting-maid, laughing, as she glided out of the apartment.

"She will not be so frantic," said Bertalda, in a voice of inquiry and agreeably surprised, "as to cause the stone cover of the fountain to be taken off this very evening?"

That instant they heard the tread of men already passing along the court-yard, and could see from the window where the officious girl was leading them directly up to the fountain, and that they carried levers and other instruments on their shoulders.

"It is certainly my will," said Bertalda with a smile, "if it does not take them too long." And, pleased with the thought, that the merest hint from her was now sufficient to accomplish what had formerly been refused with a painful reproof, she looked down upon their operations in the bright moonlight of the castle court.

The men seized the enormous stone, as if they must exert all their strength in raising it; some one of their number indeed would occasionally sigh, when he recollected they were destroying the work of their former beloved mistress. Their labour, however, was much lighter than they had expected. It seemed as if some power, from within the fountain itself, aided them in raising the stone.

"It certainly appears," said the workmen to one another in astonishment, "as if the confined water were become a jet or spouting fountain." And the stone rose more and more, and, almost without the assistance of the work-people, rolled slowly away upon the pavement with a hollow sound. But an appearance, from the opening of the fountain, filled them with awe, as it rose like a white column of water: at first they imagined it to be a spouting fountain in good earnest, until they perceived the rising form to be a pale female, veiled in white. She wept bitterly, raised her hands above her head, and wrung them with anguish, as with slow and solemn step she moved toward the castle. The servants shrunk back, and fled from the fountain; while the bride, pale and motionless with horror, stood with her maidens at the window from which she had been viewing what passed without. When the figure had now come close beneath their room, it looked up to them and uttered the low moaning of misery, and Bertalda thought she recognized through the veil the pale features of Undine. But the mourning form passed on, as sad, reluctant, and lingering, as if going to the place of execution. Bertalda screamed to her maids to call the knight: not one of them dared to stir from her place; and even the bride herself became again mute, as if trembling at the sound of her own voice.

While they continued standing at the window, overpowered with terror and motionless as statues, the mysterious wanderer entered the castle, ascended the well-known stairs, and traversed the well-known halls, her tears ever flowing in silent woe. Alas, with what different emotions had she once passed through these rooms!

The knight had in the mean time dismissed his attendants. Half undressed and in deep dejection, he was standing before a large mirror; a wax taper burned dimly beside him. At this moment he heard a low tapping at his door, the least perceptible touch of a finger. Undine had formerly tapped in this way, when she wished to amuse him with her endearing sportiveness.

"It is all illusion! a mere freak of fancy!" said he to himself. "I must to my nuptial bed."

"You must, indeed, but to a cold one!" he heard a voice, choked with sobs, repeat from without; and then he saw in the mirror, that the door of his room was slowly, slowly opened, and the white wanderer entered, and gently secured it behind her.

"They have opened the fountain," said she in a low tone, "and now I am here and you must die."

He felt in the shock and death-pause of his heart, that this must indeed be his doom; but, covering his eyes with his hands, he cried: "Do not, in my death-hour, do not drive me to distraction with terror. If you have a visage of horror behind that veil, do not lift it! Take my life, but let me not see you."

"Alas!" replied the wanderer, "will you not then look upon me once more? I am as beautiful now as when you wooed me on the peninsula!"

"O would to God it were so!" sighed Huldbrand, "and that I might die by a kiss from you!"

"Most willingly do I grant your wish, my dearest love," said she. And as she threw back her veil, her dear face met his view, smiling with celestial beauty. Trembling with love and the awe of approaching death, the knight stooped to give and receive the embrace. She kissed him with the holy kiss of Heaven; but she relaxed not her hold, pressing him more passionately in her arms, and weeping as if she would weep away her soul. Tears rushed into the knight's eyes, while a thrill both of bliss and agony* shot through his heart, until he at last expired, sinking softly back from her fair arms, and resting upon the pillow of his couch, a corse.

"I have wept him to death!" said she to some domestics, who met her in the anti-chamber; and passing through the terrified group, she went slowly out and disappeared in the fountain.

* The expression of the original is, "lieblichen Wehe," '*a blissful agony*, or '*pang*.' This union of opposite qualities, however bold the conception producing it, and however suited to express the death-pang under such circumstances, forms a *curious felicity*, rather too violent to be often admitted in English. Phrases of this kind are more familiar in German.

CHAPTER XIX.

How the Knight Huldbrand was buried.

Father Heilmann had returned to the castle, as soon as the death of the lord of Ringstetten was made known in the neighbourhood; and he arrived at the very hour when the monk, who had married the unfortunate couple, was hurrying from the door, overcome with dismay and horror.

When father Heilmann was informed of this, he replied: "It is all well; and now come the duties of my office, in which I have no need of an assistant."

He then began to console the bride, now become a widow, small as was the advantage her worldly and light-minded spirit derived from his kindness.

The old fisherman, on the other hand, though severely afflicted, was far more resigned in regard to the fate of his son-in-law and the calamity of his daughter; and while Bertalda could not refrain from accusing Undine as a murderess and sorceress, the old man calmly said: "The event, after all, could not have happened otherwise. I see nothing in it but the judgment of God; and no one, I am sure, could have his heart more pierced by the death of Huldbrand, than she who was obliged to accomplish his doom, the poor forsaken Undine!"

He then assisted in arranging the funeral solemnities, as suited the rank of the deceased. The knight was to be interred in a village church-yard, in whose consecrated ground were the graves of his ancestors: a place which they, as well as himself, had endowed with rich privileges and gifts. His shield and helmet lay upon his coffin, ready to be lowered with it into the grave, for lord Huldbrand of Ringstetten had died the last of his race: the mourners began their sorrowful march, lifting the melancholy wail of their dirges amid the calm unclouded heaven; father Heilmann preceded the procession, bearing a lofty crucifix, while Bertalda followed in her misery, supported by her aged father.

While proceeding in this manner, they suddenly saw, in the midst of the dark-habited mourning females in the widow's train, a snow-white figure, closely veiled, and wringing its hands in the wild vehemence of sorrow. Those next to whom it moved, seized with a secret dread, started back or on one side; and owing to their movements, the others, next to whom the white stranger now came, were terrified still more, so as to produce almost a complete disarrangement of the funeral train. Some of the military escort ventured to address the figure, and attempt to remove it from the procession, but it seemed to vanish from under their hands, and yet was immediately seen advancing again, with slow and solemn step, among the followers of the body. At last, in consequence of the shrinking away of the attendants, it came close behind Bertalda. It now moved so slowly, that the widow was not aware of its presence, and it walked meekly on behind, neither suffering nor creating disturbance.

This continued until they came to the church-yard, where the procession formed a circle round the open grave. Then it was that Bertalda perceived her unbidden companion, and prompted half by anger and half by terror, she commanded her to depart from the knight's place of final rest. But the veiled female, shaking her head with a gentle refusal, raised her hands toward Bertalda, in lowly supplication, by which she was greatly moved, and could not but remember with tears, how Undine had shown such sweetness of spirit on the Danube, when she held out to her the coral necklace.

Father Heilmann now motioned with his hand, and gave order for all to observe perfect stillness, that over the body, whose mound was well-nigh formed, they might breathe a prayer of silent devotion. Bertalda knelt without speaking; and all knelt, even the grave diggers who had now finished their work.

But when they rose from this breathing of the heart, the white stranger had disappeared. On the spot where she had kneeled, a little spring, of silver brightness, was gushing out from the green turf, and it kept swelling and flowing onward with a low murmur, till it almost encircled the mound of the knight's grave; it then continued its course, and emptied itself into a calm lake, which lay by the side of the consecrated ground. Even to this day, the inhabitants of the village point out the spring;—and they cannot but cherish the belief, that it is the poor deserted Undine, who in this manner still fondly encircles her beloved in her arms.

END OF UNDINE.

SINTRAM AND HIS COMPANIONS.

A NORTHERN TALE.

FROM THE GERMAN OF THE

BARON DE LA MOTTE FOUQUÉ.

NOTICE OF SINTRAM.

FROM THE AUTHOR'S PREFACE TO HIS SELECTED WORKS.

"FOLKO of Montfauçon was and is peculiarly endeared to my heart as a true type of that old French chivalric glory which now only emerges in individual appearances, for instance, beautifully, in the Vendéan wars, which, though failing in victory, were rich in honors. With these feelings, the poet could not forbear from arraying him in the colours of his own escutcheon, and assigning to him the emblems of the same, and even in some measure denoting him by his own ancestral name; for Foulqué we were called in old times, which was probably derived, according to our Norman descent, from the Northlandish name Folko, or Fulko; and a castle 'Montfauçon' was among our ancient possessions. But here that only properly concerns the noble pair, Folko and Gabrielle, as interwoven in the tale of 'Sintram.' The tale itself is the offspring of my own fantasy, immediately suggested by Albrecht Durer's admirable wood cut of 'The Knight, Death and Satan,' the birthday gift of a former friend, with the happy proposal that I should frame from it a romance or a ballad. It became more than this; and the present tale shows it to be so, being supported by divers traditions, in part derived to me orally, of the Germanic northern customs in war and festivity, and in many other relationships beside. The legend indicated at the conclusion of the information respecting Sintram, of the terrific stories of the north, transformed into southern splendour and mirthful dreams, would really then have been executed, and arose more clearly from the fantastic tones of a congenial harpsichord-player, who accidentally met the poet. Partly, however, other avocations, partly interruptions from without, have hitherto driven the project into the back ground. But it still lives within me; and now again, from the powerful, and yet child-like harmonies of the Northman Ole Bull, seems to stir more vigorously and brightly than before. Who knows what yet may happen? Meanwhile here gushes from me a song of salutation to one who, honored by me as master, is not less dear to me as a man:—

Profoundly dreampt a youth on Norland waste;
But no—it is not waste where fairy rings
Reflect the past as well as future things,
When love and woe in boding tones are drest.

They greeted him, they kissed him, and retreated;
They left for him an instrument of sound,
Whose forceful strings with highest deeds could bound,
And yet with childish frolics be entreated.

He wakes—the gift he seizes, comprehending
Its sweet mysterious pleasure how to prove,
And pours it forth in pure harmonious blending.

O may'st thou, ever victor, joyful move,
Thou Northland sailor, on life's voyage wending,
Conscious of God within thee and above."

FOUQUÉ

SINTRAM AND HIS COMPANIONS.

CHAPTER I.

In the Castle of Drontheim there were many knights assembled to hold council on the affairs of the kingdom; and after their debate, they remained till past midnight carousing together around the huge stone table in the vaulted hall. A rising storm drove the snow wildly against the rattling windows, all the thick oak doors groaned, the massive locks shook, the castle clock slowly and heavily struck the hour of one.

At that instant a boy, pale as death, with disordered hair and closed eyes, rushed into the hall, uttering a wild scream of terror. He stopped behind the richly-carved seat of the mighty Biorn, clung to the knight with both his hands, and shrieked in a piercing voice, "My knightly father! Death and another are closely pursuing me."

An awful stillness reigned suddenly in the whole assembly, broken only by the agonized shrieks of the boy. But one of Biorn's numerous retainers, an old esquire, known by the name of Rolf the Good, advanced towards the terrified child, took him in his arms, and half chanted this prayer: "Oh, Father! help Thy servant! I believe, and yet I cannot believe." The boy, as if in a dream, at once loosened his hold of the knight; and the good Rolf bore him from the hall unresisting, yet still shedding hot tears, and murmuring confused sounds.

The lords and knights looked at one another in mute amazement, until the mighty Biorn said, in a fierce but scornfully-deriding tone, "Do not suffer yourselves to be disturbed by the appearance of that strange being. He is my only son; and has been in this state since he was five years old: he is now twelve. I am, therefore, accustomed to see him so, though, at the first, I too was disquieted by it. The attack comes upon him only once in the year, and always at this same time. But forgive me for having spent so many words on my poor Sintram, and let us pass on to some worthier subject for our discourse."

Again there was silence during some minutes. Then a solitary voice began here and there to attempt renewing their former conversation, but without success. Two of the youngest and most joyous spirits began a drinking song; but the storm howled and raged so wildly without, that their mirth was soon checked. And now they all sat silent and motionless in the lofty hall; the lamp flickered under the vaulted roof; the whole party of knights looked like pale, lifeless images, dressed up in gigantic armour.

Then arose the chaplain of the castle of Drontheim, the only priest among the knightly throng, and said, "Sir Biorn, our eyes and thoughts have all been directed to you and your son in a wonderful manner; but so it has been ordered by the providence of God. You perceive that we cannot withdraw them, and you would do well to tell us exactly what you know concerning the fearful state in which we have seen your boy. Perchance, such a solemn narration, as I look forward to, might be of much use to our disturbed minds."

Biorn cast a look of displeasure on the priest, and answered, "You are more concerned in the history, than either you or I could desire. Excuse me, if I am unwilling to trouble these light-hearted warriors with such a rueful tale."

But the chaplain approached nearer to the knight, and said, in a firm yet very mild tone, "Sir knight, up to this moment it rested with you to relate, or not to relate it: but now that you have so strangely hinted at the share which I have had in your son's calamity, I must positively request that you will repeat word for word now every thing came to pass. My honor demands such an explanation, and that will weigh with you as much as with me."

In stern compliance, Biorn bowed his haughty head, and began the following narration:—"This time seven years I was keeping the Christmas-feast with my assembled followers. We have many venerable old customs which have descended to us by inheritance from our forefathers; as, for instance, that of placing a gilded boar's head on the table, and making thereon knightly vows of daring and wondrous deeds. Our chaplain there, who in those days used frequently to visit me, was never a friend to keeping up such traditions of the ancient heathen world. Men of his sort were not much in favor in those olden times."

"My excellent predecessors," interrupted the chaplain, "were infinitely more concerned in obtaining the favour of God, than that of the world, and they were not unsuccessful in their aim. By that means they converted your ancestors; and if I can in like manner be of service to you, even your jeering wili not vex me."

With looks yet darker, and an involuntary shudder, the knight resumed: "Yes, yes; I know all your promises and threats concerning an invisible Power; and how they are meant to persuade us to part more readily with whatever of this world's goods we may possess. There was a time when such belonged to me! Occasionally a strange fancy seizes me, and I feel as if ages had passed over since then, and as if I were alone the survivor, so fearfully is every thing changed. But now I recall to my mind, that the greater part of this noble company knew me in my days of happiness, and have seen my wife, my lovely Verena."

He pressed his hands on his eyes, and many thought that he wept. The tempest was now lulled; the soft light of the moon shone through the windows, and her beams played on his wild features. Suddenly he started up, so that his heavy armor rattled with a fearful sound, and he cried out in a thundering voice, "Shall I turn a monk, because she has become a nun?

No, crafty priest; your webs are too thin to catch flies of my sort."

"I have nothing to do with webs," said the chaplain. "In all openness and sincerity have I put heaven and hell before you during the space of six years; and you gave full consent to the step which the holy Verena took. But what all that has to do with your son's sufferings, I have yet to learn; and I wait for your further narration."

"You may wait long enough for that," said Biorn, with a sneer. "Sooner shall ——"

"Swear not!" said the chaplain in a loud commanding tone; and his eyes flashed almost fearfully.

"Hurra!" cried Biorn in wild affright; "Hurra! Death and his companion are let loose!" and he dashed madly out of the chamber, and down the steps. The loud wild notes of his horn were heard summoning his retainers, and presently afterwards the clatter of horses' feet on the frozen court-yard gave token of their departure.

The knights retired, silent and shuddering; while the chaplain remained alone at the huge stone table, engaged in earnest prayer.

CHAPTER II.

After some time had elapsed, the good Rolf returned with slow and soft steps, and started with surprise at finding the hall deserted. The chamber where he had been occupied in quieting and soothing the unhappy child, was in so distant a part of the castle that he had heard nothing of the knight's hasty departure. The chaplain related to him all that had passed, and then said: "But my good Rolf, I much wish to ask you concerning those strange words, with which you seemed to lull poor Sintram to rest. They sounded like sacred words, and no doubt they are, but I could not understand them. 'I believe, and yet I cannot believe.'"

"Reverend Sir," answered Rolf, "I remember that from my earliest years no history in the Gospels has taken such hold of me, as that of the child possessed with a devil, which the disciples were not able to cast out; but when our Saviour came down from the mountain where he had been transfigured, He broke the bonds wherewith the evil spirit had held the miserable child bound. I always felt as if I must have known and loved that boy, and been his playfellow in his happy days: and when I grew older, then the distress of the father on account of his lunatic son laid heavy at my heart. It must surely have all been a foreboding of the wretched state of our young lord, whom I love as if he were my own child; and now the words of the weeping father in the Gospel often come into my mind, 'I believe, Lord, help Thou mine unbelief;' and something of the sort I may very likely have repeated to-day, as a chant or a prayer. Reverend Father, when I reflect how one dreadful imprecation of the father has kept its withering hold on the son, all seems dark before me; but, God be praised! faith and hope again bring light into my mind."

"Good Rolf," said the priest, "I cannot clearly understand what you say about the unhappy Sintram; for I do not know when and how this affliction came upon him. If no oath or solemn promise binds you to secresy, will you make known to me all that is connected with it."

"Most willingly," replied Rolf. "I have long desired to have an opportunity of so doing; but you have been almost always separated from us. I dare not now leave the sleeping boy any longer alone, and to-morrow, at the earliest dawn, I must take him to his father. Will you come with me to our poor Sintram's room?"

The chaplain at once took up the small lamp which Rolf had brought with him, and they set off together along the vaulted passage. When they reached the distant chamber, they found the suffering child fast asleep. As the light of the lamp fell on his countenance, it showed his ashy paleness. The chaplain stood gazing at him for some time, and at length said

"Certainly from his birth his features were always sharp and strongly-marked, but now they are almost fearfully so for such a child. And yet, in spite of the strange expression they give, I cannot help having a kindly feeling towards him, whether I will or not."

"Most true, dear Sir," answered Rolf. And it was evident how his whole heart rejoiced at any words which betokened affection or compassion for his beloved young lord. He proceeded to place the lamp where its light could not disturb the sleeping child, and seating himself close by the priest, he began to speak in the following terms:

"During that Christmas-feast of which my lord was talking to you, he and his followers discoursed much concerning the German merchants, and the best means of keeping down the increasing pride and power of the larger trading-towns. At length Biorn laid his impious hand on the golden boar's head, and swore to put to death without mercy every German trader whom fate, in what way soever, might bring alive into his power. The gentle Verena turned pale, and would have interposed—but it was too late, the fearful word was uttered. And immediately afterwards, as though the great Enemy of souls were determined at once to secure with fresh bonds the wretched being who was thus devoted to him, a warder came into the hall to announce that two citizens of a trading-town in Germany, an old man and his son, had been shipwrecked on this coast, and were now without the gates, asking hospitality of the lord of the castle. The knight could not refrain from shuddering; but he thought himself bound by his rash vow, and by that accursed remnant of heathenism. We, his retainers, were commanded to assemble in the castle-yard, armed with sharp spears, which were to be hurled at the defenceless strangers at the first signal made to us. For the first, and I trust the last time in my life, I refused to obey the commands of my lord; my refusal was uttered in a loud voice, and with the firmest determination. The Almighty, who alone knows whom He will accept, and whom He will reject, gave me at that moment the strength and resolution I needed. And Biorn might perceive whence the refusal of his faithful old servant arose, and that it was worthy of respect. He said to me, half in anger and half in scorn: 'Go up to my wife's apartments: her attendants are running to and fro, perhaps she is ill. Go up, Rolf the Good, and remain with the women, who seem the fittest company for you.' I thought to myself, 'Jest on;' but I went silently the way that he had pointed out to me. On the stairs I was met by two strange and very awful-looking beings, whom I had never seen before; and I am still at a loss to think how they got into the castle. One of them was a great, tall man, frightfully pallid and thin; the other was a dwarf-like man, with a most hideous countenance and features. Indeed, when I collected my thoughts and looked carefully at him, it appeared to me ——"

Low moanings, and convulsive movements of the boy, here interrupted the narrative. Rolf and the chaplain hastened to his bed-side, and perceived that his countenance wore an expression of fearful agony, and that he was struggling in vain to open his eyes. The priest made the sign of the Cross over him, and immediately peace seemed to be restored, and his sleep again became calm and quiet: they both returned softly to their seats.

"You see," said Rolf, "that it will not do to attempt a more precise description of those two awful beings. Suffice it to say, that they went down into the court-yard, and that I proceeded to my lady's apartments. I found the gentle Verena almost fainting with terror and overwhelming anxiety, and I hastened to restore her with some of those remedies which the knowledge God has given me of the healing virtues of many herbs and minerals enabled me to apply. But scarcely had she recovered her senses, when, with that air of calm resolve which you know belongs to her, she desired me to conduct her down to the court-yard, saying that she must either put a stop to the fearful doings of this night, or herself fall a sacrifice. Our way took us by the little bed of the sleeping Sintram. Alas! I cannot keep from tears when I think how evenly his gentle breath then came and went, and how sweetly he smiled in his peaceful slumbers."

The old man put his hands to his eyes, and wept bitterly; but soon he resumed his sad story. "As we approached the lowest window of the staircase, we could hear distinctly the voice of the elder merchant, and on looking out, the light of the torches shewed me his noble features, as well as the bright youthful countenance of his son. "I take Almighty God to witness,' cried he, 'that I had no evil thought against this house! But surely I must have fallen unawares amongst heathens; it cannot be that I am in a Christian knight's castle: and if you are indeed heathens, then kill us at once. And you, my beloved son, be patient and of good courage; in heaven we shall learn why it was ordained that we should meet our fate here without one chance of escape.' I thought I could see those two fearful ones amidst the throng of armed retainers The pale one had a huge curved sword in his hand, the little one held a spear notched in a strange fashion. Verena tore open the window, and the silvery tones of her voice were heard above the storm of that wild night, as she cried out—'My dearest lord and husband, for the sake of your only child, have pity on those harmless men! Save them from a bloody death, and resist the temptation of the Evil Spirit.' The knight answered in his fierce wrath—but I cannot repeat his words. He staked his child on the desperate cast; he called death and the devil to see that he kept his word:—but, hush! the boy is again moaning. Let me bring the dark tale quickly to a close. Biorn commanded his followers to strike, casting on them those fierce looks which have gained him the title of Biorn of the Fiery Eyes; while at the same time the two frightful strangers seemed to bestir themselves in the crowd with more activity than before. Then Verena called out, in the extremity of her anguish, 'Help, O God, my Saviour!' Those two dreadful figures disappeared, and the knight and his retainers, as if seized with blindness, rushed wildly one against the other, but without doing injury to themselves, or yet succeeding in striking the merchants, who had so nearly fallen victims to Biorn's savage cruelty. They bowed reverently towards Verena, and with calm thanksgivings departed through the castle gates, which at that moment had been burst open by a violent gust of wind, and now gave a free passage to any who would go forth. The lady and I were yet standing bewildered on the stairs, when I fancied I saw the two fearful forms glide close by me, but there was such a cloudy, unreal look about them, that I doubted, till Verena called to me: 'Rolf, did you see a tall pale man, and a little hideous one with him, pass just now up the staircase?' I flew after them; but, alas! when I reached the poor boy's room, I found him already in the same state in which you saw him a few hours ago. Ever since, the attack has come on him regularly at this time, and he is in all respects fearfully changed. The lady of the castle did not fail to discern the avenging hand of Heaven in this calamity; and as the knight, her husband, instead of shewing signs of repentance, added each day to the number of his violent deeds, she resolved to take refuge in a cloister; and tnere, by unremitting prayer, to obtain mercy in time and eternity for herself and her unhappy child."

Rolf was silent; and the chaplain said, after some moments' reflection: "I now understand why, six years ago, Biorn confessed his guilt to me in general terms, and consented that his wife should take the veil. Some faint compunction must then have stirred within him, and perhaps the traces of it may yet exist. Anyhow it was impossible that so tender a flower as Verena could remain longer in such rough keeping. But who is there now to watch over and protect our poor Sintram?"

"The prayers of his mother are his safeguard," answered Rolf. "Reverend Sir, when the first dawn of day appears, as it does now, and when the morning breeze plays lightly around, they always bring to my mind the soft-beaming eyes of my lady, and I again seem to hear the sweet tones of her voice.

"And let us add our devout supplications to the Lord," said the chaplain: and he and Rolf knelt in silent and earnest prayer by the bed of the pale sufferer, who soon began to smile as he lay still dreaming.

CHAPTER III.

THE rays of the sun shining brightly into the room, awoke Sintram, and raising himself up, he looked angrily at the chaplain, and said: "So there is a priest in the castle! And yet that accursed dream continues to torment me even in his very presence! A pretty sort of Priest he must be!"

"My child," answered the chaplain in the mildest tone, "I have prayed for you most fervently, and I shall never cease doing so—but God alone is Almighty."

"You speak very impertinently to the son of the great knight, Biorn," cried Sintram. "'My child!' indeed! If those horrible dreams had not been again haunting me, you would make me laugh heartily."

"My young lord," said the chaplain, "I am by no means surprised that you should not recognize me, for in truth neither should I know you again." And his eyes filled with tears as he spoke.

The good Rolf looked sorrowfully in the boy's face, saying, "Ah! my dear young master, you are so much better than you would make people believe. Why did you speak in that way? Your memory is so good, that you must surely recollect your kind old friend the chaplain, who used formerly to be constantly at the castle, and to bring you so many presents—bright coloured pictures of saints, and beautiful songs?"

"I know all that very well," replied Sintram thoughtfully. "My blessed mother was alive in those days."

"Our gracious lady is still living, God be praised!" said the good Rolf.

"But she does not live for us, poor sick creatures that we are!" cried Sintram. "And why will you not call her blessed? Surely she knows nothing about my dreams?"

"Yes, she does know of them," said the chaplain, "and she prays to God on your behalf. But take heed, and restrain that wild, haughty temper of your's. It might, indeed, come to pass that she no longer knew anything about your dreams, and that would be if you were to die; and then the holy angels would also cease to know any thing of you."

Sintram fell back on his bed as if thunderstruck: and Rolf said with a gentle sigh, "You should not speak so severely to my poor sick child, Reverend Sir."

The boy again sat up, and with streaming eyes he turned towards the chaplain, saying in a kind and gentle tone: "Let him do as he pleases, you good tender-hearted Rolf; he knows very well what he is about. Would you reprove him if I were slipping down a rocky precipice, and he were to catch me roughly by the hair of my head in order to save me?"

The priest looked at him with emotion, and was about to give utterance to some kind expression, when Sintram suddenly sprang off the bed and asked after his father. As soon as he heard of the knight's departure, he would not remain another hour in the castle; and when both the chaplain and the old esquire expressed their fears lest a rapid journey should be hurtful to him before he had shaken off the effects of his late attack, he said to them: "Believe me, Reverend Sir, and good old Rolf, if I were not subject to these hideous dreams, there would not be a bolder youth in the whole world; and even as it is, I am not so far behind the very best. Besides, till another year has passed, there is no fear of my dreams again troubling me."

Rolf obeyed a somewhat imperious sign from his young master, and went to prepare the horses. No sooner were they brought out, than the boy threw himself unto his saddle, and taking a courteous leave of the chaplain, he dashed along the frozen valley that lay between the snow-clad mountains. He had not ridden far, in company with his old attendant, when he heard a strange indistinct sound proceeding from a neighbouring cleft in the rock; it was partly like the clapper of a small mill, but mingled with that were hollow groans, and other tones of distress. They directed their horses towards the place whence the sounds came, and a wonderful sight presented itself before them.

A tall man, deadly pale, in a pilgrim's garb, was striving with violent though unsuccessful efforts, to work his way out of the snow, and to get up the mountain; and at each exertion which he made, a quantity of bones, which were hanging loosely all about his garments, rattled one against the other, and caused the mysterious sound already mentioned. Rolf, much terrified, crossed himself, while the bold Sintram called out to the stranger, "What art thou doing there? Give an account of thy solitary labours."

"I live in death," replied that other one with a fearful grin.

"Whose are those bones which hang about thee?"

"They are relics, young Sir."

"Art thou a pilgrim?"

"I have no rest, no quiet; I go up and down the land."

"Thou must not perish here in the snow before my eyes."

"That I will not."

"Thou must come up and sit on my horse."

"That I will do."

And all at once he started up out of the snow with surprising strength and agility, and sprang on the horse behind Sintram, clasping him tight in his long arms. The animal, startled by the rattling of the bones, and as if seized with madness, rushed away through the most trackless passes. The boy soon found himself alone with his strange companion; for Rolf, breathless with fear, spurred on his horse in vain, and remained far behind them. After slipping down the steep mountain side, which was entirely covered with snow, into a narrow defile, the horse seemed somewhat to slacken his pace, but yet continued to snort and foam as before, and could not be controlled. Still, his headlong course being now changed into a rough irregular trot, Sintram was able to breathe more freely, and to begin the following discourse with his unknown companion.

"Draw thy garment closer round thee, thou pale man: the bones will then rattle less, and I shall be able to curb my horse."

"It would be of no avail, boy; it would be of no avail. The bones must rattle."

"Do not clasp me so tight with thy long arms, they are so cold."

"It cannot be helped, boy; it cannot be helped. Be content. For my long cold arms are not pressing yet on thy heart."

"Do not breathe on me so with thy icy breath. All my strength is departing."

"I must breathe, boy; I must breathe. But do not complain. I am not blowing thee away."

The strange dialogue here came to an end; for to Sintram's surprise, he found himself on an open plain, over which the sun was shining brightly, and at no great distance before him he descried his father's castle. While he was doubting as to whether he might invite the unearthly pilgrim to rest there, this one put an end to his hesitation by throwing himself suddenly off the horse, whose wild course was checked by the shock. Raising his fore-finger, he said to the boy:

"I know old Biorn of the Fiery Eyes well: perhaps but too well. Commend me to him. It will not need to tell him my name; he will recognize me by the description you can give of me." So saying, the ghastly stranger turned aside into a thick firwood, and disappeared amongst the tangled branches.

Slowly and thoughtfully Sintram rode on towards his father's castle, his horse being now again quiet and almost exhausted. He scarcely knew how much he ought to relate of his wonderful adventure, and he also felt oppressed with anxiety for the good Rolf, who had remained so far behind. He found himself at the castle-gate sooner than he had expected; the drawbridge was lowered, the doors were thrown open; an attendant led the youth into the great hall, where Biorn was sitting all alone at a huge table, with many flagons and glasses before him, and suits of armor ranged on either side of him. It was his daily custom, by way of company, to have the armor of his ancestors, with closed vizors, placed all round the table at which he sat. The father and son began conversing as follows:

"Where is Rolf?"

"I do not know, father: I lost sight of him in the mountains."

"I will have Rolf shot, if he cannot take better care than that of my only child."

"Then, father, you will have your only child shot at the same time, for without Rolf I cannot live; and if even one single dart is aimed at him, I will be there to receive it, and to shield his true and faithful heart."

"Is it so?—Then Rolf shall not be shot, but he shall be driven from the castle."

"In that case, father, you will see me go away also; and I will give myself up to serve him in forests, in mountains, in caves."

"Is it so?—Well, then, Rolf must remain here."

"That is just what I think, father."

"Were you riding quite alone?"

"No, father; but with a strange pilgrim: he said that he knew you very well—perhaps, too well." And thereupon Sintram began to relate and to describe all that had passed with the pale man.

"I know him also very well," said Biorn. "He is half crazed and half-wise, as we sometimes are astonished at seeing that people can be. But do you, my boy, go to rest after your wild journey. I give you my word that Rolf shall be kindly received if he arrives here; and that if he does not come soon he shall be sought for in the mountains."

"I trust to your word, father," said Sintram, with a mixture of pride and humility in his tone; and he proceeded to obey the command of the grim lord of the castle.

CHAPTER IV.

It was getting towards evening when Sintram awoke. He saw the good Rolf sitting at his bedside, and looked up in the old man's kind face with a smile of unusual innocent brightness. But soon again his dark brows were knit, and he asked: "How did my father receive you, Rolf? Did he say a harsh word to you?"

"No, my dear young lord, he did not—indeed, he did not speak to me at all. At first he looked very wrathful; but he controlled himself, and ordered a servant to bring me food and wine to refresh me, and afterwards to take me to your room."

"He might have kept his word better. But he is my father, and I must not judge him too severely. I will now go down to the evening meal." So saying, he sprang up and threw on his furred mantle. But Rolf stopped him, and said in a tone of entreaty: "My dear young master, you would do better to take your meal to-day alone here in your own apartment. For there is a guest with your father, in whose company I should be very sorry to see you. If you will remain here I will entertain you with pleasant tales and songs."

"There is nothing in the world which I should like better, dear Rolf," answered Sintram, "but it does not befit me to shun the company of any man. Tell me, whom should I find with my father?"

"Alas!" said the old man, "you have already found him in the mountain. Formerly, when I used to ride about the country with Biorn, we often met with him, but I was forbidden to tell you any thing about him; and this is the first time that he has ever come to the castle."

"Oh. the crazy pilgrim!" replied Sintram; and he stood some moments buried in thought, and apparently weighing the whole matter in his mind. At last rousing himself he said: "Dear old friend, I would most willingly stay here with you this evening and listen to your stories and songs, and all the pilgrims in the world should not make me leave this quiet room. But one thing must be considered. I feel a kind of dread of that pale, tall man, and by such fears no true knight's son can ever suffer himself to be overcome. So do not be angry, dear Rolf, if I determine to go and look that strange Palmer in the face." And he shut the door of the chamber behind him, and with firm and echoing steps proceeded to the hall.

The pilgrim and the knight were sitting opposite to each other at the great table, on which many lights were burning; and it was fearful, amongst all the lifeless armour, to see those two tall grim men move, and eat, and drink. As the pilgrim looked up on the boy's entrance, Biorn said: "You know him already: he is my only child, and your fellow-traveller this morning." The Palmer fixed an earnest look on Sintram, and answered, shaking his head: "I do not know what you mean." Then the boy burst forth impatiently: "It must be confessed that you deal very unfairly by us! You say that you know my father but too well, and now it appears that you do not know me at all. Who allowed you to ride on his horse, and in return had his good steed driven almost wild? Answer if you can!"

Biorn put on a somewhat displeased look, but was in truth delighted at any such outbreak of his son's unruly temper; while the pilgrim shuddered as if terrified and overcome by some secret irresistible power. At length with a trembling voice he said these words: "Yes, yes, my dear young lord, you are surely quite right; you are perfectly right in every thing which you may please to assert."

Then the lord of the castle laughed aloud, and said: "Why, you strange pilgrim, what is become of all your wonderfully fine speeches and warnings now? Has the boy all at once struck you dumb and powerless? Beware, you prophet messenger, beware!" But the Palmer cast a fearful look on Biorn, which seemed to quench the light of his fiery eyes, and said in thundering accents: "Between me and thee. old man, the case stands quite otherwise. We have nothing to reproach each other with. And now suffer me to sing a song to you on the lute." He stretched out his hand, and took down from the wall an old worn out lute which was hanging there, and having with surprising skill and rapidity put it in a state fit to be used, he struck some chords, and the low melancholy tones of the instrument seemed well adapted to the words he began to sing:

"The flow'ret was mine own, mine own,
But I have lost its fragrance rare,
And knightly name and freedom fair,
Thro' sin, thro' sin alone.

The flow'ret was thine own, thine own,
Why cast away what thou didst win?
Thou knight no more, but slave of sin,
Thou'rt fearfully alone!"

"Have a care!" shouted he at the close in a pealing voice, as he pulled the strings with such tremendous force that they all broke, and a cloud of dust rose from the instrument, which spread round him like a mist. Sintram had been watching him narrowly whilst he was singing, and more and more did he feel convinced that it was impossible that this man and his fellow-traveller of the morning could be one and the same person. Every doubt was removed when the stranger again looked round at him with the same timid, anxious air, and with many excuses and low reverences replaced the lute in its former position, and then ran out of the hall as if bewildered with terror; his manner forming a strange contrast with the proud and stately deportment which he had assumed towards Biorn.

The eyes of the boy were now directed to his father, and he perceived that he had sunk back senseless in his seat, as though he had been struck by a sudden blow. Sintram's cries summoned Rolf and other attendants, but it was only by their united exertions that they succeeded in restoring their lord to animation; his looks were still wild and disordered, but he suffered himself to be taken to rest without making any opposition.

CHAPTER V.

A LONG illness followed this sudden attack, and during the course of it, the stout old knight, in the midst of his delirious ravings, did not cease to affirm confidently that he must and should recover at last. He would laugh proudly when his fever fits came on, and rebuke them for daring to attack him so needlessly. Then he would murmur to himself: "That was not the right one yet; there must still be another one out in the cold mountains."

At such expressions Sintram involuntarily shuddered; they seemed to confirm his idea that the being who had ridden with him, and he who had sat at table in the castle, were two quite distinct persons: and he knew not why, but this thought was an inexpressibly awful one to him.

Biorn recovered, and appeared to have entirely forgotten his adventure with the Palmer. He hunted in the mountains, he carried on his usual wild warfare with his neighbours, and Sintram became his almost constant companion; whereby each year the youth acquired a fearful increase of strength of body, with an equal fierceness of spirit. Every one trembled at the sight of his sharp pallid features, his dark rolling eyes, his tall, muscular, and somewhat lean form,—and yet no one hated him, not even those whom he distressed or injured to gratify his wildest humours This might arise in part out of regard to old Rolf, who seldom left him for long, and who always held a softening influence over him; but also many of those who had known the Lady Verena before she retired from the world, affirmed that a faint reflection of the heavenly expression which had lighted up her features, could often be traced in those of her son, however unlike they might be in form,—and that by this their hearts were won.

Once, just at the beginning of spring, Biorn and his son were hunting in the neighbourhood of the sea coast, over a tract of country which did not belong to them; drawn thither less by the love of sport than by the wish of bidding defiance to a chieftain whom they detested, and thus exciting a feud. At that season of the year, when his winter dreams had just passed off, Sintram was always unusually fierce, and disposed for warlike adventures,—and this day he was enraged at the chieftain for not coming forth from his castle to attack the intruders with armed force, and he cursed the cowardly patience and love of peace which kept his enemy thus quiet. Just then one of his wild companions rushed towards him, shouting joyfully: "Be content, my dear young lord! I will wager that all is coming about as we and you wish; for as I was pursuing a wounded deer down to the sea-shore, I perceived a sail in sight, and a vessel filled with armed men making for the shore. Doubtless your enemy is intending to take you by surprise by coming in this way."

Sintram, full of joy at the news, called his followers together as secretly as possible, being resolved this time to take on himself alone the whole direction of the engagement which was likely to follow; and then to rejoin his father, and astonish him with the sight of captured foes, and other tokens of victory.

The hunters, thoroughly acquainted with every cliff and rock, concealed themselves near the landing-place, and soon the strange vessel was seen approaching nearer and nearer, till at length it came to anchor, and its crew began to disembark in unsuspicious security. At the head of them appeared a knight of high degree, in polished steel armour richly inlaid with gold. His head was bare, for he carried his golden helmet in his left hand, and as he looked around him with the air of one accustomed to command, none could fail to admire his noble countenance shaded by dark brown locks, and animated by the bright smile which played around his well-shaped mouth.

A feeling came across Sintram that he must have seen this knight somewhere in by-gone times, and he stood motionless for a few moments. But suddenly he raised his hand, to make the preconcerted signal of attack. In vain did the good Rolf, who had just succeeded in getting up to him, whisper in his ear that these could not be the foes whom he had taken them for, but that they were entire strangers, and evidently of no mean race. "Let them be who they may," replied the wild youth, "they have been the cause of my coming here, and they shall pay dearly for having so deceived me. Say not another word, if you value your life." And immediately he gave the signal; a thick shower of javelins followed, and the Norwegian warriors rushed forth with flashing swords. They soon found that they had to do with adversaries as brave, or braver than they could have desired. More fell on the side of these who made than of those who received the assault, and the strangers appeared to have a surprising knowledge of the mode of fighting which belonged to those northern regions. The knight clad in steel armour had not had time to put on his helmet, but it seemed as if he in no-wise needed such protection, for his good sword afforded him sufficient defence even against the spears and darts which were incessantly hurled at him, as with rapid skill he received them on the shining blade, and dashed them far away shivered into fragments.

Sintram could not at the first onset penetrate to where this valiant chief was standing, as all his followers, eager after such a noble prey, thronged closely round him; but now the way was cleared enough for him to spring towards the brave stranger, shouting a war cry, and brandishing his sword above his head. "Gabrielle!" cried the knight, as he dexterously parried the heavy blow which was descending, and with one powerful sword-thrust he laid his youthful antagonist prostrate on the ground, then placing his knee on Sintram's breast, he drew forth a dagger and held it at his throat. The men-at-arms ranged themselves around—Sintram felt that no hope remained for him. He determined to die as it became a bold warrior, and without giving one sign of emotion, he looked on the fatal weapon with a steady gaze.

As he lay with his eyes cast upwards, he fancied that he saw an apparition of a lovely female form in a bright attire of blue and gold. "Our ancestors told truly of the Valkyrias," murmured he. "Strike then, thou unknown conqueror."

But with this the knight did not comply, neither was it a Valkyria who had so suddenly appeared, but the beautiful wife of the stranger, who having advanced to the edge of the vessel, had thus met the upraised look of Sintram. "Folko," cried she, in the softest tone, "thou knight without reproach! I know that thou wilt spare a vanquished foe." The knight sprang up, and with courtly grace assisted the youth to rise, saying, "You owe your life and liberty to the noble lady of Montfauçon. But if you are so far lost to all sense of honour as to wish to resume the combat, here am I—let it be yours to begin."

Sintram sank on his knees overwhelmed with shame and remorse; for he had often heard speak of the high renown of the French knight, Folko of Montfauçon, who was distantly allied to his father's house, and of the grace and beauty of his gentle lady, Gabrielle.

CHAPTER VI.

The lord of Montfauçon looked with astonishment at his strange adversary; and as he gazed on him, recollections arose in his mind of that northern race from whom he was descended, and with whom he had always maintained friendly relations. His eye fell on a golden bear's claw, with which Sintram's cloak was fastened, and the sight of that made all clear to him.

"Have you not," said he, "a valiant and far-famed kinsman called the Sea-king Arinbiorn, whose helmet is adorned with golden vulture wings? And is not your father the knight Biorn? For surely the bear's claw on your mantle must be the cognizance of your house." Sintram gave a sign of assent, but his deep sense of shame and humiliation did not allow him to speak.

The knight of Montfauçon raised him from the ground, and said gravely, yet gently: "We are then of kin the one to the other; but I could never have believed that any one of your noble house would attack a peaceful man without provocation, nay, even lie in wait to surprise him."

"Slay me at once," answered Sintram, "if indeed I am worthy to die by the hand of so renowned a knight—I can no longer endure the light of day." "Because you have been overcome?" asked Montfauçon. Sintram shook his head. "Or is it rather because you have committed an unknightly action?"

The glow of shame that overspread the youth's countenance answered this question. "But you should not on that account wish to die," resumed Montfauçon. "You should rather wish to live that you may prove your repentance, and make your name illustrious by many noble deeds. For you are endowed with a bold spirit and with strength of limb, and also with the quick eye of one fitted to command. I should have made you a knight this very hour, if you had borne yourself as bravely in a good cause, as you have just now done in a most unworthy one. See to it, that there may not be much delay in your receiving that high honour. I trust to your fulfilling the promise of good which is discernible in you."

A joyous sound of music interrupted his discourse. The Lady Gabrielle, bright as the morning, had now come down from the ship, surrounded by her maidens, and having been informed by Folko in a few words who his late adversary was, she spoke of the combat as if it had only been a fair and honourable passage of arms, saying, "You must not be cast down, noble youth, because my wedded lord has won the prize, for be it known to you that in the whole world there is but one knight who can boast of not having been overcome by the baron of Montfauçon. And who can say," continued she sportively, "whether even that would have happened, had he not set himself to win back the magic ring from me, from me his lady-love, destined to him, as well by the choice of my own heart, as by the will of Heaven."

Folko bent his head smiling over the snow-white hand of his lady, and then desired the youth to conduct them to his father's castle. Rolf undertook to superintend the disembarking of the horses and valuables of the strangers, filled with joy at the thought that an angel in woman's form had appeared to exercise a softening influence over his beloved young master, and perhaps even to free him from that curse under which he had so long suffered.

Sintram sent messengers all around to seek for his father, and to announce to him the arrival of his noble guests. They therefore found the old knight in his castle, with every thing prepared for their reception. Gabrielle could not enter the vast, dark-looking building without a slight shudder, which was increased when she saw the rolling fiery eyes of its lord; even the pale dark-haired Sintram seemed to her to assume a more fearful appearance, and she sighed to herself: "Oh! what an awful abode have you brought me to visit, my own true knight!

Oh that we were once again in my sunny Gascony, or in your knightly Normandy!"

But the grave yet courteous reception they met with, the deep respect paid to her grace and beauty, and to the high fame of Folko, helped to re-assure her; and ere long her buoyant spirit took pleasure in observing all the strange novelties by which she was surrounded. And besides, it could only be for a passing moment that any womanly fears found a place in her breast when her lord was near at hand—for well did she know what effectual protection that brave baron was ever ready to afford to all those who were near to him, or anyway committed to his charge.

Soon afterwards Rolf passed through the great hall in which Biorn and his guests were seated, conducting their attendants, who had charge of the baggage, to the apartments allotted to strangers—and Gabrielle, catching sight of her favourite lute, desired it might be brought to her, in order that she might see if the precious instrument had suffered any damage. As she bent over it with earnest attention, and her taper fingers ran up and down the strings, a smile, bright as the summer's dawn, lighted up the countenances of Biorn and his son, and both said with an involuntary sigh: "Ah! if you would but play on that lute, and sing to it! It would be too enchanting!" The lady looked up at them well pleased, and smiling her assent, she began this song:—

"Songs and flowers are returning
And radiant skies of May,
Earth her choicest gifts is yielding,
But one is past away.

The spring that clothes with tend'rest green,
Each grove and sunny plain,
Shines not for my forsaken heart,
Brings not my joys again.

Warble not so, thou nightingale,
Upon thy blooming spray,
Thy sweetness now will burst my heart,
I cannot bear thy lay.

For flowers and birds are come again,
 And breezes mild of May,
But treasured hopes and golden hours
 Are lost to me for aye!"

The two Norwegians sat plunged in melancholy thought; but gradually Sintram's eyes began to brighten with a milder expression, his cheeks glowed, every feature relaxed, till those who looked at him could have fancied they saw a glorified spirit. The good Rolf who had stood listening to the song, rejoiced from his heart as he gazed at him, and devoutly raised his hands in pious gratitude to heaven. But Gabrielle's astonishment did not suffer her to take her eyes off Sintram. At last she said to him: "I should much like to know what it is that has so struck you in that little song. It is merely a simple lay of the spring, full of the images which that sweet season never fails to call up in the minds of my countrymen."

"But is your home really so lovely, so wondrously full of poetry and its delights?" cried the enraptured Sintram. "Then I am no longer surprised at your heavenly beauty, at the empire you have already gained over my hard, wayward heart! For from such a paradise angelic messengers would surely be sent to comfort and enlighten the dark desolate world without." And so saying he fell on his knees before the lady in an attitude of deep humility. Folko looked on all the while with an approving smile, whilst Gabrielle, in much embarrassment, seemed hardly to know how she should treat the half-wild, yet courteous young stranger. After a little hesitation, however, she extended her fair hand to him, and said as she gently raised him: "Any one who listens with such delight to music, must surely know how to awaken its strains himself. Take my lute, and let us hear one of your spirit-stirring songs."

But Sintram drew back, and would not take the instrument, and he said: "Heaven forbid that my rough untutored hand should touch those delicate strings! For even were I to begin with some soft strains, yet before long the wild spirit which dwells in me would break out, and the beautiful instrument would assuredly be injured or destroyed. No, no, suffer me rather to fetch my own huge harp, strung with bears' sinews set in brass, for in truth I do feel myself inspired to play and sing."

Gabrielle murmured a half-frightened assent, and Sintram having brought his harp, began to strike it loudly, and to sing these words with a voice no less powerful:

"Sir Knight, Sir Knight, oh! whither away
With thy snow-white sail on the foaming spray?"
Sing heigh, sing ho, for the land of flowers!

"Too long have I trod upon ice and snow,
I seek the bowers where roses blow."
Sing heigh, sing ho, for the land of flowers!

He steered on his course by night and day
Till he cast his anchor in Naples Bay.
Sing heigh, sing ho, for that land of flowers!

There wandered a Lady upon the strand,
Her fair hair bound with a golden band.
Sing heigh, sing ho, for that land of flowers!

"Hail to thee! hail to thee! Lady bright,
Mine own shalt thou be ere morning light."
Sing heigh, sing ho, for that land of flowers!

"Not so, Sir Knight," the Lady replied,
"For you speak to the Margrave's chosen bride."
Sing heigh, sing ho, for that land of flowers!

"Your lover may come with his shield and spear,
And the victor shall win thee, Lady dear!"
Sing heigh, sing ho, for that land of flowers!

"Nay, seek for another bride, I pray,
Most fair are the maidens of Naples Bay."
Sing heigh, sing ho, for that land of flowers!

"No, Lady, for thee my heart doth burn,
And the world cannot now my purpose turn."
Sing heigh, sing ho, for that land of flowers!

Then came the young Margrave, bold and brave,
But low was he laid in a grassy grave.
  Sing heigh, sing ho, for that land of flowers!

And then the fierce Northman joyous cried,
"Now shall I possess lands, castle and Bride!"
  Sing heigh, sing ho, for that land of flowers!

Sintram's song was ended, but his eyes glared wildly, and the vibrations of the harp-strings still resounded in a marvellous manner. Biorn's attitude was again erect, he stroked his long beard and rattled his sword as if in great delight at what he had just heard. The wild song and the strange aspect of the father and son made Gabrielle tremble more than ever, but a glance towards the Lord of Montfauçon again quieted her fears, for there he sat with a calm smile on his lips, as composed in the midst of all the noise as though it had only been caused by a passing autumnal storm.

CHAPTER VII.

Some weeks had passed since this, when one day, as the shadows of evening were beginning to fall, Sintram entered the garden of the castle in a very disturbed state of mind. Although the presence of Gabrielle never failed to sooth and calm him, yet if she left the apartment for even a few instants, the fearful wildness of his spirit seemed to return with renewed strength. On this occasion, after having in the kindest manner read legends of the olden times to his father Biorn during great part of the day, she had retired to her own chamber. The sweet tones of her lute could be distinctly heard in the garden below, but the sounds only drove the agitated youth farther and farther into the deep shades of the ancient trees which surrounded the garden. Stooping suddenly to avoid some over-hanging branches, he started at finding himself close to something which he had not perceived before, and which at first sight he took for a small bear standing on its hind legs, with a wonderfully long and crooked horn on its head. He drew back in surprise and fear, a shrill voice addressed these words to him: "Well, my brave young knight, whence do you come? whither are you going? and wherefore are you so terrified?" And then he became aware that what he saw was a little old man so wrapped up in a rough garment of fur, that scarcely one of his features was visible, and wearing in his cap a strange looking long feather. "But whence do *you* come? and whither are *you* going?" returned the angry Sintram. "For you are the person to whom such questions should be addressed. What business have you in our domains, you hideous little being?"

"Well, well," sneered the other one, "I am thinking that I am quite big enough as I am. And as to the rest, why should you object to my being here hunting for snails? Snails cannot surely be included in the game which your high mightinesses consider that you alone have a right to pursue? Now it happens that I know how to prepare from them an excellent high-flavoured beverage; and I have taken a sufficient number for to-day: marvellous fat little animals, with wise faces like a man's, and long twisted horns on their heads. Would you like to see them? Look here!"

And then he began to unfasten and fumble about his fur-garment, till Sintram, filled with disgust and horror, said. "Psha! I detest such animals! Be quiet, and tell me at once, who, and what you yourself are." "Are you so bent upon knowing my name?" replied the little man. "Let it content you to hear that I am Master of all secret knowledge, and well-versed in the most intricate depths of ancient history. Ah! my young Sir, if you would only hear some of the things I have to tell! But you are too much afraid!"

"Afraid of you!" cried Sintram, with a wild laugh.

"Many a better man than you has been so before now," muttered the Little Master, "but they did not like being told of it any more than you do."

"To prove that you are mistaken," said Sintram, "I will remain here with you till the moon has risen high in the heavens. But you must relate to me one of your stories the while."

The little man nodded his head with a look of much satisfaction, and as they paced together up and down a retired walk shaded by lofty elm-trees, he began discoursing as follows:—

"Many hundred years ago a young knight called Paris of Troy lived in that sunny land of the south where are found the sweetest songs, the brightest flowers, and the most beautiful ladies. You know a song that tells of that fair land, do you not, young Sir? 'Sing heigh, sing ho, for that land of flowers.'" Sintram gave a sign of assent, and sighed deeply. "Now," resumed the little Master, "it happened that Paris led that kind of life which is not uncommon in those countries, and of which their poets often sing—he would pass whole months together in the garb of a peasant, making the woods and mountains resound to the tones of his lute, and watching the flocks which he led to pasture. Here one day three beautiful goddesses appeared to him, who were disputing about a golden apple—and they appealed to him to decide which of them was the most beautiful, as to her the golden prize was to be adjudged. The first had power to give thrones and sceptres and crowns to whom she would—the second could give wisdom and knowledge—and the third knew how to prepare love-charms which could not fail of securing the affections of the fairest of women. Each one in turn proffered her choicest gifts to the young shepherd, in order that, tempted by them, he might give the prize to her. But as beauty charmed him more than anything else in the world, he decided that the third goddess should win the golden apple—her name was Venus. The two others departed in great displeasure, but Venus bid him put on his knightly armour, and his helmet adorned with waving feathers, and then she conducted him to a famous city called Sparta, where ruled the noble King Menelaus. His young wife Helen was the loveliest woman on earth, and the goddess offered her to Paris in return for the golden apple. He was most ready to have her, and wished for nothing better; but he asked how he was to gain possession of her."

"Paris can have been but a sorry knight," interrupted Sintram. "Such things are easily settled. The husband is challenged to a single combat, and he that is victorious, carries off the wife."

"But King Menelaus was exercising hospitality towards the young knight," said the narrator.

"Listen to me, Little Master," cried Sintram, "he might have asked the goddess for some other beautiful woman, and then have mounted his horse, or weighed anchor, and departed in search of her."

"Yes, yes, it is very easy to say so," replied the old man. "But if you only knew how bewitchingly lovely this Queen Helen was. After seeing her, no admiration was left for any one else." And then he began a glowing description of the charms of this wondrously beautiful princess, giving to her every one of Gabrielle's features with such exactness, that Sintram, overcome with emotion, was obliged to lean against a tree to support himself. The Little Master stood opposite to him, grinning, and he asked, "Well now, could you have advised that poor knight Paris to fly from her?"

"Tell me at once what happened next," stammered Sintram.

"The goddess acted honourably towards Paris," continued the old man. "She declared to him that if he would carry away the lovely princess to his own city Troy, he might do so, and thus cause the ruin of his whole house and of his country; but that during ten years he would be able to defend Troy against his enemies and live happy in the love of his fair lady."

"And he took her on those terms, unless he was a fool!" cried the youth.

"To be sure he accepted them," whispered the Little Master. "I would have done so in his place! And do you know, young Sir, it once fell out that the appearance of things was exactly like what we now see. The newly risen moon, partly veiled by clouds, was shining dimly through the thick branches of the trees in the silence of the evening. Leaning against a tree, as you are now doing, there stood the young enamoured knight Paris, and at his side the enchantress Venus, but so disguised and transformed, that she did not look much more attractive than I do. And by the silvery light of the moon, the form of the beautiful beloved one was seen sweeping by amidst the whispering boughs." He was silent, and, as if to realize his deluding words, Gabrielle just then appeared, musing as she walked alone down the alley of elms. "Awful being, by what name shall I call you? What is it that you would drive me to?" muttered the trembling Sintram.

"Do not you remember your father's strong fortress on the Rocks of the Moon?" replied the old man. "The castellan and the garrison are entirely devoted to you. It could well stand a ten years' siege, and the postern gate which leads to it is open, as was that of the royal citadel of Sparta for the happy Paris." The youth looked, and perceived in fact that a gate in the garden-wall, which was usually closed, had now been left open, and that the distant mountains lighted up by the moon might be clearly seen through it. "And if he did not accept, he was a fool," said the Little Master, with a grin, echoing Sintram's former words. At that moment, Gabrielle drew near to him. She was within reach of his grasp, had he made the least movement; and the moon as it shone on her heavenly countenance, gave new charms to it. The youth had already bent forwards.

"My Lord and God, I pray
Turn from his heart away
This world's turmoil.
And call him to Thy light,
Be it through sorrow's night,
Through pain or toil."

These words were sung by old Rolf at that very time, as he lingered on the banks of the lake by the castle, seeking a relief to his anxious thoughts concerning Sintram in the fervent supplications he addressed to the Almighty. The sounds reached Sintram's ear; he stood as if spell-bound, and made the sign of the Cross. Immediately the Little Master fled away, jumping uncouthly on one leg through the gates and shutting them after him with a loud noise.

Sintram approached the terrified Gabrielle, and said as he offered his arm to support her: "Suffer me to lead you back to the castle. The nights in these northern regions are often wild and fearful."

CHAPTER VIII.

THEY found the two knights within sitting together, after their evening repast. Folko was relating stories in his usual mild and cheerful manner, and Biorn was listening with a moody air, but yet as if against his will the dark cloud might pass away under the influence of his companion's bright and gentle courtesy. Gabrielle saluted the baron with a smile, and signed to him to continue his discourse, as she took her place next to Biorn, with the watchful kindness which ever marked her bearing towards him. Sintram the while stood by the hearth, abstracted and melancholy, and the embers, as he stirred them, cast an unnatural gleam over his pallid features.

"And of all the German trading towns," continued Montfauçon, "the largest and richest is Hamburgh. In Normandy the merchants of this city are always received with a hearty welcome, and those excellent people never fail to prove themselves our friends when we seek their advice and assistance. When I first visited Hamburgh, every honour and respect was paid me. I found its inhabitants engaged in a war with a neighbouring prince, and immediately I devoted my sword to their service, and that not without success."

"Your sword! your knightly sword!" interrupted Biorn, and more than the wonted fire flashed from his eyes. "You turned it against a knight, and on behalf of shopkeepers!"

"Sir knight," replied Folko calmly, "the barons of Montfauçon have ever been used to take the side which they esteemed the right one in combats, without consulting indifferent bystanders, and as I have received this good custom from my forefathers, so do I wish to hand it on to my remotest descendants. If you do not esteem this a wise practice, you are at liberty to speak your opinion freely. But I cannot suffer you to say anything against the people of Hamburgh after I have declared them to be my friends and allies."

Biorn cast down his fierce eyes to the ground, and their wild expression seemed to fade away. He said in a subdued tone: "Proceed, noble baron. You are right, and I am wrong." Then Folko stretched out his hand to him across the table, and resumed his narration: "Amongst all my beloved Hamburghers the dearest to me are two very remarkable men—a father and son. What have they not seen and done in the remotest corners of the earth! and how has every talent been devoted to the good of their native town! My life has by the blessing of God been not unfruitful in deeds of renown, but in comparison with the wise Gotthard Lenz and his stout-hearted son Rudlieb, I look upon myself as nothing but an esquire who has perhaps some few times attended knights to tourneys, and besides that has never gone out of his own forests. They have carried the light of religion, and with it happiness and peace, to savage nations whose very names are unknown to me, and the wealth which they have brought back from those distant climes has all been given to promote the common welfare as unhesitatingly as if no other use could possibly be devised for it. On their return from their long and perilous sea voyages, they hasten to an hospital which has been founded by them and of which they undertake the entire charge. Then they proceed to select the most fitting spots whereon to erect new towers and fortresses for the defence of their beloved country. Next they repair to the houses where strangers and travellers receive hospitality at their cost—and then they return to their own abode, where guests are entertained with a splendour worthy of a king's palace, and yet with the unassuming simplicity of manners which is thought only to belong to the shepherd's cot. Many a tale of their wondrous adventures serves to enliven these sumptuous feasts. Amongst others, I remember to have heard my friends relate one at the thought of which I still shudder. Possibly I may gain some more complete information on the subject from you. It appears that several years ago, just about the time of the Christmas festival, Gotthard and Rudlieb were shipwrecked on the coast of Norway, during a violent winter's tempest; they could never exactly ascertain the situation of the rocks on which their vessel stranded; but so much is certain, that very near the sea-shore stood a huge castle to which the father and son betook themselves, seeking for that assistance and shelter which Christian people are ever willing to afford each other in case of need. They went alone, leaving their followers to watch the ship. The castle gates were thrown open, and they thought all was well. But on a sudden the court-yard was filled with armed men, who with one accord aimed their sharp iron-pointed spears at the defenceless strangers, whose dignified remonstrances and mild entreaties were only heard in sullen silence or with scornful jeerings. After a while a knight came down the stairs, his eyes, so to speak, flashing fire, they hardly knew whether to think they saw some fearful apparition, or a wild heathen—he gave a signal, and the fatal spears closed around them. At that instant the soft tones of a woman's voice fell on their ear; she was calling on the Saviour's holy name for aid; at the sound, the wild figures in the court-yard rushed madly one against the other, the gates burst open, and Gotthard and Rudlieb fled away, catching a glimpse as they went of an angelic face which appeared at one of the windows of the castle. They made every exertion to get their ship again afloat, preferring to trust themselves to the treacherous sea, rather than to remain on that barbarous coast, and at last they landed in Denmark after encountering many perils and dangers. They have always said that it must have been a Heathen's castle in which they were so cruelly treated, but I am rather disposed to think it was some ruined fortress, long deserted by men, in which evil spirits were wont to hold their nightly assemblies, for is it possible to imagine that even a Heathen could be found with so much of a demon's temper as to meet strangers, asking for hospitality, with deadly weapons, instead of the refreshment and shelter they needed?"

Biorn gazed fixedly on the ground, as though he were turned into stone—but Sintram came towards the table, and said: "Father, let us seek out this wicked abode, and let us level it to the ground. I cannot tell how, but I feel quite sure that the accursed deed we have just heard of is alone the cause of my frightful dreams." Enraged at his son's words, Biorn rose up, and would perhaps again have uttered some dreadful imprecation, but Heaven decreed otherwise, for just at that moment the pealing notes of a trumpet were heard, which drowned the angry tones of his voice; the great doors opened slowly, and a herald entered the hall. He bowed reverently, and then said: "I am sent by Jarl Eric the aged. He returned two days ago from his expedition to the Grecian seas. His wish had been to take vengeance on the island which is called Chios, where fifty years ago his father was slain by the soldiers of the Emperor. But your kinsman, the sea-king Arinbiorn, who was lying there at anchor, tried to pacify him and to turn him from his purpose—to this Jarl Eric would not listen—so the sea-king said next that he would never suffer Chios to be laid waste, because it was an island where the lays of an old Greek bard, called Homer, were excellently sung, and where moreover a very choice wine was made. Words proving of no avail, a combat ensued, in which Arinbiorn had so much the advantage that Jarl Eric lost two of his ships, and only with difficulty escaped in one which had already sustained great damage. Eric the aged has now resolved to take revenge on some of the sea-king's race, since Arinbiorn himself is rarely to be found. Will you, Biorn of the Fiery Eyes, at once pay as large a penalty in cattle and goods of whatever description, as it may please the Jarl to demand? Or will you prepare to meet him with an armed force at Niflung's Heath seven days hence?"

Biorn bowed his head quietly, and replied in a mild tone: "Seven days hence at Niflung's Heath." He then offered to the herald a golden goblet full of rich wine, and added: "Drink that, and then carry off with thee the cup which thou hast emptied."

"The Baron of Montfauçon likewise sends greeting to thy chieftain Jarl Eric," interposed Folko, "and engages to be also at Niflung's Heath, as the hereditary friend of the sea-king's house, and also as being the kinsman and guest of Biorn of the Fiery Eyes."

The herald was seen to tremble at the name of Montfauçon, he bowed very low, cast an anxious, reverential look at the baron, and left the hall. Gabrielle looked on her knight with a smile that spoke of entire trust in his valour, when she heard him pledge himself to appear in the field, and she only asked, "Where shall I remain whilst you go forth to battle, Folko?" "I had hoped," answered Biorn, "that you would be well contented to stay in this castle, lovely lady; I leave my son to guard you and attend on you." Gabrielle hesitated an instant, and Sintram, who had resumed his position near the fire, muttered to himself as he fixed his eyes on the bright flames which were flashing up: "Yes, yes, so it will probably happen. I can fancy that king Menelaus had just left Sparta on some warlike expedition when the young knight Paris met the lovely Helen that evening in the garden." But Gabrielle, shuddering, although she knew not why, said quickly: "Remain here without you, Folko? And how could I bear to forego the joy of seeing you win fresh laurels? or the honour of tending you, should you chance to receive a wound?" Folko bent his head in acknowledgment of his lady's anxious tenderness, and replied: "Come with your own true knight, since such is your pleasure, and be to him a bright guiding star. It is a good old northern custom that ladies should be present at knightly combats, and no true warrior of the north will fail to respect the place whence beams the light of their eyes. Unless indeed," continued he, with an inquiring look at Biorn, "unless Jarl Eric has degenerated from his valiant forefathers?"

"His honour may be relied on," said Biorn, confidently.

"Then array yourself, my fairest love," said the delighted Folko, "array yourself, and come forth with us to the battle-field, to behold and judge our knightly deeds."

"Come forth with us to the battle-field," echoed Sintram. in a sudden transport of joy.

And they all dispersed; Sintram betaking himself again to the wood, while the others retired to rest.

CHAPTER IX.

It was a wild, dreary tract of country that which bore the name of Niflung's Heath. According to tradition, the young Niflung, son of Hogni, the last of his race, had there ended in sadness and obscurity a life which no warlike deeds had rendered illustrious. Many ancient monuments of the dead were still standing round about, and in the few oak-trees scattered here and there over the plain, huge eagles had built their nests—the beating of their heavy wings as they fought together, and their wild screams, were heard far off in regions more thickly peopled by man, and at the sound children would tremble in their cradles, and old men quake with fear as they sat over the blazing hearth.

As the seventh night, the last before the day of combat, was just beginning, two large armies were seen descending from the hills in opposite directions: that which came from the west was commanded by Eric the aged, that from the east by Biorn of the Fiery Eyes. They appeared thus early in compliance with the custom which required that adversaries should always present themselves at the appointed field of battle before the time named, in order to prove that they rather sought than dreaded the hour of trial. Folko immediately chose out the most convenient spot for the tent of blue and gold to be pitched, which was to shelter his gentle lady; whilst Sintram, in the character of herald, rode over to Jarl Eric to announce to him that the beauteous Gabrielle of Montfauçon was there guarded by his father's warriors, and would the next morning be present as a judge of the combat.

Jarl Eric bowed low on receiving this intelligence, and ordered his bards to strike up a lay, the words of which ran as follows:—

"Warriors bold of Eric's band,
Gird your glittering armour on,
Stand beneath to-morrow's sun,
In your might.

Fairest dame that ever gladdened
Our wild shores with beauty's vision,
May thy bright eyes o'er our combat,
Judge the right.

Tidings of yon noble stranger
Long ago have reached our ears,
Wafted upon southern breezes,
O'er the wave.

Now midst yonder hostile ranks,
In his warlike pride he meets us,
Folko comes! Fight, men of Eric,
True and brave!"

These wondrous tones floated over the plain, and reached the tent of Gabrielle. It was no new thing to hear her knight's fame celebrated on all sides, but now that she listened to his praises bursting forth in the stillness of night from the mouth of his enemies, she could scarcely refrain from kneeling at the feet of the mighty chieftain. But he with courteous tenderness prevented her from sinking into that lowly posture, and pressing his lips fervently on her snow-white hand, he said: "My deeds, oh lovely lady, belong to thee, and not to me!"

No sooner had the darkness of night passed away, and the red streaks in the east announced the arrival of the appointed morning, than the whole plain seemed alive with preparations for the combat: knights put on their rattling armour, war-horses began to neigh impatiently, the morning-draught went round in gold and silver goblets, while war-songs and the harps of the bards resounded far and near. A joyous march was heard in Biorn's camp, as Montfauçon, with his troops and retainers, all clad in bright steel armour, conducted their lady up to a neighbouring hill, where she would be safe from the spears which would soon be flying in all directions, and whence she could command a complete view of the battle-field. The morning sun lighted up her lovely features, adding radiance to her surpassing beauty, and as she came in view of the camp of Jarl Eric, his soldiers lowered their weapons, whilst the chieftains bent their proud heads which were covered with huge helmets. Two of Montfauçon's pages remained in attendance on the lady Gabrielle, well content to exchange their hopes of gaining renown in the battle-field for the far greater honour of being chosen to fulfil this office. Both armies passed in front of her, saluting her as they went; they then placed themselves in array, and the fight began.

The spears flew from the hands of the stout northern warriors, rattling against the broad shields under which they sheltered themselves, or sometimes clattering as they met in the air; at intervals, on one side or the other, a man was struck, and fell bathed in his blood. After a short pause, the knight of Montfauçon advanced with his troop of Norman horsemen—even as he dashed past, he did not fail to lower his shining sword to salute Gabrielle, and then, with a loud exulting war-cry, which burst from the lips of all, they charged the left wing of the enemy. Eric's foot-soldiers, kneeling firmly in close ranks, received them with fixed javelins—many a noble horse fell wounded to death, and in falling brought his rider with him to the ground—others again crushed their foes under them as they writhed in mortal agonies. In the midst of the confusion and bloodshed, Folko and his war-steed escaped unhurt, and followed by a small band of chosen men, he dashed through the hostile ranks. Already were they falling into disorder, already were Biorn's warriors giving shouts of victory, when a troop of horse, headed by Jarl Eric himself, advanced against the valiant Baron of Montfauçon; and whilst his Normans, hastily assembling round their leader, assisted him in repelling this unexpected attack, the enemy's infantry were gradually forming themselves into a thick impenetrable mass, which rolled on in formidable strength. All these movements seemed to be directed by a warrior in the centre, whose loud piercing shout was heard at every instant. And scarcely were the troops formed into this close array, when suddenly they spread themselves out on all sides, carrying every thing before them with the irresistible force of the burning torrent from a volcano.

Biorn's soldiers, who had thought themselves on the point of enclosing their enemies, gave way at once before this wondrous onset. The knight himself in vain attempted to stem the tide of fugitives, and with difficulty escaped being carried away by it.

Sintram stood looking on this scene of confusion with mute indignation; friends and foes passed by him, all equally avoiding him, and dreading to come in contact with one whose aspect was so fearful, nay almost unearthly, in his motionless rage. He aimed no blow either to right or left, his powerful battle-axe hung idly at his side. But his eye flashed fire, and seemed to be piercing the enemy's ranks through and through, in the endeavor to find out who it was that had conjured up this sudden warlike spirit. At length he discovered the object of his search. A small man clothed in strange-looking armor, with large golden horns in his helmet, and a long visor, advancing in front of it, was leaning on a two-edged curved spear, and seemed to be looking with derision at the hasty flight of Biorn's troops as they were pursued by their victorious foes. "That is he," cried Sintram, "he who would bring me to disgrace before the eyes of Gabrielle!" And with the swiftness of an arrow he flew towards him, uttering a wild shout of defiance. The combat was fierce, but not of long duration. To the wondrous dexterity of his adversary, Sintram opposed his far superior strength and height, and he dealt such a tremendous blow on the horned helmet that a stream of blood rushed forth, the small man fell as if stunned, and after some frightful convulsive movements, his limbs appeared to stiffen in death.

His overthrow gave the signal for that of all Eric's army. Even those who had not seen him fall, suddenly lost their courage, and again retreated in confusion, or ran in wild affright on the very spears of their enemies. At the same time Montfauçon was dispersing Jarl Eric's cavalry, after a desperate conflict, and had taken their chief prisoner with his own hand. Biorn of the Fiery Eyes stood victorious in the middle of the field of battle. The day was won.

CHAPTER X.

In full view of both armies, with glowing cheeks and looks of modest humility, Sintram was conducted by the brave baron of Montfauçon up the hill where Gabrielle stood in all the lustre of her beauty. Both warriors bent the knee before her, and Folko said with much solemnity: "Lady, this valiant youth of a noble race has borne away the palm of victory to-day. I pray you to let him receive from your fair hand the reward to which he is so justly entitled."

Gabrielle bowed courteously, took off her scarf of blue and gold, and fastened to it a bright sword which a page brought to her on a cushion of cloth of silver. She then with a smile presented her precious gift to Sintram, who was bending forward to receive it, when suddenly Gabrielle drew back, and turning to Folko, she said: "Noble baron, should not he, on whom I bestow a scarf and sword, be first admitted into the order of knighthood?" Folko sprang up, and bowing low before his lady, gave the youth the accolade with solemn earnestness. Then Gabrielle buckled on his sword, saying: "Take this for the honour of God and the service of noble ladies, young knight. I saw you fight, I saw you conquer, and my fervent prayers were offered up for you. Fight and conquer often again as you have done this day, that the fame of your deeds may be wafted even to my far distant country." And at a sign from Folko, she offered her cheek for the new knight to kiss. Thrilling all over, and full of a holy joy, Sintram arose in deep silence, and tears streamed down his cheeks, whilst the shout of the assembled troops greeted the enraptured youth with stunning applause. Old Rolf stood silently on one side, and as he saw the mild beaming expression in his beloved pupil's countenance, he calmly and piously returned thanks.

The strife is now at an end—rich blessings are showered down—the evil foe is slain."

Biorn and Jarl Eric had the while been talking together with eagerness but not with animosity. The conqueror now led his vanquished enemy up the hill, and presented him to the baron and Gabrielle, saying: "Instead of two enemies, you now see two sworn allies, and I request you, my beloved guests and kinsfolk, to receive him graciously as one who, from henceforward, belongs to us." "He was ever one with you in heart," added Eric, smiling; "I have indeed sought for revenge of former wrongs, but I have now had enough of defeats both by sea and land. Yet I thank Heaven, that neither in the Grecian seas, nor on Niflung's Heath, have I shown myself wanting in valor." The lord of Montfauçon assented cordially, and the terms of peace were agreed on with entire good will. Jarl Eric then addressed Gabrielle in so courtly a manner that she could not refrain from looking on the gigantic old warrior with a smile of astonishment, and she gave him her hand to kiss.

Meanwhile Sintram was standing apart, speaking earnestly to his good Rolf, and at length he was heard to say: "But before all, be sure that you bury that wonderfully brave knight whom my battle-axe laid low. Choose out the greenest hill for his resting-place, and the loftiest oak to shade his grave. Also I wish you to open his visor and to examine his countenance carefully, lest the blow should only have deprived him of motion, not of life; and moreover, that you may be able to give me an exact description of him to whom I owe the noblest, most precious prize ever adjudged to man."

Rolf departed to execute his orders. "Our young knight is speaking there of one amongst the slain, of whom I should like to hear more," said Folko, turning to Jarl Eric. "Who was the wonderful chieftain who rallied your troops in so masterly a manner, and who at last fell under Sintram's powerful weapon?"

"You ask me more than I know how to answer," replied

Jarl Eric. "About three nights ago, this stranger made his appearance amongst us. I was sitting with my chieftains and warriors round the hearth, forging our armour, and singing the while. Suddenly, above the din of our hammering and our singing, we heard so loud a noise that it silenced us in a moment, and we sat motionless as if we had been turned into stone. The sound continued equally stunning, and at last we made out that it must be caused by some person blowing a huge horn outside the castle, in order to obtain admittance. I went down myself to the gate, and as I passed through the court-yard I perceived that all my dogs were so terrified by the extraordinary noise as to be howling and crouching in their kennels, instead of barking at the intruders. I scolded them, and called to them, but even the fiercest would not follow me. 'Then,' thought I to myself, 'I must shew you the way to set to work;' so I grasped my sword firmly, I set my torch on the ground close beside me, and I let the gates fly open without further delay. For I well knew that it would be no easy matter for any one to effect an entrance against my will. A loud laugh greeted me, and I heard these words: 'Well, well, what mighty preparations are these before one small man is allowed to find the shelter he seeks!' And in truth I did feel myself redden with shame when I saw the small stranger standing opposite to me, quite alone. I called to him to come in at once, and offered my hand to him; but he still showed some displeasure, and would not give me his in return. As he went up, however, he became more friendly, he showed me the golden horn on which he sounded that blast, and which he carried screwed on his helmet, as well as another exactly like it. When he was sitting with us in the hall, he behaved in a very strange manner—sometimes he was merry, sometimes cross, by turns courteous and rude in his demeanour, without any one being able to see a motive for such constant changes. I longed to know where he came from, but how could I ask my guest such a question? He told us as much as this, that he was starved with cold in our country, and that his own was much warmer. Also he appeared well acquainted with the city of Constantinople, and related fearful stories of how brothers, uncles and nephews, nay even fathers and sons, had been known there to drive each other from the throne, and to exercise such cruelties as putting out eyes, and cutting out tongues when they stopped short of murdering their opponents. At length he said his own name; it sounded harmonious, like a Greek name, but none of us could remember it. Before long, he displayed his skill as an armourer. He understood marvellously well how to handle the red-hot iron, and how to form it into weapons of a more murderous nature than any I had ever before seen. I would not suffer him to go on making them, for I was resolved to meet you in the field with such arms only as you would yourselves bear, and as we are all used to in our northern countries. Then he laughed, and said he thought it would be quite possible to be victorious without their aid, provided address and dexterity were not wanting, and so forth; if only I would entrust the command of my infantry to him, I might depend upon success. It occurred to me that he who was so skilled in forging arms must also wield them well—yet I required some proof of his powers. Sir knight, he came off victorious in trials of strength, more surprising than any you could imagine—and although the fame of young Sintram as a bold and brave warrior is spread far and wide, yet I can scarce believe that he really succeeded in slaying such an one as my Greek ally showed himself to be."

He would have continued speaking, but the good Rolf here made his appearance hastening towards them, followed by a few attendants, the whole party looking so ghastly pale that all eyes were involuntarily fixed on them, and every one waited anxiously to hear what tidings they brought. Rolf stood still, silent and trembling.

"Take courage, my old friend!" cried Sintram. "Whatever you may have to tell will come forth clear and true from your honest lips." "My dear master," began the old man, "be not angry, but as to burying that strange warrior whom you slew, it is a thing impossible. Would that we had never opened that wide, hideous visor! For so horrible a countenance grinned at us from underneath it, so distorted by death, and with such a fiendish expression, that we hardly kept our senses. We could not by any possibility have touched him. I would rather be sent to kill wolves and bears in the desert, and look on whilst fierce birds of prey feast on their carcasses."

All present shuddered, and were silent—till Sintram nerved himself to say: "Dear good old man, why use such wild words as I never till now heard you utter? But tell me, Jarl Eric, did your ally present such an awful appearance while he was yet alive?"

"I do not call it to mind," answered Jarl Eric, looking inquiringly at his companions who were standing around. They said the same thing as their lord; but on further questioning, it appeared that neither the chieftain, nor the knights, nor the soldiers, could say exactly what the stranger was like.

"We must then find it out for ourselves, and bury the corpse," said Sintram; and he signed to the assembled party to follow him. All did so, except the lord of Montfauçon, whom the whispered entreaty of Gabrielle kept at her side. He lost nothing by remaining behind: for though Niflung's Heath was searched from one end to the other many times, yet the body of the unknown warrior was never again discovered.

CHAPTER XI.

THE joy and serenity which came over Sintram's soul on this day appeared to be much more than a passing gleam. If still an occasional thought of the knight Paris and the fair Helen would for a moment make his heart beat wildly, it needed but one look at his scarf and sword to restore calmness within. "What can any man wish for more than has been already bestowed on me?" would he say to himself at such times, in deep emotion. And thus it went on for a long while.

The autumn, so beautiful in those northern climes, had already begun to redden the leaves of the old oaks and elms round the castle, when one day it chanced that Sintram found himself seated in company with Folko and Gabrielle, in almost the very same spot in the garden where he had before met that mysterious being whom, without knowing why, he had named the Little Master. But on this day in what a different light did every thing appear! The sun was sinking slowly over the sea,—the mist of an autumnal evening was rising from the fields, and wreathing itself round the hill on which stood the huge castle. Gabrielle, placing her lute in Sintram's hands, said to him: "Dear youth, I no longer fear entrusting my delicate favourite to you, now that you are become so mild and gentle. Let me again hear you sing that lay of the land of flowers, for I am sure that it will now sound much sweeter than when you accompanied it with the vibrations of your fearful harp."

The young knight bowed as he prepared to obey the lady's commands. With a grace and softness hitherto strangers to him, the wild strains flowed from his lips, and appeared to lose their former character, and to change into harmony to which angels might have listened. Tears stood in Gabrielle's eyes;

and Sintram, as he gazed on the bright pearly drops, poured forth tones of yet richer sweetness. When the last notes were sounded, Gabrielle's angelic voice was heard to echo them, and as she repeated

"Sing heigh, sing ho, for that land of flowers,"

Sintram put down the lute, and raised his thankful eyes towards the stars, which were now stealing out and studding the whole face of the sky. Then Gabrielle, turning towards her lord, murmured these words: "Oh, how long have we been wandering far away from our own sunny hills and bright gardens! Oh! for that land of the sweetest flowers!"

Sintram could scarce believe that he heard aright, so suddenly did he feel himself as if shut out from paradise. But his faint hopes of being mistaken were crushed by the assurance of Folko, that he would endeavour to fulfil his lady's wishes with all possible speed, and that their ship was lying off the shore ready to put to sea. She thanked him with a kiss imprinted softly on his forehead; and leaning on his arm she bent her steps towards the castle.

The wretched Sintram, neglected and forgotten, remained behind, motionless as if he had been turned to stone. At length, when the darkness of night had spread itself over the whole sky, he started up wildly, ran up and down the garden as if all his former madness had taken possession of him, and then rushed out, and wandered upon the hills in the pale moonlight. There he dashed his sword against the trees and bushes, so that all around was heard a sound of crashing and falling, the birds of night flew about him screeching in wild alarm, and the deer, startled by the noise, sprung away to take refuge in the thickest coverts.

On a sudden old Rolf appeared, returning home from a visit to the chaplain of Drontheim, to whom he had been relating with tears of joy, how Sintram was subdued by Gabrielle's mild influence, and how they might venture to hope that his evil dreams would never again disturb his mind. And now the sword of the furious youth had well-nigh wounded the old man in some of its fearful thrusts to right and left. He stopped short, and, clasping his hands, he said with a deep sigh: "Alas, my beloved Sintram, my foster-child! what madness has seized you, and made you thus wild and frantic?"

The youth stood awhile as if spell-bound, he looked in his old friend's face with a fixed and melancholy gaze, and his eyes became dim, like expiring watch-fires seen through a thick cloud of mist. At length he sighed forth these words, almost inaudibly: "Good Rolf, good Rolf, depart from me! I have been cast out of your garden of delight; and if sometimes a light breeze blows open its golden gates so that I can look in and see the sunny spot where heavenly inhabitants wander to and fro, then immediately a cruel cutting wind arises, which shuts to the gates, and I remain without, to pass a never-ending winter in cheerless desolation."

"Beloved young knight, oh! listen to me;—listen to the voice of the good Spirit within you! Do you not bear in your hand that very sword which the bright lady you serve girded you with? Does not her scarf wave over your wildly beating heart? Do you not recollect how you used to say, that no mortal could wish for more than had been bestowed on yourself?"

"Yes, Rolf, I have said that," replied Sintram, sinking on the mossy turf, drowned in bitter tears. The old man wept also. Before long the youth stood again erect, his tears ceased to flow, his countenance assumed a cold terrible expression, and he said: "You see, Rolf, I have passed such blessed peaceful days, and I thought within myself that the powers of evil would never again have dominion over me. So, perchance, it might have been, just as much as daylight would always last were the sun never to go below the horizon. But ask the poor benighted earth, wherefore she looks so dull and dark! Bid her again smile as she was wont to do! Old man, she cannot smile;—and now that the gentle compassionate moon has disappeared behind the clouds with her sadly-soothing funeral veil, she cannot even weep. And in this hour of darkness, all that is wild and awful wakes up into life! So do not stop me, I tell thee, do not stop me! Hurrah! I am rushing behind the pale moon!" His voice changed to a hoarse murmur at these last words. He tore away from the trembling old man, and rushed through the forest. Rolf knelt down, and prayed and wept silently.

CHAPTER XII.

Where the sea-beacn was wildest, and the cliffs most steep and rugged, and close by the remains of three shattered oaks, which probably marked a place where, in darker times, human victims had been sacrificed, now stood Sintram, leaning, as if exhausted, on his drawn sword, and gazing intently on the dancing waves. The moon had again shone forth, and as her pale beams fell on his motionless figure through the quivering branches of the trees, he might have been taken for some fearful idol image. Suddenly some one, hitherto unnoticed by him, half-raised himself out of the withered grass, uttered a faint groan, and again lay down. This marvellous conversation then arose between the two:

"Thou that movest thyself so strangely amid the grass, dost thou belong to the living or to the dead?"

"That is as you may choose to take it. I am dead to heaven and joy—I live for hell and anguish."

"I could fancy that I had already heard thee speak."

"Oh, yes, thou surely hast."

"Art thou a troubled spirit? and was thy life-blood poured out here in ancient times?"

"I am a troubled spirit;—but no man ever has, or ever can shed my blood. I have been cast down—oh! into a frightful abyss!"

"And wert thou killed by the fall?"

"I am living now,—and I shall live longer than thou."

"I could almost fancy that thou wert the crazy pilgrim with the dead men's bones hanging about him."

"I am not he, although we often consort together,—and, indeed, in the most friendly manner. But to let you into a secret, he considers me to be mad. If I sometimes urge him, and say to him, 'Take!'—then he hesitates, and points upwards towards the stars. And, again, if I say, 'Take not!'—then, to a certainty, he seizes on it in some awkward manner, and so he spoils my best joys and pleasures. But, in spite of all this, we remain as before, bound by a close alliance, and even by a degree of relationship."

"Give me thy hand, and let me help thee up."

"Ho, ho! my active young sir, that might bring you no good. Yet, in fact, you have already helped to raise me. Give heed to what is going on around."

The movements of Sintram's unknown companion seemed to become stranger each minute; thick clouds swept wildly over the moon and the stars, and Sintram's thoughts grew no less wild and stormy, while far and near an awful howling could be heard amidst the trees and the grass. At length the mysterious being arose from the ground. As if to gratify a fearful curiosity, the moon looked out from behind a cloud, and the sudden gleam of light showed the horror-stricken Sintram that his companion was none other than the Little Master.

"Avaunt," cried he, "I will listen no more to your evil stories about the knight Paris. They would end by driving me quite mad."

"My stories about Paris are not needed for that!" grinned the Little Master. "It is enough that the Helen of your affections should be journeying towards Montfauçon. Believe me, madness has already taken possession of every part of you. But what should you say were she to remain? For that, however, you must show me more courtesy than you have of late." Therewith he raised his voice towards the sea, as if fiercely rebuking it, so that Sintram could not keep from shuddering and trembling before the hideous dwarf. But he checked himself, and grasping his sword-hilt with both hands, he said contemptuously: "You and Gabrielle! what acquaintance do you pretend to have with Gabrielle?"

"Not much," was the reply. And the Little Master might be seen to quake with fear and rage, as he continued: "I cannot well bear to hear the name of your Helen; do not din it in my ears ten times in a breath. But if the tempest should increase? If the foaming waves should swell, and roll on till they form an impenetrable barrier round the whole coast of Norway? The voyage to Montfauçon must in that case be altogether given up, and your Helen would remain here at least through the long, long, dark winter!"

"If! if!" replied Sintram, with scorn. "Is the sea your bond-slave? Are tempests obedient to you?"

"They are rebels, accursed rebels," muttered the Little Master. "You must lend me your aid, Sir Knight, if I am to subdue them; but you have not the heart for such a service."

"Boaster, evil boaster!" answered the youth. "What is that you require of me?"

"It is not much, Sir Knight, nothing at all for one who has strength and ardour of soul. You need only look at the sea steadily for one half-hour, without ever ceasing to wish intensely that it should foam and rage and swell, and never again become quiet until winter has laid its icy hold upon your mountains. Then king Menelaus will be effectually prevented from undertaking a voyage to Montfauçon. And now give me a lock of your black hair, which is blowing so wildly about your head, looking like ravens' or vultures' wings."

The youth drew his sharp dagger, madly cut off a lock of his hair, threw it to the strange being, and according to his directions began gazing on the sea, and wishing ardently that a storm should arise. And soon the water began to be slightly agitated with a motion almost as imperceptible as the murmuring of one disturbed by uneasy dreams, who would gladly be at rest and yet cannot. Sintram was on the point of giving up, when the moonbeams fell on the white sails of a ship which was going rapidly in a southerly direction. A pang shot through his heart, as he was thus forcibly reminded of Gabrielle's departure; he wished again with all his power, and fixed his eyes intently on the watery expanse. "Sintram," a voice might have said to him, "ah! Sintram, can you be indeed the very same who but so lately was gazing in deep emotion on the tearful eyes of Gabrielle?"

And now the waves were seen to heave and swell, and the howling tempest swept over the ocean; the breakers, white with foam, became visible in the moonlight. Then the Little Master threw the lock of Sintram's hair up towards the clouds, and as it was blown to and fro by the blast of wind, the storm burst in all its fury, so that sea and sky were covered with one thick cloud, and far off might be heard the cries of distress from many a sinking vessel.

Just then the crazy pilgrim with the dead-men's bones rose up in the midst of the waves, close to the shore; his height appeared gigantic as he rocked to and fro in a fearful manner; the boat in which he was standing was entirely hid from sight by the raging waves which rose all around it.

"You must save him, Little Master, you must anyhow save him," cried Sintram, his voice rising in a tone of angry entreaty above the roaring of the winds and waves—but the dwarf replied with a laugh: "Be quite at ease on his account, he will be able to save himself. The waves can do him no harm. Do you see? They are only begging of him, and therefore they jump up so boldly round him. And he gives them bountiful alms; very bountiful, that I can assure you."

Accordingly the pilgrim was seen to throw some bones in the sea, and to pass on his way without suffering damage. Sintram felt his blood run cold with horror, and he rushed wildly towards the castle. His companion had either fled or vanished away.

CHAPTER XIII.

Biorn and Gabrielle and Folko of Montfauçon were sitting round the great stone table, from which, since the arrival of his noble guests, the lord of the castle had caused those suits of armour to be removed that formerly had been his companions—they were placed all together in a heap in one of the adjoining apartments. At this time, while the storm was beating so furiously against doors and windows, it seemed as if the ancient armour were also stirring in the next room, and Gabrielle several times half rose from her seat in great alarm, fixing her eyes on the small iron door, as though she expected to see an armed spectre issue therefrom, bending down his plumed helmet as he passed underneath the low vaulted door-way. The knight Biorn smiled grimly, and said, as if reading her thoughts: "Oh! he will never again come out thence, I have put an end to that for ever." His guests looked at him inquiringly, as if anxious to understand his meaning; and with a strange air of unconcern, as though the storm had awakened all the fierceness of his soul, he began the following history:

"I was once a happy man myself; I could smile, as you do—and I could rejoice in the clear morning air, as you do; that was before the hypocritical chaplain had so worked on the pious scruples of my lovely wife, as to induce her to shut herself up in a cloister, and leave me alone with my ungovernable child. That was not fair usage on the part of the fair Verena. Well, so it was, that in the first days of her dawning beauty, before I knew her, many knights sought her hand, amongst whom was Sir Weigand the Slender; and towards him the gentle maiden showed herself the most favourably inclined. Her parents were well aware that Weigand's rank and station were little below their own, and that his fame as a warrior without reproach promised to stand high, so that before long it was generally known that Verena and he were betrothed to each other. It happened one day that they were walking together in the garden of her father's castle, at the time when a shepherd was driving his flock up the mountain beyond. The maiden took a fancy to a little snow-white lamb which she saw frolicking about, and wished to have it. Weigand flew out of the garden, overtook the shepherd, and offered him two pieces of gold for the lamb. But the shepherd would not part with it, and scarcely listened to the knight, going quietly the while up the mountain side. Weigand persevered, but failing in his attempts, he lost patience, and at last uttered some threat. The shepherd, who was not wanting in the pride and stubbornness of all our northern peasants, threatened in return. Suddenly Weigand's sword glittered above his head—the stroke should have fallen lightly—but who can control a fiery horse, or an angry warrior's arm? The shepherd's head seemed cleft asunder by the blow, he rolled bathed in blood down to the very bottom of the precipice—his terrified flock dispersed on the mountains. The little lamb alone took refuge in the garden, and, all sprinkled with its master's blood, it laid itself down at Verena's feet, as if asking for protection. She took it up in her arms, and from that moment never suffered Weigand to appear again in her presence. She continued to cherish the little lamb, and seemed to take pleasure in nothing else in the world, while she became each day more and more pale, like the lilies, and her every thought was devoted to Heaven. She would soon have taken the veil, but just then I came to aid her father in a war in which he was engaged, and saved him from his too powerful enemies. As a reward of my services, he prevailed on his daughter to give me her fair hand. The overwhelming weight of his affliction would not suffer the unhappy Weigand to remain in his own country—he went as a pilgrim to Asia, whence our forefathers came, and there he performed wondrous deeds of valour, not omitting acts of humiliation and penitence. I could not hear him spoken of in those days without my heart being strangely moved with compassion. Years rolled by, and he returned, meaning to erect a church or monastery on that mountain, towards the west, whence the walls of my castle are distinctly seen. It was said that he wished to become a priest there, but it fell out otherwise. For some pirates having sailed from the southern seas towards our coasts, and having heard mention made of this monastery which was in progress, their chief hoped to find much gold in the possession of those who were building it, or to get a large ransom for them, if he should succeed in surprising them, and carrying them off. He could not have known much about the valour of northern warriors! However, he soon arrived, and having landed in the creek under the black rocks, he led his men through a by-path up to the building, surrounded it, and thought in himself that the game was now in his hands. Ha! then out rushed Weigand and his builders, and fell upon them with swords, and hatchets, and hammers. The heathens fled away to their ships, closely pursued by Weigand. In passing by our castle, he caught a sight of Verena on the terrace, and, for the first time during so many years, she bestowed a courteous and kind salutation on the victorious warrior. At that moment a dagger, hurled by one of the pirates in the midst of his hasty flight, struck Weigand's uncovered head, and he fell to the ground bleeding and insensible. We completed the rout of the heathens: then I directed the wounded knight to be brought into the castle; and my Verena's pale cheeks glowed as lilies do in the light of the morning sun, and Weigand opened his eyes with a smile when he was brought near her. He refused to be taken into any room but the small one close to this, where the armour is now placed; for he said that he felt as if it were a cell like that which he hoped soon to inhabit in the quiet cloister he was erecting. All was done conformably to his desire; my sweet Verena nursed him, and he appeared at first to be advancing favourably towards recovery, but his head continued weak, and liable to be confused by the slightest emotion—his steps were faltering, and his cheeks colourless. We would not suffer him to depart. When we were sitting here together in the evening, he used always to come tottering into the hall through the low doorway; and my heart was sad, and wrathful too, when the soft eyes of Verena beamed so sweetly on him, and a glow like that of the evening sky lighted up her pale countenance. But I bore it, and I could have borne it to the end of our lives,—when, alas! Verena shut herself up in a cloister!"

His head fell so heavily on his folded hands, that the stone table groaned under it, and he remained a long while motionless as a corpse. When he again raised himself up, his eyes glared as he looked round the hall, and he said to Folko: "Your beloved Hamburghers, Gotthard Lentz, and Rudlieb his son, they have much to answer for! Who bid them come and be shipwrecked so close to my castle?"

Folko cast a piercing look on him, and a fearful inquiry was on the point of escaping his lips, but another look at the trembling Gabrielle caused him to refrain, at least for the present moment, and the knight Biorn continued his narrative:

"Verena was with her nuns, I was left alone, and my despair had driven me to the mountains and the forest during the whole day. Towards evening I returned to my deserted castle, and scarcely was I in the hall, when the little door creaked on its hinges, and Weigand, who had slept through all, crept towards me and asked: 'Where can Verena be?' Then I became like one out of his senses, and I shouted, 'She is gone mad, and so am I, and you also, and now we are all mad!' Merciful Heaven, the wound on his head burst open, and a dark red stream flowed over his face—alas! how different from the redness which overspread it when Verena met him at the castle gate,—and he rushed forth, raving mad, into the wilderness without, and ever since has wandered all around, as a crazy pilgrim."

He was silent, and so were Folko and Gabrielle,—all three pale and cold, like images of the dead. At length the fearful narrator added in a low voice, and as if he were quite exhausted: "He has visited me since that time, but he will never again come through the low door-way. Have I not established peace and order in my castle?"

CHAPTER XIV.

Sintram had not returned home, when the inhabitants of the castle betook themselves to rest in great disturbance of mind No one thought of him, for every heart was filled with strange forebodings of evil, and with undefined anxiety. Even the firm heroic spirit of the knight of Montfauçon did not escape the general agitation.

Old Rolf still remained without, weeping in the forest, heedless of the storm which beat on his unprotected head, while he waited for his young master. But he had gone a very different way; and when the morning dawned, he entered the castle from the opposite side.

Gabrielle's slumbers had been but too sweet during the whole night. It had seemed to her that angels with golden wings had blown away the wild histories she had listened to the evening before, and had wafted to her the bright flowers, the sparkling sea, and the green hills of her own home. She smiled, and drew her breath calmly and softly, whilst the supernatural tempest raged and howled through the forests, and kept up a fearful conflict with the troubled sea. But, in truth, when she awoke in the morning, and heard the crashing of the storm still continuing, and saw the clouds still hiding the face of the heavens, she could have wept for anxiety and sadness, especially when she heard from her maidens that Folko had already left their apartment clad in full armour as if prepared for a combat. At the same time she could distinguish the sound of the heavy tread of armed men in the echoing halls, and, on inquiring, found that the knight of Montfauçon had assembled all his retainers to be in readiness to protect their lady.

Wrapped in a cloak of ermine, she stood trembling like a tender flower which has just sprung up out of the snow, and is exposed to the rude blasts of a winter's storm. At that moment Sir Folko entered the room, arrayed in his brilliant armour, and in peaceful guise carrying his golden helmet, with the long shadowy plumes in his hand. He saluted Gabrielle with an air of cheerful serenity, and, at a sign from him, his attendants retired—the men-at-arms without were heard quietly dispersing

"Lady," said he, as he took his seat beside her on a couch to which he led her, already re-assured by his presence; "Lady, will you forgive your knight for having left you to endure some moments of anxiety, whilst he was obeying the call of honour and the stern voice of duty. Now all is set in order, quietly and peacefully; dismiss your fears and every thought that has troubled you, as things that have no longer any existence."

"But you and Biorn?" asked Gabrielle.

"On the word of a knight," replied he, "all is as it should be." And thereupon he began to talk over indifferent subjects with his usual ease and vivacity; but Gabrielle, bending towards him, said, with deep emotion:

"Oh Folko, my knight, the guiding star of my life, my pro tector, and my dearest hope on earth, tell me all, if you may. If you are bound by a promise to keep any thing secret, I ask no more. You know that I am of the race of Portamour, and I would ask nothing from my knight which could cast even a breath of suspicion on his spotless shield."

Folko thought gravely for one instant, then looking at her with a bright smile, he said: "It is not that, Gabrielle, but can you bear what I have to disclose? Will you not sink down at the tidings, as a slender fir gives way under a mass of snow?"

She raised herself with a somewhat proud air, and said: "I have already reminded you of the name of my father's house. Let me now add that I am the wedded wife of the Baron of Montfauçon."

"Then so let it be," replied Folko solemnly; "and if that must come forth openly which should ever have remained hidden in the darkness which belongs to such deeds of wickedness at least the horror of longer expectation shall not be added to it. Know then, Gabrielle, that the wicked knight who attempted the destruction of my friends Gotthard and Rudlieb, is none other than our kinsman and host, Biorn of the Fiery Eyes."

Gabrielle shuddered and covered her eyes with her fair hands; but at the end of a moment she looked up with a bewildered air, and said: "I have heard wrong surely, although it is true that yesterday evening such a thought flashed across my mind. For did not you say awhile ago that all was settled and at peace between you and Biorn? Between the brave baron and such a man after such a crime?"

"You heard aright," answered Folko, looking with fond delight on the delicate, yet noble spirited being beside him. "This morning with the earliest dawn I went to him and challenged him to a mortal combat in the neighbouring valley, if he were the man to whose cruelty Gotthard and Rudlieb had so well nigh fallen victims. He was already completely armed, and merely saying, 'I am he,' he led the way towards the forest. But when we stood alone at the place of combat, he flung away his shield down a giddy precipice, then his sword was hurled after it, and next with gigantic strength he tore off his coat of mail, and said: 'Now fall on, thou minister of vengeance, for I am a man laden with guilt, and I dare not fight with thee.' How could I then attack him? A strange kind of truce was agreed on between us,—he is to be my vassal to a certain extent, and yet I solemnly forgave him in my own name and in that of my friends. He was contrite, and yet no tear was in his eye, no word of penitence on his lips. He is only kept under by the power with which I am endued by having right on my side, and it is on that tenure that Biorn is my vassal. I know not, lady, whether you can bear to see us together on these terms; if not, I will ask for hospitality in some other castle—there are none in Norway which would not receive us joyfully and honourably, and this wild autumnal storm may put off our voyage for many a day. Only I feel persuaded of this, that if we depart directly and in such a manner, the heart of this savage man will break."

"Where my noble lord remains, there am I content to remain also under his protection," replied Gabrielle, and again her heart glowed with rapture at the greatness of her knight.

CHAPTER XV.

The noble lady had just unbuckled her knight's armour with her own fair hands,—for it was only on the field of battle that pages or esquires were permitted to perform that office for Montfauçon,—and now she was throwing over his shoulders his mantle of blue velvet embroidered with gold, when the door opened gently, and Sintram, entering the room, saluted them with an air of deep humility. Gabrielle received him kindly as she was wont, but, suddenly turning pale, she looked away and said: "Oh! Sintram, what has happened to you? And how can one single night have so fearfully altered you?"

Sintram stood still, thunderstruck, and feeling as if he himself did not know what had befallen him. Then Folko took him by the hand, led him towards a bright polished shield, and said very earnestly: "Look here at yourself, young knight!"

No sooner had Sintram cast a glance at the mirror than he drew back with horror. He fancied that he saw the Little Master before him with that single upright feather sticking out of his cap; but he at length perceived that the mirror was only showing him his own image and none other, and that it was owing to the lock of hair cut off by his own dagger that his whole appearance had become so strange, nay, even unearthly, as he was obliged to confess himself.

"Who has done that to you," asked Folko in a tone yet more grave and solemn. "And why does your disordered hair stand on end?"

Sintram knew not what to answer. He felt as if he were standing to be judged, and as if his sentence could be none other than a shameful degradation from his knightly rank. Suddenly Folko drew him away from the shield, and taking him towards the window against which the storm was beating he asked: "Whence comes this tempest?"

Still Sintram kept silence. His limbs began to tremble under him, and Gabrielle, pale and terrified, whispered: "Oh Folko, my knight, what has happened? Oh tell me; are we come into an evil enchanted castle?"

"The land of our Northern ancestors," replied Folko with solemnity, "is full of mysterious knowledge. But we may not, for all that, call its people enchanters; still this youth has good cause to watch himself narrowly; he whom the Evil One has touched by so much as one hair of his head. . . ."

Sintram heard no more; with a deep groan he staggered out of the room. As he left it, he met old Rolf, still almost benumbed by his exposure to the cold and storms of the night. Now in his joy at again seeing his young master, he did not remark his altered appearance; but as he accompanied him to his sleeping room, he said: "Witches and spirits of the tempest must have taken up their abode on the sea-shore. I am certain that such wild storms never arise without some magical arts."

Sintram fell into a fainting-fit, from which Rolf could with difficulty recover him sufficiently to appear in the great hall at the mid-day repast. But before he went down, he caused a mirror to be brought, and having again surveyed himself therein with grief and horror, he cut close round all the rest of his long black hair, so that he made himself look almost like a monk, and thus he joined the party already assembled round the table. They all looked at him with surprise, but old Biorn rose up and said fiercely: "Are you going to betake yourself to a cloister as well as the fair lady, your mother?"

A commanding look from the Baron of Montfauçon checked any farther outbreak, and, as if in apology, Biorn added with a forced smile: "I was only thinking if any accident had befallen him, like Absalom's, and if he had been obliged to save himself from being strangled by parting with all his hair."

"You should not jest on sacred subjects," answered the Baron severely, and all were silent. No sooner was the repast ended than Folko and Gabrielle, with grave and courteous salutation, retired to their own apartments.

CHAPTER XVI.

After this time a great change took place in the mode of living of the inhabitants of the castle. Those two bright beings, Folko and Gabrielle, spent most part of the day in their apartments, and when they appeared below, their intercourse with Biorn and Sintram was marked by a grave dignified reserve on their part and by humility mixed with fear on that of their hosts. Nevertheless, Biorn could not endure the thought of his guests seeking shelter in any other knight's abode. Once that Folko said a word on the subject, something like a tear stood in the wild man's eye—his head sank, and he said in a scarcely audible voice: "It must be as you please: but I feel that if you go, I shall fly to the caves and rocks in despair."

And thus they all remained together; for the storm continued to rage with such increasing fury over the sea, that no thought of embarking could be entertained, and the oldest man in Norway could not call to mind having witnessed such an autumn. The priests examined all the Runic books, the bards looked through their store of lays and tales, and yet they could find no record of the like. Biorn and Sintram braved the tempest; but during the few hours in which Folko and Gabrielle showed themselves, the father and son were always in the castle, in respectful attendance upon them; the rest of the day—nay, even frequently, the whole night long, they rushed through the forests and over the rocks in pursuit of bears. Folko, the while, summoned to his aid all the brightness of his fancy, all the courtly grace he was endowed with, in order to make Gabrielle forget that she was living in this wild castle and that the long hard northern winter was setting in, which would keep her there an ice-bound prisoner for many a month. Sometimes he would relate tales of deep interest; then he would play the liveliest airs to induce Gabrielle to tread a measure with her attendants; then, again, handing his lute to one of the women, he would himself take a part in the dance, never failing to express by his gestures his homage and devotion to his lady. Another time he would have the spacious halls of the castle prepared for his armed retainers to go through their warlike exercises and trials of strength, and Gabrielle always adjudged the reward to the conqueror. Folko often joined the circle of combatants; but always took care to deprive no one of the prize, by confining his efforts merely to parrying the blows aimed at him. The Norwegians, who stood around as spectators, used to compare him to the demi-god Baldur, one of the heroes of their old traditions, who was wont to let the darts of his companions be all hurled against him, conscious that he was invulnerable, and trusting in his own inherent strength.

At the close of one of these martial exercises, old Rolf advanced towards Folko, and beckoning him with an humble look, he said softly: "They call you Baldur the brave, the good—and they are right. But even the good and brave Baldur did not escape death. Take heed to yourself." Folko looked at him with surprise. "Not that I know of any treacherous design against you," continued the old man; "or that I can even foresee the likelihood of any being formed. God forbid that a Norwegian should feel such a fear. But when you stand before me in all the brightness of your glory, the fleetingness of everything earthly is brought strongly to my mind, and I cannot refrain from saying, 'Take heed, noble baron! oh, take heed! There is nothing, however great, which does not come to an end.'"

"Those are wise and pious thoughts," replied Folko, calmly, "and I will treasure them in my inmost heart."

The good Rolf spent frequently some time with Folko and Gabrielle, and seemed to form a connecting link between the two widely-differing parties in the castle. For how could he have ever forsaken his own Sintram! It was only in their wild hunting expeditions, when they had no regard to the storms and tempests which were raging, that he no longer was able to follow his young lord.

At length the icy reign of winter began in all its glory. The season was sufficient of itself to prevent a return to Normandy being thought of, and therefore the storm which had been raised by magical art, was lulled. The hills and valleys shone brilliantly in their white attire of snow, and Folko used sometimes, with skates on his feet, to draw his lady in a light sledge over the glittering frozen lakes and streams. On the other hand, the bear-hunts of the lord of the castle and his son assumed a still more desperate and to them enjoyable aspect.

About this time,—when Christmas was drawing near, and Sintram was seeking to overpower his apprehensions of the fearful dreams which were wont to trouble him then, by the most daring expeditions,—about this time, Folko and Gabrielle chanced to be standing together on one of the terraces of the castle. The evening was mild; the snow-clad fields were glowing in the red light of the setting sun; from below there were heard men's voices singing songs of ancient heroic times, while they worked in the armourer's forge. At last the songs died away, the beating of hammers ceased, and without the speakers being visible, or there being any possibility of distinguishing them by their voices, the following discourse was distinctly heard:—

"Who is the bravest amongst all those whose race derives its origin from our renowned land?"

"It is Folko of Montfauçon."

"Rightly said; but, tell me, is there any danger from which even this bold baron draws back?"

"In truth there is one thing,—and we who have never left Norway, face it quite willingly and joyfully."

"And that is?"

"A bear-hunt in winter, over trackless plains of snow, down frightful ice-covered precipices."

"Truly thou answerest aright, my comrade. He who knows not how to fasten our skates on his feet, how to turn in them to the right or left at a moment's warning, he may be a valiant knight in other respects, but he had better keep away from our hunting parties, and remain with his timid wife in her apartments." At which the speakers were heard to laugh as if well pleased, and then to betake themselves again to their armourers' work.

Folko stood long buried in thought. A glow beyond that of the evening sky reddened his cheek. Gabrielle also remained silent, revolving in her mind that for which she was unable to find words. At last she took courage, and embracing her beloved, she said: "To-morrow you will go forth to hunt the bear, will you not? and you will bring the spoils of the chase to your lady?"

The knight gave a joyful sign of assent; and the rest of the evening was spent in dances and music.

CHAPTER XVII.

"SEE, my noble lord," said Sintram the next morning, when Folko had expressed his wish of going out with him, "these skates of ours give such wings to our course that we go down the mountain-side more swiftly than the wind, and even in going up again we are too quick for any one to be able to pursue us, and on the plains no horse can keep up with us, and yet they can only be worn with safety by those who are well practised. It seems as though some strange spirit dwelt in them, which is fearfully dangerous to any that have not learnt the management of them in their childhood."

Folko answered somewhat proudly: "Do you suppose that this is the first time that I have been amongst your mountains? Years ago I have joined in this sport, and, thank Heaven! there is no knightly exercise which does not speedily become familiar to me."

Sintram did not venture to make any further objections, and still less did old Biorn. They both felt relieved when they saw with what skill and ease Folko buckled the skates on his feet, without suffering any one to assist him. This day they hunted up the mountain, in pursuit of a fierce bear which had often before escaped from them. Before long it was necessary that they should separate into different parties, and Sintram offered himself as companion to Folko, who, touched by the humble manner of the youth, and his devotion to him, forgot all that had disturbed him latterly in the pale, altered being before him, and agreed heartily to his proposal. As now they continued to climb higher and higher up the mountain, and saw from many a giddy height the rocks and crags below them looking like a vast expanse of sea suddenly turned into ice whilst tossed by a violent tempest the noble Montfauçon drew his breath more freely. He poured forth war-songs and love-songs in the clear mountain air, and the startled echoes repeated from rock to rock the lays of his southern home. He sprang lightly from one precipice to another, making use skilfully of the staff with which he was furnished for support, and turning now to the right, now to the left, as the fancy seized him, so that Sintram was fain to exchange his former anxiety for a wondering admiration, and the hunters, whose eyes had never been taken off the baron, burst forth with loud applause, proclaiming far and wide this fresh proof of his prowess.

The good fortune which usually accompanied Folko's deeds of arms, seemed still unwilling to leave him. After a short search, he and Sintram found distinct traces of the savage animal they were pursuing, and with beating hearts they followed the track so swiftly, that even a winged enemy would have been unable to escape from them. But the creature whom they sought did not attempt a flight—he lay sulkily ensconced in a cavern near the top of a steep precipitous rock, infuriated by the shouts of the hunters, and only waiting in his lazy fury for some one to be bold enough to climb up to his retreat, that he might tear him to pieces. Folko and Sintram had now reached the foot of this rock, the rest of the hunters being dispersed over the far-extending plain. The track led the two companions up the rock, and they set about climbing on the opposite sides of it, that they might be the more sure of not missing their prey. Folko reached the lonely topmost point first, and cast his eyes around. A wide, boundless tract of country, covered with untrodden snow, was spread before him, melting in the distance into the lowering clouds of the gloomy evening sky. He almost thought that he must have missed the traces of the fearful animal; when close beside him from a cleft in the rock, issued a long growl, and a huge black bear appeared on the snow, standing on its hind legs, and with glaring eyes it advanced towards the baron. Sintram the while was struggling in vain to make his way up the rock against the masses of snow which were continually slipping down upon him.

Rejoicing in an adventure such as he had not encountered for years, and which now appeared new to him, Folko of Montfauçon levelled his hunting spear, and awaited the attack of the wild beast. He suffered it to approach so near that its fearful claws were almost upon him; then he made a thrust, and the spear was buried deep in the bear's breast. But the furious beast still pressed on with a fierce growl, kept up on its hind legs by the cross iron of the spear, and the knight was forced to use all his strength not to lose his footing and to resist the savage assault; and the whole time there was the grim face of the bear all covered with blood, close before him, and sounding in his ear was its deep savage growl, which told of its thirst for blood, even in the midst of its death-struggles. At length the bear's resistance grew weaker, and the dark blood streamed upon the snow; one powerful thrust hurled him backwards over the edge of the precipice. At the same instant, Sintram stood by the baron of Montfauçon. Folko said, drawing a deep breath: "But I have not yet the prize in my hands, and have it I must, since fortune has given me a claim to it. Look, one of my skates seems to be out of order. Do you think, Sintram, that it is in such a state as not to hinder me in sliding down to the foot of the precipice?"

"Let me go instead," said Sintram. "I will bring you the head and the claws of the bear."

"A true knight," replied Folko with some displeasure, "never leaves his work to be finished by another. What I ask is, whether my skate is still fit for use?"

As Sintram bent down to look, and was on the point of saying "No!" he suddenly heard a voice close to him, saying "Why, yes! to be sure; there is no doubt about it."

Folko thought that Sintram had spoken, and darted off with the swiftness of an arrow, whilst his companion looked up in great surprise. The abhorred features of the Little Master met his eyes. As he was going to address him with angry words, he heard the sound of the baron's fearful fall down the precipice, and he stood still in silent horror. There was a breathless silence also in the abyss below.

"Now, why do you delay?" said the Little Master, after a pause. "He is dashed to pieces. Go back to the castle, and take the fair Helen to yourself."

Sintram shuddered. Then his detestable companion began to extol Gabrielle's charms in such glowing, deceiving words, that the heart of the youth swelled with a torrent of emotions he had never before known. He only thought of him who was now lying at the foot of the rock as of an obstacle removed from his way to Paradise; he turned towards the castle.

But a cry was heard below: "Help! help! my comrade! I am yet alive, but I am sorely wounded."

Sintram's will was changed, and he called to the baron: "I am coming."

But the Little Master said: "Nothing can be done to help king Menelaus; and the fair Helen knows it already. She is only waiting for knight Paris to comfort her." And with detestable craft he wove in that tale with what was actually happening, bringing in the most highly wrought praises of the lovely Gabrielle; and alas! the blinded youth harkened to him, and fled away! Again he heard far off the baron's voice calling to him: "Knight Sintram, knight Sintram, you on whom I bestowed that noble order, haste to me and help me! The she-bear and her whelps will be upon me, and I cannot use my right arm! knight Sintram, knight Sintram, haste to help me!"

His cries were overpowered by the furious speed with which the two were carried along on their skates, and by the evil words of the Little Master, who was mocking at the late proud bearing of king Menelaus towards the miserable Sintram. At last he shouted: "Good luck to you, she-bear! good luck to your whelps! There is a glorious meal for you! Now you will destroy the fear of Heathendom, him at whose name the Moorish women weep, the mighty Baron of Montfauçon. Never again, oh! dainty knight, will you shout at the head of your troops, 'Mountjoy St. Denys!'" But scarce had this holy name passed the lips of the Little Master, than he set up a howl of anguish, writhing himself with horrible contortions, and wringing his hands, and he ended by disappearing in a storm of snow which then arose.

Sintram planted his staff firmly in the ground, and stopped. How strangely did the wide expanse of snow, the distant mountains rising above it, and the dark green fir woods,—how strangely did they all look at him in cold reproachful silence! He felt as if he must sink under the weight of his sorrow and his guilt. The bell of a distant hermitage came floating sadly over the plain. With a burst of tears he exclaimed, as the darkness grew thicker around him: "My mother! my mother! I had once a beloved tender mother, and she said I was a good child!" A ray of comfort came to him as if brought on an angel's wing; perhaps Montfauçon was not yet dead! and he flew like lightning along the path which led back to the steep rock. When he got to the fearful place, he stooped and looked anxiously down the precipice. The moon which had just risen in full majesty helped him with her light. The knight of Montfauçon, pale and covered with blood, was supporting himself on one knee, and leaning against the rock—his right arm, which had been crushed in his fall, hung powerless at his side; it was plain that he had not been able to draw his good sword out of the scabbard. But, nevertheless, he was keeping the bear and her young ones at bay by his bold threatening looks, so that they only crept round him, growling angrily; every moment ready for a fierce attack, but as often driven back affrighted at the majestic air by which he conquered even when defenceless.

"Oh! what a knight would here have perished!" groaned Sintram, "and through whose guilt?" At that instant his spear flew with so true an aim that the bear fell weltering in her blood; the young ones ran away howling.

The baron looked up with surprise. His countenance beam

ed as the light of the moon fell upon it, with a grave and stern, yet mild expression, like some angelic vision. He made a sign to Sintram to come to him, and the youth slid down the side of the precipice, full of anxious haste. He was going to attend to the wounded knight, but Folko said: "First cut off the head and claws of the bear which I slew. I promised to bring the spoils of the chase to my lovely Gabrielle. Then come to me, and bind up my wounds. My right arm is broken." Sintram obeyed the baron's commands. When the tokens of victory had been secured, and the broken arm bound up, Folko desired the youth to help him back to the castle.

"Oh Heavens!" said Sintram in a low voice, "if I dared to look in your face! or only knew how to come near you!"

"You were indeed going on in an evil course," said Montfauçon, gravely; "but how could we, any of us, stand before God, did we not bring repentance with us! Anyhow you have saved my life, and let that cheer your heart."

The youth with tenderness and strength supported the baron's left arm, and they both went their way silently into the moonlight.

CHAPTER XVIII.

Sounds of wailing were heard from the castle as they approached; the chapel was solemnly lighted up: within it knelt Gabrielle, lamenting for the death of the knight of Montfauçon.

But how quickly was the scene changed, when the noble baron, pale, indeed, and wounded, yet having escaped the dangers that beset his life, stood smiling at the entrance of the holy building, and said in a low, gentle voice: "Look up Gabrielle, and be not affrighted: for by the honor of my race your knight still lives." Oh! with what joy did Gabrielle's eyes sparkle, as she turned to her knight and then raised them again to heaven; the tears which still streamed from them having now their source in the deep joy of thankfulness! With the help of two pages, Folko knelt down beside her, and they both offered up a silent prayer of thanksgiving for their present happiness.

When they all left the chapel, the wounded knight being tenderly supported by his lady, Sintram was standing without in the darkness, himself as gloomy as the night, and like a bird of the night shunning the sight of man. Yet he came trembling forward into the torch-light, laid the bear's head and claws at the feet of Gabrielle, and said: "The noble Folko of Montfauçon presents the spoils of to-day's chase to his lady."

The Norwegians burst forth with shouts of joyful surprise at the stranger knight, who in the very first hunting expedition had slain the most fearful and dangerous beast of their mountains.

Then Folko looked around with a smile as he said: "And now none of you must jeer at me, if I stay at home for a short time with my timid wife."

Those who the day before had talked together in the armourer's forge, came out from the crowd, and bowing low, they replied: "Noble baron, who could have thought that there was no knightly exercise in the whole world, in which you would not show yourself far above all other men?"

"The pupil of old Sir Hugh may be somewhat trusted," answered Folko kindly. "But now, you bold northern warriors, bestow some praises also on my deliverer, who saved me from the claws of the she-bear, when I was lying under the rock wounded by my fall."

He pointed to Sintram, and the general shout was again raised, and old Rolf, his eyes dim with tears of joy, bent his head over his foster-son's hand. But Sintram drew back shuddering.

"Did you but know," he said, "whom you see before you, all your spears would be aimed at my heart; and perhaps that would be the best thing that could befal me. But I spare the honour of my father and of his race, and for this time I will not make a confession. Only this much must you hear, noble warriors."

"Young man," interrupted Folko, with a reproving look, 'already again so wild and fierce? I desire that you will hold your peace about your dreaming fancies."

Sintram was silenced for a moment, but hardly had Folko begun to move towards the steps of the castle, than he cried out: "Oh no, no, noble wounded knight, stay yet awhile; I will serve you in everything that your heart can desire; but this once I cannot obey you. Brave warriors, you must and shall know so much as this: I am no longer worthy to live under the same roof with the noble baron of Montfauçon and his angelic lady Gabrielle. And you, my aged father, farewell: take no further heed of me. I intend to live in the stone fortress on the rocks of the Moon, until a change of some kind comes over me."

There was that in his way of speaking against which no one dared to urge any opposition, not even Folko himself.

The wild Biorn bowed his head humbly, and said: "Do according to your pleasure, my poor son; for I much fear that you are right."

Then Sintram walked solemnly and silently through the castle gate, followed by the good Rolf. Gabrielle led her exhausted lord up to their apartments.

CHAPTER XIX.

THAT was a mournful journey on which the youth and his aged foster-father went towards the Rocks of the Moon, through the wild tangled paths of the snow-covered vallies. Rolf from time to time sang some verses of hymns, in which comfort and peace were promised to the penitent sinner, and Sintram thanked him for them with looks of grateful sadness. Otherwise neither of them spoke a word.

At length, when the dawn of day was approaching, Sintram broke silence by saying: "Who are those two, sitting yonder by the frozen stream? A tall man, and a little one. Their own wild hearts must have driven them also forth into the wilderness. Rolf, do you know them? The sight of them makes me shudder."

"Sir," answered the old man, "your disturbed mind deceives you. Where you are looking, there stands a lofty fir-tree, and the old weather-beaten stump of an oak, half-covered with snow, which gives them a somewhat strange appearance. There are no men sitting yonder."

"But, Rolf, look there! Look again carefully! Now they move, they whisper together."

"Sir, the morning breeze moves the branches, and whistles in the sharp pine-leaves, and in the yellow oak-leaves, and rustles the crisp snow."

"Rolf, now they are both coming towards us. Now they are standing before us; they are quite close."

"Sir, it is we who get nearer to them as we walk on, and the setting moon throws such long gaint-like shadows over the plain."

"Good evening!" said a hollow voice, and Sintram knew it

was the crazy pilgrim, near to whom stood the malignant dwarf, looking more hideous than ever.

"You are right, Sir knight," whispered Rolf, as he drew back behind Sintram, and made the sign of the Cross on his breast and forehead.

The bewildered youth, however, advanced towards the two figures, and said: "You have always taken wonderful pleasure in being my companions. What do you expect will come of it? And do you choose to go now with me to the stone fortress? There I will tend you, poor pale pilgrim; and as to you, frightful Master, most evil dwarf, I will make you shorter by the head, to reward you for your deeds yesterday."

"That would be a fine thing," sneered the Little Master; "and perhaps you imagine that you would be doing a great service to the whole world? And indeed, who knows? Something might be gained by it! Only, poor wretch, you cannot do it."

The pilgrim meantime was waving his pale head to and fro thoughtfully, saying: "I believe truly, that you would willingly have me, and I would go to you willingly, but I may not yet. Have patience awhile; you will yet surely see me come, but at a distant time, and, first, we must again visit your father together, and then also you will learn to call me by my right name, my poor friend."

"Beware of disappointing me again!" said Little Master to the pilgrim in a threatening voice; but he, pointing with his long, shrivelled hand towards the sun, which was just now rising, said: "Stop either that sun or me, if you can!"

Then the first rays fell on the snow, and Little Master ran down a precipice, scolding as he went, but the pilgrim walked on in the bright beams, calmly and with great solemnity, towards a neighboring castle on the mountain. It was not long before its chapel bell was heard tolling for the dead.

"For Heaven's sake," whispered the good Rolf to his knight, "for Heaven's sake, Sir Sintram, what kind of companions have you here? One of them cannot bear the light of God's blessed sun, and the other has no sooner set a foot in a dwelling, than the passing-bell is heard from thence. Could he have been a murderer?"

"I do not think that," said Sintram. "He seemed to me the best of the two. But it is a strange wilfulness of his not to come with me. Did I not invite him kindly? I believe that he can sing well, and he should have sung to me some gentle lullaby. Since my mother has lived in a cloister, no one sings lullabies to me any more."

At this tender recollection his eyes were bedewed with tears. But he did not himself know what he had said besides, for there was wildness and confusion in his spirit. They arrived at the Rocks of the Moon, they mounted up to the stone fortress. The castellan, an old, gloomy man, who was all the more devoted to the young knight from his dark melancholy and wild deeds, hastened to lower the drawbridge. Greetings were exchanged in silence, and in silence did Sintram enter, and those joyless gates closed with a crash behind the future recluse.

CHAPTER XX.

YES, truly, a recluse, or at least something like it, did poor Sintram now become! For towards the time of the approaching Christmas Festival his fearful dreams came over him, and seized him so fiercely, that all the esquires and servants fled with shrieks out of the castle, and would never venture back again. No one remained with him except Rolf and the old castellan. After a while, indeed, Sintram became calm, but he went about looking so pallid and subdued, that he might have been taken for a wandering corpse. No comforting of the good Rolf, no devout soothing lays, were of any avail; and the castellan, with his fierce, scarred features, his head almost entirely bald from a huge sword-cut, his stubborn silence, seemed like a yet darker shadow of the miserable knight. Rolf often thought of going to summon the holy chaplain of Drontheim, but how could he have left his lord alone with the gloomy castellan, a man who at all times raised in him a secret horror. Biorn had long had this wild strange warrior in his service, and honoured him on account of his unshaken fidelity and his fearless courage, without the knight or any one else knowing whence the castellan came, or indeed exactly who he was. Very few people knew by what name to call him, but that was the more needless since he never entered into discourse with any one. He was the castellan of the stone fortress on the Rocks of the Moon, and nothing more.

Rolf committed his deep heartfelt cares to the merciful God, trusting that He would soon come to his aid, and the merciful God did not fail him. For on Christmas eve the bell at the drawbridge sounded, and Rolf, looking over the battlements, saw the chaplain of Drontheim standing there, with a companion indeed that surprised him,—for close beside him appeared the crazy pilgrim, and the dead men's bones on his dark mantle shone very strangely in the glimmering star-light; but the sight of the chaplain filled the good Rolf too full of joy to leave room for any doubt in his mind—for, thought he, whoever comes with *him*, cannot but be welcome! And so he let them both in with respectful haste, and ushered them up to the hall where Sintram, pale and with a fixed look, was sitting under the light of one flickering lamp. Rolf was obliged to support and assist the crazy pilgrim up the stairs, for he was quite benumbed with cold.

"I bring you a greeting from your mother," said the chaplain, as he came in, and immediately a sweet smile passed over the young knight's countenance, and its deadly pallidness gave place to a bright, soft glow.

"Oh Heaven!" murmured he, "does then my mother yet live, and does she care to know anything about me?"

"She is endowed with wonderful presentiment of the future," replied the chaplain, "and all that you ought either to do or to leave undone is pictured in various ways in her mind, during a half-waking trance, but with most faithful exactness. Now she knows of your deep sorrow, and she sends me, the Father Confessor of her convent, to comfort you, but at the same time to warn you, for, as she affirms, and as I am also inclined to think, many strange and heavy trials lie before you."

Sintram bowed himself towards the chaplain with his arms crossed over his breast, and said with a gentle smile: "Much have I been favoured, more, a thousand times more, than I could have dared to hope in my best hours, by this greeting from my mother, and your visit, reverend sir; and all after falling more fearfully low than I had ever fallen before. The mercy of the Lord is great, and how heavy soever may be the weight and punishment which he may send, I trust with his grace to be able to bear it."

Just then the door opened, and the castellan came in with a torch in his hand, the red glare of which made his face look the colour of blood. He cast a terrified glance at the crazy pilgrim, who had just sunk back in a swoon, and was supported on his seat and tended by Rolf; then he stared with astonishment at the chaplain, and at last murmured: "A strange meeting! I believe that the hour for confession and reconciliation is now arrived."

"I believe so, too," replied the priest, who had heard his low whisper; "this seems to be truly a day rich in grace and peace. That poor man yonder, whom I found half frozen by the way, would make a full confession to me at once, before he followed me to a place of shelter. Do as he has done, my dark-browed warrior, and delay not your good purpose for one instant."

Thereupon he left the room with the castellan, who gave a sign of compliance, but he turned back to say: "Sir knight, and your esquire! take good care the while of my sick charge."

Sintram and Rolf did according to the chaplain's desire, and when at length their cordials made the pilgrim open his eyes once again, the young knight said to him with a friendly smile: "Do you see? you are come to visit me after all. Why did you refuse me when a few nights ago I asked you so earnestly to come? Perhaps I may have spoken wildly and hastily. Did that scare you away?"

A sudden expression of fear came over the pilgrim's countenance, but soon he again looked up at Sintram with an air of gentle humility, saying: "Oh my dear lord, I am most entirely devoted to you—only never speak to me of former passages between you and me. I am terrified whenever you do it. For, my lord, either I am mad and have forgotten all that is past, or that being has met you in the wood, whom I look upon as my all-powerful twin-brother."

Sintram laid his hand gently on the pilgrim's mouth, as he answered: "Say nothing more about that matter. I most willingly promise to be silent."

Neither he nor old Rolf could understand what appeared to them so awful in the whole matter; but both shuddered.

After a short pause, the pilgrim said: "I would rather sing you a song, a soft, comforting song. Have you not a lute here?"

Rolf fetched one, and the pilgrim, half-raising himself on the couch, sang the following words:—

When death is coming near,
When thy heart shrinks in fear,
And thy limbs fail,
Then raise thy hands and pray
To Him who smooths thy way
Through the dark vale.

Seest thou the eastern dawn,
Hear'st thou in the red morn
The angel's song?
O lift thy drooping head
Thou who in gloom and dread
Hast lain so long.

Death comes to set thee free,
O meet him cheerily
As thy true friend,
And all thy fears shall cease,
And in eternal peace
Thy penance end.

"Amen," said Sintram and Rolf, folding their hands; and whilst the last chords of the lute still resounded, the chaplain and the castellan came slowly and gently into the room. "I bring a precious Christmas gift," said the priest. "After many sad years, hope of reconciliation and peace of conscience are returning to a noble, but long disturbed mind. This concerns you, beloved pilgrim; and do you, my Sintram, with a joyful trust in God, take encouragement and example from it."

"More than twenty years ago," began the castellan at a sign from the chaplain, "more than twenty years ago I was a stout and active herdsman, and I drove my flock up the mountains. A young knight followed me, whom they called Weigand the Slender. He wanted to buy of me my favourite little lamb for his fair bride, and offered me much red gold for it. I sturdily refused. The over-boldness of youth carried us both away. A stroke of his sword hurled me senseless down the precipice."

"Not killed?" asked the pilgrim in a scarce audible voice.

"I am no ghost," replied the castellan somewhat morosely; and then after an earnest look from the priest he continued more humbly: "I recovered slowly and in solitude, with the help of remedies which were easily found by me, a herdsman, in our productive vallies. When I came back into the world, no man knew me with my scarred face, and my head which had become bald. I heard a report going through the country, that, on account of this deed of his, Sir Weigand the Slender had been rejected by his fair betrothed Verena, and how he had pined away, and she had wished to retire into a convent, but her father had persuaded her to marry the great knight Biorn. Then there came a fearful thirst for vengeance into my heart, and I disowned my name and my kindred and my home, and entered the service of the mighty Biorn as a strange wild man, in order that Weigand the Slender should always be deemed a murderer, and that I might feed on his anguish. So have I fed upon it for all these long years. I have revelled frightfully in his self-imposed banishment, in his cheerless return home, in his madness. But to-day"—and hot tears gushed from his eyes—"but to-day God has broken the hardness of my heart; and dear Sir Weigand, look upon yourself no more as a murderer, and say that you will forgive me, and pray for him who has done you so fearful an injury, and"——Sobs choked his words. He fell at the feet of the pilgrim, who with tears of joy pressed him to his heart, in token of forgiveness.

CHAPTER XXI.

THE joy of this hour passed from its first overpowering brightness, to the calm, thoughtful aspect of daily life, and Weigand, now restored to health, laid aside the mantle with dead men's bones, saying: "I had chosen for my penance to carry these fearful remains about with me, in the idea that perhaps some of them might have belonged to him whom I have murdered. Therefore I used to search for them round about in the deep beds of the mountain torrents, and in the high nests of the eagles and vultures. And while I was searching I sometimes—could it have been only an illusion?—I seemed to meet a being who was very like myself, but far, far more powerful, and yet still paler and more haggard."—An imploring look from Sintram stopped the flow of his words. With a gentle smile, Weigand bowed towards him, and said: "You know now all the deep, unutterably deep sorrow which preyed upon me. My fear of you, and my yearning love for you, are no longer without explanation to your kind heart. For, dear youth, though you may be like your fearful father, you have also the kind gentle heart of your mother, and its reflection brightens your pallid, stern features, like the glow of a morning sky which lights up ice-covered mountains and valleys. But alas! how long have you lived alone even amidst your fellow-creatures! And how long is it since you have seen your mother, my dearly-loved Sintram?"

"I feel, too, as though a spring were gushing up in the barren wilderness of my heart," replied the youth; "and I should perchance be altogether restored, could I but keep you long with me, and weep with you, dear friend. But I have that within me which says that you will very soon be taken from me."

"I believe, indeed," said the pilgrim, "that my song the

other day was very near my last, and that it contained a prediction full soon to be accomplished in me. But, as the soul of man is always like the thirsty ground, the more blessings God has bestowed on us, the more earnestly do we look out for new ones, so would I crave for one more ere my life closes, as I would fain hope, in happiness. Yet indeed it cannot be granted me," added he, with a faltering voice, "for I feel myself too utterly unworthy of such high grace."

"But it will be granted!" said the chaplain joyfully. "He that humbleth himself shall be exalted, and I fear not to take him who is now cleared from the stain of murder, to receive a farewell from the holy and forgiving countenance of Verena."

The pilgrim stretched both his hands up towards Heaven, and an unbroken thanksgiving seemed to pour from his beaming eyes, and to brighten the smile that played on his lips.

Sintram looked sorrowfully on the ground, and sighed gently to himself: "Alas! happy he who dared go also!"

"My poor, good Sintram," said the chaplain in a tone of the softest kindness, "I understand you well, but the time is not yet come. The powers of Evil will again raise up their wrathful heads within you, and Verena must check both her own and your longing desires, until all is pure in your spirit as in her's. Comfort yourself with the thought that God looks mercifully upon you, and that the joy so earnestly sought for, will not fail to come—if not here, most assuredly beyond the grave."

But the pilgrim, as though awaking out of a trance, rose with energy from his seat, and said: "Do you please to come forth with me, reverend chaplain? Before the sun appears in the heavens, we could reach the convent-gates, and I should not be far from Heaven."

In vain did the chaplain and Rolf remind him of his weakness: he smiled, and said that there could be no question about it, and he girded himself, and tuned the lute which he had asked leave to take with him. His decided manner overcame all opposition, almost without words: and the chaplain had already prepared himself for the journey, when the pilgrim looked with much emotion at Sintram, who, oppressed with a strange weariness, had sunk half asleep on a couch, and he said: "Wait a moment. I know that he wants me to give him a soft lullaby." The pleased smile of the youth seemed to say yes, and the pilgrim, touching the strings with a light hand, sang these words:—

"Sleep peacefully, dear boy,
Thy mother sends the song
That whispers round thy couch,
To lull thee all night long.
In silence and afar,
For thee she ever prays,
And longs once more in fondness
Upon thy face to gaze.

And when thy waking cometh,
Then in thy every deed,
In all that may betide thee,
Unto her words give heed.
O listen for her voice,
If it be yea or nay,
And though temptation meet thee,
Thou shalt not miss the way.

If thou canst listen rightly,
And nobly onward go,
Then pure and gentle breezes
Around thy cheeks shall blow.
Then on thy peaceful journey
Her blessing thou shalt feel,
And though from thee divided,
Her presence o'er thee steal.

O safest, sweetest, comfort!
O blest and living light!
That strong in Heaven's power
All terrors put to flight!
Rest quietly, sweet child,
And may the gentle numbers
Thy mother sends to thee,
Waft peace unto thy slumbers."

Sintram fell into a deep sleep, smiling and breathing softly. Rolf and the castellan remained by his bed, whilst the two travellers pursued their way in the quiet starlight.

CHAPTER XXII.

The dawn had almost appeared, when Rolf, who had been asleep, was awoke by low singing, and as he looked round, he perceived with surprise that the sounds came from the lips of the castellan, who said, as if in explanation: "So does Sir Weigand sing at the convent-gates, and they are kindly opened to him." Upon which old Rolf fell asleep again, uncertain whether what had passed had been a dream or a reality. After awhile the bright sunshine awoke him again, and when he rose up, he saw the countenance of the castellan wonderfully illuminated by the red light of the morning sun, and altogether those features, once so fearful, were shining with a soft, nay, almost child-like mildness of expression. The mysterious man seemed to be the while listening to the motionless air, as if he were hearing a most pleasant discourse, and as Rolf was about to speak, he made him a sign of entreaty to remain quiet, and he continued in his eager, listening attitude.

At length he sank slowly and contentedly back in his seat, whispering: "God be praised! She has granted his last prayer; he will be laid in the burial-ground of the convent, and now he has forgiven me from the bottom of his heart. I can assure you, that he is having a peaceful end."

Rolf did not dare ask a question, or awake his lord; he felt as if one already departed had spoken to him.

The castellan remained still for a long space of time, always with a bright smile on his face. At last he raised himself up a little, again listened, and said: "It is over. The sound of the bells is very sweet. We have overcome. Oh! how soft and easy does the good God make it to us!" And so it came to pass. He stretched himself back as if weary, and his soul was freed from his care-worn body.

Rolf now gently awoke his young knight, and pointed to the smiling face of the dead. And Sintram smiled too; he and his good esquire fell on their knees and prayed to God for the departed spirit. Then they rose up, and bore the cold body to the vaulted hall, and watched by it with holy candles until the return of the chaplain. That the pilgrim would not come back again, they very well knew.

Towards mid-day, accordingly, the chaplain returned alone. He could scarcely do more than confirm what was already known to them. He only added a comforting and hopeful greeting from Sintram's mother to her son, and told that the blissful Weigand had fallen asleep like a tired child, whilst Verena with calm tenderness held a crucifix before him.

"And in eternal peace our penance end!"

sang Sintram gently to himself, and they prepared a last resting-place for the now so peaceful castellan, and laid him therein with all the due solemn rites.

The chaplain was obliged soon afterwards to depart, but when bidding Sintram farewell, he again said kindly to him: "Your dear mother knows assuredly, how gentle, and calm, and good, you are now become!"

CHAPTER XXIII.

In the castle of Sir Biorn of the Fiery Eyes, Christmas eve had not passed so brightly and happily, but yet there too all had gone visibly according to God's will.

Folko, at the entreaty of the lord of the castle, had allowed Gabrielle to support him into the hall, and the three now sat at the round stone-table whereon a sumptuous meal was laid. On either side, there were long tables, at which sat the retainers of both knights, in full armour, according to the custom of the north. Torches and lamps lighted the lofty hall with an almost dazzling brightness.

The deepest shades of night had now gathered around, and Gabrielle softly reminded her wounded knight to withdraw. Biorn heard her and said: "You are right, fair lady, our knight needs rest. Only let us first keep up one more old honourable custom."

And at his sign four attendants brought in with pomp a great boar's head, which looked as if cut out of solid gold, and placed it in the middle of the stone-table. Biorn's retainers rose with reverence, and took off their helmets; Biorn himself did the same.

"What means this?" asked Folko very gravely.

"What your forefathers and mine have done on every Yule Feast," answered Biorn. "We are going to make vows on the boar's head, and then pass the goblet round to their fulfilment."

"We no longer keep what our ancestors called the Yule Feast," said Folko; "we are good Christians, and we keep holy Christmas-tide."

"We may observe the one without leaving off the other," answered Biorn. "I hold my ancestors too dear to forget their knightly customs. Those who think otherwise may act according to their wisdom, but that shall not hinder me. I swear by the golden boar's-head"———And he stretched out his hand towards it.

But Folko called out, "In the Name of our Holy Saviour, forbear. Where I am, and still have breath and will, none celebrate the rites of the wild heathens."

Biorn of the Fiery Eyes glared angrily at him. The men of the two barons separated from each other, with a hollow sound of rattling armour, and ranged themselves in two bodies on either side of the hall, each behind its leader. Already here and there helmets were fastened and visors closed.

"Bethink thee yet what thou art doing," said Biorn. "I was about to vow an eternal union with the house of Montfauçon, nay, even to bind myself to do it grateful homage, but if thou disturbest me in the customs which have come to me from my forefathers, look to thy safety, and the safety of all that is dear to thee. My wrath no longer knows any bounds."

Folko made a sign to the pale Gabrielle to retire behind his followers, saying to her: "Be of good cheer, my noble wife, weaker Christians have borne, for the sake of God and of His holy Church, greater dangers than now seem to threaten us. Believe me, the lord of Montfauçon is not so easily overcome."

Gabrielle obeyed, something comforted by Folko's fearless smile, but this smile inflamed yet more the fury of Biorn. He again stretched out his hand towards the boar's head, as if about to make some dreadful vow, when Folko snatched a gauntlet of Biorn's off the table, with which he, with his unwounded left arm, struck such a powerful blow on the gilt idol that it fell crashing to the ground, shivered to pieces. Biorn and his followers stood as if turned to stone. But soon swords were grasped by armed hands, shields were taken down from the walls, and an angry threatening murmur sounded through the hall.

At a sign from Folko, one of his faithful retainers brought him a battle-axe; he swung it high in the air with his powerful left hand, and he stood looking like an avenging angel as he spoke these words through the tumult with awful calmness: "What seek ye, O ye deluded Northmen? What wouldst thou, sinful lord? You are indeed become heathens, and I hope to show you that it is not in my right arm alone that God has put strength for victory. But if you can yet hear, listen to my words. Biorn, on this same accursed, and now, by God's help, shivered boar's head, thou didst lay thy hand when thou didst swear to sacrifice any inhabitants of the German towns that should fall into thy power. And Gotthard Lenz came, and Rudlieb came, driven on these shores by the storm. What didst thou then do, savage Biorn? What did you do at his bidding, you who were keeping the Yule-feast with him? Try your fortune on me. The Lord will be with me as he was with those holy men. To arms! and—" (he turned to his warriors,)—"let our battle-cry be Gotthard and Rudlieb!"

Then Biorn let drop his drawn sword; then his followers paused, and none among the Norwegians dared lift his eyes from the ground. By degrees they one by one began to disappear from the hall; and at last Biorn stood quite alone opposite to the baron and his followers. He seemed hardly aware that he had been deserted, but he fell on his knees, stretched out his shining sword, pointed to the broken boar's head, and said. "Do with me as you have done with that; I deserve no better. I ask but one favour, only one; do not disgrace me, noble baron, by seeking shelter in another castle while you remain in Norway."

"I do not fear you," answered Folko, after some thought, "and as far as may be, I freely forgive you." Then he drew the sign of the Cross over the wild form of Biorn, and left the hall with Gabrielle. The retainers of the house of Montfauçon followed him proudly and silently.

The high spirit of the fierce lord of the castle was now quite broken, and he watched with increased humility every look of Folko and Gabrielle. But they withdrew more and more into the happy solitude of their own apartments, where they enjoyed in the midst of the sharp winter a bright spring-tide of love and happiness. The wounded condition of Folko did not hinder the evening delights of songs and music and poetry—but rather a new charm was added to them when the tall, handsome knight leant on the arm of his delicate lady, and they thus, changing as it were their deportment and duties, walked slowly through the torch-lit halls, scattering their kindly greetings like flowers among the crowds of men and women.

All this time little or nothing was heard of poor Sintram. The last wild outbreak of his father had increased the terror with which Gabrielle remembered the self-accusations of the youth; and the more resolutely Folko kept silence, the more did she fear that some dreadful mystery lay beneath. Indeed a secret shudder came over the knight when he thought on the pale, dark-haired youth. Sintram's repentance had bordered on settled despair; no one knew even what he was doing in the fortress of Evil-Report on the Rocks of the Moon. Strange rumours were brought by the retainers who had fled from it, that the Evil Spirit had obtained complete power over Sintram, that no man could stay with him, and that the fidelity of the dark and mysterious castellan had cost him his life.

Folko could hardly drive away the fearful imagination that the lonely young knight was become a wicked magician.

And perhaps indeed evil spirits did flit about the banished Sintram, but it was without his calling them up. In his dreams he often saw the wicked enchantress Venus, in her golden chariot drawn by winged cats, pass over the battlements of the stone fortress, and heard her say, mocking him: "Foolish Sintram, foolish Sintram, hadst thou but listened to the Little Master's words! Thou wouldst now be in Helen's arms, and the Rocks of the Moon would be called the Rocks of Love, and the stone fortress would be the garden of roses. Thou wouldst have lost thy pale face and black tangled hair,—for thou art only enchanted, dear youth,—and thine eyes would have beamed more softly, and thy cheeks bloomed more freshly, and thy hair would have been more golden than was that of prince Paris, when men wondered at his beauty. Oh! how Helen would have loved thee!" Then she showed him, in a mirror, his own figure kneeling before Gabrielle, who sank into his arms blushing as the morning. When he awoke from such dreams, he would seize in eager haste the sword and scarf which his lady had given him, as a shipwrecked man seizes the plank which is to save him, and while the hot tears fell upon it, he would murmur to himself: "There was indeed one hour in my sad life when I was happy, and deserved it."

Once he sprang up at midnight after one of these dreams. only this time with a more thrilling horror than usual; for it had seemed to him that the features of the enchantress Venus had changed towards the end of her speech, as she looked down upon him with marvellous scorn, and she appeared to him almost to assume those of the hideous Little Master. The youth had no better means of calming his distracted mind than to throw the sword and scarf of Gabrielle over his shoulders, and to hasten forth under the solemn starry canopy of the wintry sky. He walked in deep thought backwards and forwards under the leafless oaks, and the snow-laden firs, which grew on the high ramparts.

Then he heard a sorrowful cry of distress sound from the moat; it was as if some one were attempting to sing, but was stopped by excess of grief. Sintram exclaimed, "Who's there?" and all was still. When he was silent and again began his walk, the frightful groanings and moanings were heard afresh, as if they came from a dying person. Sintram overcame the horror which seemed to hold him back, and began in silence to climb down into the deep dry moat, which was cut in the rock He was soon so low down that he could no longer see the stars shining; he saw a shrouded form move beneath him,—and sliding rapidly down the remainder of the steep descent, he stood near the groaning figure; it ceased its lamenta tions, and began to laugh like a maniac from beneath its long folded iemale garments.

"Oh, ho, my comrade! Oh, ho, my comrade! You are now going a little too fast: well, well, it is all right: and see now, you stand no higher than I, my pious valiant youth! Take it patiently,—take it patiently!"

"What do you want with me? Why do you laugh? why do you weep?" asked Sintram impatiently.

"I might ask you the same question," answered the dark figure, "and you would be less able to answer me, than I to answer you. Why do you laugh? why do you weep?—Poor creature! But I will show you a remarkable thing in your fortress, of which you know nothing. Give heed!"

And the shrouded figure began to scratch and scrape at the stones till a little iron door opened, and showed a long passage which led into the deep darkness.

"Will you come with me?" whispered the strange being: "it is the shortest way to your father's castle. In half an hour we shall come out of this passage, and we shall be in your beauteous lady's apartment. King Menelaus shall lie in a magic sleep,—leave that to me,—and then you will take the slight delicate form in your arms, and you will bring her to the Rocks of the Moon; so you will recover all that seemed lost by your former wavering."

Then Sintram might have been seen to stagger. He was shaken to and fro by the fever of passion and the stings of conscience · but at last, pressing the sword and scarf to his heart, he cried out: "Oh! that fairest, most glorious hour of my life! If I lose all other joys, I will hold fast that brightest hour!"

"A bright, glorious hour!" said the figure from under its veil, like an evil echo. "Do you know whom you then conquered? A good old friend, who only showed himself so sturdy in order to give you the glory of overcoming him. Will you convince yourself? Will you look?"

The dark garments of the little figure flew open, and Sintram saw the dwarf warrior in strange armour with the gold horn on his helmet, and the curved spear in his hand; the very same whom Sintram thought he had slain on Niflung's Heath, now stood before him, and grinned as he said: "You see, my friend, every thing in the wide world is made up of dreams and froth; wherefore hold fast the dream which delights you, and sip up the froth which refreshes you! Hasten to that underground passage, it leads up to your angel Helen. Or would you first know your friend yet better?"

His visor opened, and the hateful face of the Little Master glared upon the knight. Sintram asked, as if in a dream: "Art thou also that wicked enchantress Venus?"

"Something like her," answered the Little Master, laughing, "or rather she is something like me. And if you will only get disenchanted, and recover the beauty of prince Paris,—then, O prince Paris," and his voice changed to an alluring song, "then, O prince Paris, I shall be fair like you!"

At this moment the good Rolf appeared above on the rampart; a consecrated taper in his lantern shone down into the moat, as he sought for the young knight. "In God's name, Sir Sintram," he called out, "what have you to do there with the spectre of him whom you slew on Niflung's Heath, and whom I never could bury?"

"Do you see? do you hear?" whispered the Little Master, and drew back into the darkness of the underground passage. "The wise man up there knows me well. You see your heroic feat came to nothing. Come, take the joys of life while you may!"

But Sintram sprang back with a strong effort into the circle of light made by the shining of the taper from above, and cried out: "Depart from me, unquiet spirit! I know well that I bear a name on me, in which thou canst have no part."

Little Master rushed, in fear and rage, into the passage, and, yelling, shut the iron door behind him. It seemed as if he could be still heard groaning and roaring.

Sintram climbed up the wall of the moat, and made a sign to

his foster-father not to speak to him—he only said: "One of my best joys, yes, the very best, has been taken from me—but by God's help, I am not yet wholly lost."

In the earliest light of the following morning, he and Rolf stopped up the entrance to the perilous passage with huge blocks of stone.

CHAPTER XXIV.

The long northern winter was at last ended; the fresh, green leaves rustled merrily in the woods, patches of soft moss appeared amongst the rocks, the valleys were clothed with grass, the brooks sparkled, the snow melted from all but the highest mountain-tops, and the bark which was ready to carry away Folko and Gabrielle danced on the sunny waves. The baron, who was now quite recovered, and strong and fresh as though his health had sustained no injury, stood one morning on the shore with his fair lady, and, full of glee at the prospect of returning to their home, the noble pair looked on with satisfaction at their attendants, who were busied in the ship with preparations for the voyage.

Then said one of them, in the midst of a confused sound of talking: "But what has appeared to me the most fearful and the most strange thing in this northern land, is the stone fortress on the Rocks of the Moon: I have never indeed been inside it, but when I used to see it in our huntings, towering above the tall fir-trees, there came a tightness over my breast, as if some unearthly beings were dwelling in it. And a few weeks ago, when the snow was yet lying hard in the valleys, I came unawares quite close upon the strange building. The young knight Sintram was walking alone on the ramparts as the shades of twilight stole on, like the spirit of a departed knight, and he drew from the lute which he carried such soft melancholy tones, and he sighed so deeply and sorrowfully . . ."

The voice of the speaker was drowned in the noise of the crowd, and as he also just then reached the ship with his package, which had been hastily fastened up, Folko and Gabrielle could not hear the rest of his speech. But the fair lady looked on her knight with eyes dim with tears, and sighed: "Is it not behind those mountains that the Rocks of the Moon lie? The unhappy Sintram makes me sad at heart."

"I understand you, sweet gracious lady, and the pure compassion which fills your heart," replied Folko, and instantly ordered his swift-footed steed to be brought. He placed his noble lady under the charge of his retainers, and leaping into the saddle, he pursued his way, followed by the grateful smiles of Gabrielle, along the valley which led towards the stone fortress.

Sintram was seated near the drawbridge, touching the strings of the lute, and shedding some tears on the golden chords, almost exactly as Montfauçon's esquires had described him. Suddenly a cloudy shadow passed over him, and he looked up, expecting to see a flight of cranes in the air; but the sky was clear and blue. While the young knight was still wondering, a long bright spear fell at his feet from a battlement of the armoury turret. "Take it up,—make good use of it! your foe is near at hand! Near also is the downfal of your cherished hopes of happiness!" Thus he heard it distinctly whispered in his ear; and it seemed to him that he saw the shadow of the Little Master glide close by him to a neighbouring cleft in the rock. But at the same time, also, a tall, gigantic, haggard figure passed along the valley, in some measure like the departed pilgrim, only much, very much larger, and he raised his long bony arm with an awfully threatening air, then disappeared in an ancient tomb.

At the very same instant Sir Folko of Montfauçon came swiftly as the wind up the Rocks of the Moon, and he must have seen something of those strange apparitions, for, as he stopped close behind Sintram, he looked rather pale, and he asked low and earnestly: "Sir knight, who are those two with whom you were just now holding converse here?"

"The good God knows," answered Sintram. "I know them not."

"If the good God does but know!" cried Montfauçon. "But I fear me that he knows you not, nor your deeds."

"You speak strangely harsh words," said Sintram. "Yet ever since that evening of misery,—alas! and even long before

—I have no right to complain of anything you may say or do. Dear sir, you may believe me, I know not those fearful companions; I call them not; and I know not what terrible curse it is which binds them to my footsteps. The merciful God, as I would hope, is mindful of me the while, as a faithful shepherd does not forget even the worst and most widely-strayed of his flock, but calls after it with an anxious voice in the gloomy wilderness."

Then the anger of the baron was quite melted. Two tears stood in his eyes, and he said: "No, assuredly, God has not forgotten you; only do you not forget your gracious God. I did not come to rebuke you—I came to bless you in Gabrielle's name and in my own. The Lord preserve you, the Lord guide you, the Lord lift you up. And Sintram, on the far-off shores of Normandy I shall bear you in mind, and I shall hear how you struggle against the curse which darkens your unhappy life, and if you ever obtain the victory over it, and overcome in the evil day, then you shall receive from me a token of love and reward, more precious than either you or I can understand at this moment."

The words flowed prophetically from the baron's lips; he himself was only half-conscious of what he said. With a kind salutation he turned his noble steed, and again flew down the valley towards the sea-shore.

"Fool, fool, thrice a fool!" whispered the angry voice of the Little Master, in Sintram's ear, but old Rolf was singing his morning hymn in clear tones within the castle, and the last lines were these:—

"Whom worldlings scorn,
Who lives forlorn,
On God's own word doth rest;
With heavenly light,
His path is bright,
His lot among the blest."

Then a holy joy took possession of Sintram's heart; and he looked around him yet more gladly than in the hour when Gabrielle gave him the scarf and sword, and Folko dubbed him knight.

CHAPTER XXV.

THE baron and his lovely lady were sailing across the broad sea with favouring gales of spring, nay the coast of Normandy had already appeared above the waves, but still was Biorn of the Fiery Eyes sitting gloomy and speechless in his castle. He had taken no leave of his guests. There was more of proud fear of Montfauçon, than of reverential love for him in his soul, especially since the adventure with the boar's head, and the thought was bitter to his haughty spirit, that the great baron, the flower and glory of their whole race, should have come in peace to visit him, and should now be departing in displeasure, in stern reproachful displeasure. He had constantly before his mind, and it never failed to bring fresh pangs, the remembrance of how all had come to pass, and how all might have gone otherwise; and he was always fancying he could hear the songs in which after-generations would recount this voyage of the great Folko, and the worthlessness of the savage Biorn. At length, full of fierce anger, he cast away the fetters of his troubled spirit, he burst out of the castle with all his horsemen, and began to carry on a warfare more fearful and more lawless than any in which he had yet been engaged.

Sintram heard the sound of his father's war-horn, and committing the stone fortress to old Rolf, he sprang forth ready armed for the combat. But the flames of the cottages and farms on the mountains rose up before him, and showed him, written as if in characters of fire, what kind of war his father was waging. Yet he went on towards the spot where the army was mustered, but only to offer his mediation, affirming that he would not lay his hand on his good sword in so abhorred a service, even though the stone fortress, and his father's castle besides, should fall before the vengeance of their enemies.

Biorn hurled the spear which he held in his hand against his son with mad fury. The deadly weapon whizzed past him. Sintram remained standing with his visor raised, he did not move one limb in his defence, when he said: "Father! do what you will; but I join not in your godless warfare."

Biorn of the Fiery Eyes laughed scornfully: "It seems that I am always to have a spy over me here; my son succeeds to the dainty French knight!" But nevertheless he came to himself, he accepted Sintram's mediation, made amends for the injuries he had done, and returned gloomily to his castle. Sintram went back to the Rocks of the Moon.

Such occurrences were frequent after that time. It went so far that Sintram came to be looked upon as the protector of all those whom his father pursued with relentless fury; but nevertheless, sometimes his own wildness would carry the young knight away to accompany his fierce father in his fearful deeds. Then Biorn used to laugh with horrible pleasure, and to say: "See there, my son, how the flames we have lighted blaze up from the villages, as the blood spouts up from the wounds our swords have made! It is plain to me, however much you may pretend to the contrary, that you are, and that you will ever remain, my true and beloved heir!"

After such terrible wanderings, Sintram could find no comfort but in hastening to the chaplain of Drontheim, and confessing to him his misery and his sins. The chaplain would freely absolve him after due penance had been performed, and again raise up the broken-hearted and repenting youth; but he would often say: "Oh! how nearly had you reached your last trial and gained the victory, and looked on Verena's countenance, and atoned for all! Now you have thrown yourself back for years. Think, my son, on the shortness of man's life; if you are always falling back anew, how will you ever reach the sum mit on this side the grave?"

Years came and went, and Biorn's hair was white as snow, and the youth Sintram had reached the middle age; old Rolf was now scarcely able to leave the stone fortress; and sometimes he said: "I feel it a burden that my life should yet be prolonged, but also there is much comfort in it, for I shall think that the good God has in store for me here below some great happiness; and it must be something in which you are concerned, my beloved Sir Sintram, for what else in the whole world could rejoice my heart?"

But, nevertheless, every thing remained as it was, only Sintram's fearful dreams at Christmas-time each year rather increased than diminished in horror. Again, the holy season was drawing near, and the mind of the sorely afflicted knight was more troubled than ever before. Sometimes, if he had been reckoning up the nights which were yet to elapse before it, a cold sweat would stand on his forehead, while he said: "Mark my words, dear old foster-father, this time something most awfully decisive lies before me."

One evening he felt an overwhelming anxiety about his father. It seemed to him that the Prince of Darkness was going up to Biorn's castle; and in vain did Rolf remind him that the snow was lying deep in the valleys, in vain did he suggest that the knight might be overtaken by his frightful dreams in the lonely mountains during the night-time. "Nothing can be worse to me than remaining here would be," replied Sintram.

He took his horse from the stable and rode forth in the gathering darkness. The noble steed slipped and stumbled and fell in the trackless ways, but his rider always raised him up and urged him only more swiftly and eagerly towards the object which he longed and yet dreaded to reach. Nevertheless, he might never have arrived at it, had not his faithful hound Skovmark kept with him. The dog sought out the lost track for his beloved master, and invited him into it with joyous barkings, and warned him by his howls against hidden precipices and treacherous ice under the snow. Thus they arrived about midnight at Biorn's castle. The windows of the hall shone opposite to them with a brilliant light, as though some great feast were being kept there,—and confused sounds, as of singing, met their ears. Sintram gave his horse hastily to some retainers in the court-yard, and ran up the steps, whilst Skovmark staid by the well-known horse.

A good esquire came towards Sintram within the castle, and said: "God be praised, my dear master, that you are come,—for surely nothing good is going on above. But take heed to yourself, also, and be not deluded. Your father has a guest with him,—and, as I think, a very evil one."

Sintram shuddered as he threw open the doors. A little man in the dress of a miner was sitting with his back towards him; the armour had been for some time past again ranged round the stone table, so that only two places were ever left empty. The seat opposite the door had been taken by Biorn of the Fiery Eyes; and the dazzling light of the torches fell upon his features with such a red glare, that he most fully established his right to that fearful surname.

"Father, whom have you here with you?" cried Sintram; and his suspicions rose to certainty as the miner turned round, and the detestable face of the Little Master grinned from under the dark hood he wore.

"Yes, just see, my fair son," said the wild Biorn; "you have not been here for a long while,—and so to-night this jolly comrade has paid me a visit, and your place has been taken. But throw one of the suits of armour out of the way, and put a seat for yourself instead of it,—and come and drink with us, and be merry."

"Yes, do so, Sir Sintram," said the Little Master, with a laugh. "Nothing worse could come of it than that the broken pieces of armour might clatter somewhat strangely one against the other; or, at most, that the disturbed spirit of him to whom the suit belonged, might look over your shoulder: but he would not drink up any of our wine—ghosts have nothing to do with that. So now fall to!"

Biorn joined in the laughter of the hideous stranger with wild mirth; and while Sintram was mustering up his whole strength not to lose his senses at such terrible words, and was fixing a calm steady look on the Little Master's face,—the old man cried out:

"Why do you look at him so? Is it that you fancy there is a mirror before you? Now that you are together, I do not see it so much; but awhile ago I thought that you were like enough to each other to be mistaken."

"God forbid!" said Sintram: and he walked up close to the fearful apparition, saying: "I command you, detestable stranger, to depart from this castle, in right of my authority as my father's heir,—as a consecrated knight, and as a Christian man!"

Biorn seemed as if he wished to oppose himself to this command with all his savage might. The Little Master muttered to himself: "You are not by any means the master in this house, pious knight; you have never lighted a fire on this hearth."

Then Sintram drew the sword which Gabrielle had given him,—held the cross formed by the hilt before the eyes of his evil guest,—and said calmly, but with a powerful voice: "Worship, or fly!"

And he fled! the frightful stranger,—he fled with such lightning speed, that it could scarcely be seen whether he had sprung through the window or the door. But in going he overthrew some of the armour,—the tapers went out,—and it seemed that the pale blue flame which lighted up the hall in a marvellous manner, gave a fulfilment to the Little Master's former words; and that the spirits of those to whom the armour had belonged, were leaning over the table grinning fearfully.

Both the father and the son were filled with horror,—but each chose an opposite way to save themselves. Biorn wished to have his hateful guest back again; and the power of his will was seen when the Little Master's step resounded anew on the stairs, and his hard brown hand shook the lock of the door. On the other hand, Sintram ceased not to say within himself: "We are lost, if he comes back! We are lost to all eternity, if he comes back!" And he fell on his knees, and prayed fervently from the depth of his troubled heart to Father, Son, and Holy Spirit. Then the Little Master left the door; and again Biorn willed him to return; and again Sintram's prayers drove him away. So went on this strife of wills throughout the long night; and fierce whirlwinds raged the while around the castle, till all the household thought the end of the world was come. At length the dawn of morning appeared through the windows of the hall,—the fury of the storm was lulled,—Biorn sank back powerless in slumber on his seat; —peace and hope were restored to the inmates of the castle,—and Sintram, pale and exhausted, went out to breathe the dewy air of the mild winter's morning before the castle-gates.

CHAPTER XXVI.

THE faithful Skovmark followed his master, caressing him; and when Sintram fell asleep on a stone seat in the wall, he lay at his feet, keeping watchful guard. Suddenly he pricked up his ears, looked round with delight, and bounded joyfully down the mountain. Just afterwards the chaplain of Drontheim appeared amongst the rocks, and the good beast went up to him as if to greet him, and then again ran back to the knight to announce a welcome visitor.

Sintram opened his eyes, to feel the pleasure of a child whose Christmas-gifts have been placed at his bed-side to surprise him. For the chaplain smiled at him as he had never yet seen him smile. There was in it a token of victory and blessing, or at least of the near approach of both. "You have accomplished much yesterday, very much," said the holy priest, and his hands were joined and his eyes full of bright tears. "I thank God on your behalf, my noble knight. Verena knows all, and she too blesses God. I do indeed now dare hope that the time will soon come when you may appear before her. But Sintram, Sir Sintram, there is need of haste—for the old man above requires speedy aid, and you have still a heavy—as I hope the last—yet a most heavy trial to undergo for his sake. Arm yourself, my knight, arm yourself even with temporal weapons. In truth, this time only spiritual armour is needed, but it always befits a knight as well as a monk, to wear, in the decisive moments of his life, the entire solemn garb of his station. If it so please you, we will go directly to Drontheim together. You must return thence to-night. Such is the tenor of the hidden decree, which has been dimly unfolded to Verena's foresight. Here there is yet much that is wild and distracting, and you have great need to-day of calm preparation."

With humble joy Sintram bowed his assent, and called for his horse and for a suit of armour. "Only," added he, "let not any of that armour be brought, which was last night over, thrown in the hall."

His orders were quickly obeyed. The arms which were fetched, adorned with fine engraved work, the simple helmet, formed rather like that of an esquire than a knight, the lance of almost gigantic size, which belonged to the suit,—on all these the chaplain gazed in deep thought, and with melancholy emotion. At last, when Sintram with the help of his esquires was well-nigh equipped, the holy priest spoke: "Wonderful are the ways of God's providence! See, dear Sintram, this armour and this spear were formerly those of Sir Weigand the Slender, and with them he did many mighty deeds. When he was tended by your mother in the castle, and when even your father still showed himself kind and courteous, he asked, as a favour, that his armour and his lance should be allowed to hang in Biorn's armoury,—Weigand himself, as you well know, intended to build a cloister and to live there as a monk,—and he put his old esquire's helmet with it, instead of another, because he was yet wearing that one when he first saw the fair Verena's angelic face. How wondrously does it now come to pass, that these very arms which have so long been laid aside, should have been brought to you for the decisive hour of your life! To me, as far as my short-sighted human wisdom can tell, to me it seems truly a very solemn token, but one that is full of high and glorious promise."

Sintram stood now in complete array, composed and stately, and from his tall, slender figure might have been supposed still in early youth, had not the deep lines of care which furrowed his countenance shown him to be advanced in years.

"Who has placed boughs on the head of my war-horse?" asked Sintram of the esquires with displeasure. "I am not a conqueror, nor a wedding-guest. And besides, there are no boughs now, but these red and yellow crackling leaves of the oak, dull and dead like the season itself."

"Sir knight, I know not, myself," answered an esquire, "but it seemed to me that I could not do otherwise."

"Let it be," said the chaplain. "I feel that this is also sent as a token full of meaning from the right source."

Then the knight threw himself into his saddle; the priest went beside him; and they both rode slowly and silently towards Drontheim. The faithful dog followed his master. When the lofty castle of Drontheim appeared in sight, a gentle smile spread itself over Sintram's countenance, like a gleam of sunshine on a wintry valley. "God has done great things for me," said he. "I once rushed from here, a fearfully wild boy; I now come back, a penitent man. I trust that good is yet in store for my poor troubled life."

The chaplain assented kindly, and soon afterwards the travellers passed under the echoing vaulted gateway into the castle-yard. At a sign from the priest, the retainers approached with respectful haste, and took charge of the horses; then he and Sintram went through long winding passages, and up many steps, to the remote chamber which the chaplain had chosen for his own: far away from the noise of men, and near to the clouds and the stars. There the two passed a quiet day in devout prayer, and earnest reading of Holy Scripture.

When the evening began to close in, the chaplain arose and said: "And now, my knight, get ready your horse, and mount and ride back again to your father's castle. A toilsome way lies before you, and I dare not go with you. But I can, and I will call upon the Lord for you, all through the long, fearful night. Oh, beloved instrument of the Most High, you will yet not be lost!"

Thrilling with strange forebodings, but nevertheless strong and vigorous in spirit, Sintram did according to the holy man's desire. The sun set as the knight approached a long valley, strangely shut in by rocks, through which lay the road to his father's castle.

CHAPTER XXVII.

Before entering the rocky pass, the knight, with a prayer and thanksgiving, looked back once more at the castle of Drontheim. There it was, so vast and quiet and peaceful, the bright windows of the chaplain's high chamber yet lighted up by the last gleam of the sun, which had already disappeared. In front of Sintram was the gloomy valley, looking as if prepared to be his grave.

Then there came towards him some one riding on a small horse, and Skovmark, who had gone up to the stranger as if to find out who he was, now ran back with his tail between his legs and his ears put back, howling and whining, and he crept terrified under his master's war-horse. But even the noble steed appeared to have forgotten his once so fearless and warlike ardour. He trembled violently, and when the knight would have turned him towards the stranger, he reared and snorted and plunged, and began to throw himself backwards. It was only with difficulty that Sintram's strength and horsemanship got the better of him, and he was all white with foam when Sintram came up to the unknown traveller.

"You have cowardly animals with you," said the latter, in a low smothered voice.

Sintram was unable, in the ever-increasing darkness, rightly to distinguish what kind of being he saw before him; only a very pallid face, which at first he had thought was covered with freshly fallen snow, met his eyes from amidst the long hanging garments in which the figure was clothed. It seemed that the stranger carried a small box, wrapped up; his little horse, as if wearied out, bent his head down towards the ground, whereby a bell, which hung from the wretched torn bridle under his neck, was made to give a strange sound After a short silence, Sintram replied: "Noble steeds avoid those of a worse race, because they are ashamed of them; and the boldest dogs are attacked by a secret terror at sight of forms to which they are not accustomed. I have no cowardly animals with me."

"Good, Sir knight, then ride with me through the valley."

"I am going through the valley, but I want no companions."

"But, perhaps, I want one. Do you not see that I am unarmed? And at this season, at this hour, there are frightful, unearthly beasts about."

Just then, as if to confirm the awful words of the stranger, a thing swung itself down from one of the nearest trees covered with hoar frost,—no one could say if it were a snake, or a lizard,—it curled and twisted itself, and appeared to be going to slide down upon the knight or his companion. Sintram levelled his spear, and pierced the creature through. But with the most hideous contortions it fixed itself firmly on the spear head, and in vain did the knight endeavour to rub it off against the rocks or the trees. Then he let his spear rest upon his right shoulder, with the point behind him, so that the horrible beast no longer met his sight, and he said with good courage to the stranger: "It does seem indeed that I could help you, and I am not forbidden to have an unknown stranger in my company; so let us push on bravely into the valley!"

"Help!" so resounded the solemn answer. "Not help. I, perhaps, may help thee. But God have mercy upon thee, if the time should ever come when I could no longer help thee. Then thou wouldst be lost, and I should become very frightful to thee. But we will go through the valley, I have thy knightly word for it. Come!"

They rode forward. Sintram's horse still showing signs of fear, the faithful dog still whining, but both obedient to their master's will. The knight was calm and steadfast. The snow had slipped down from the smooth rocks, and by the light of the rising moon could be seen various strange twisted shapes on their sides, some looking like snakes, and some like human faces; but they were only formed by the veins in the rock, and the half bare roots of trees which had planted themselves in that desert place with capricious firmness. High above, and at a great distance, the castle of Drontheim, as if to take leave, appeared again through an opening in the rocks. The knight then looked keenly at his companion, and he almost felt as if Weigand the Slender were riding beside him. "In God's name," cried he, "art thou not the shade of that departed knight who suffered and died for Verena?"

"I have not suffered, I have not died, but ye suffer and ye die, poor mortals!" murmured the stranger. "I am not Weigand. I am that other one, who was so like him, and whom thou hast also met before now in the wood."

Sintram strove to free himself from the terror which came over him at these words. He looked at his horse; it appeared to him entirely altered. The dry, many coloured oak-leaves on its head were waving like the flames around a sacrifice, in the uncertain moon-light. He looked down again to see after his faithful Skovmark. Fear had likewise most wondrously changed him. On the ground in the middle of the road were lying dead men's bones, and hideous lizards were crawling about, and, in defiance of the wintry season, poisonous mushrooms were growing up all around.

"Can this be still my horse on which I am riding," said the knight to himself in a low voice; "and can that trembling beast which runs at my side, be my own dog?"

Then some one called after him in a yelling voice: "Stop! Stop! Take me also with you!"

Looking round, Sintram perceived a small frightful figure, with horns, and a face partly like a wild boar and partly like a bear, walking along on its hind legs, which were those of a horse, and in its hand was a strange hideous weapon shaped like a hook or a sickle. It was the being who had been wont to trouble him in his dreams, and alas! it was also the wretched

Little Master himself, who, laughing wildly, stretched out a long claw towards the knight.

The bewildered Sintram murmured: "I must have fallen asleep! and now my dreams are coming over me!"

"You are awake," replied the rider of the little horse, "but you know me also in your dreams. For behold! I am Death." And his garments fell from him, and there appeared a mouldering skeleton, its ghastly head crowned with serpents; that which he had kept hidden under his mantle, was an hour-glass with the sand almost run out. Death held it towards the knight in his fleshless hand. The bell at the neck of the little horse gave forth a solemn sound. It was a passing-bell.

"Lord, into Thy hands I commend my spirit!" prayed Sintram; and full of earnest devotion he rode after Death, who beckoned him on.

"He has not got you yet! He has not got you yet!" screamed the fearful fiend. "Give yourself up to me rather. In one instant,—for swift are your thoughts, swift is my might, —in one instant you shall be in Normandy. Helen yet blooms in beauty as when she departed hence, and this very night she would be yours." And once again he began his unholy praises of Gabrielle's loveliness, and Sintram's heart glowed like wildfire in his weak breast.

Death said nothing more, but raised the hour-glass in his right hand yet higher and higher, and as the sand now ran out more quickly, a soft light streamed from the glass over Sintram's countenance, and then it seemed to him as if eternity in all its calm majesty were rising before him, and a world of confusion dragging him back with a deadly grasp.

"I command thee, wild form that followest me," cried he, "I command thee in the name of our Lord Jesus Christ, to cease from thy seducing words, and to call thyself by that name by which thou art recorded in Holy Writ!" A name, which sounded more fearful than a thunder-clap, burst despairingly from the lips of the Tempter, and he disappeared.

"He will return no more," said Death in a kindly tone.

"And now I am become wholly thine, my stern companion?"

"Not yet, my Sintram. I shall not come to thee till many, many years are past. But thou must not forget me the while."

"I will keep the thought of thee steadily before my soul, thou fearful yet wholesome monitor, thou awful yet loving guide!"

"Oh! I can truly appear very gentle." And so it proved indeed. His form became more softly defined in the increasing gleam of light which shone from the hour-glass, the features which had been awful in their sternness wore a gentle smile, the crown of serpents became a bright palm-wreath, instead of the horse appeared a white misty cloud on which the moonbeams played, and the bell gave forth sounds as of sweet lullabies. Sintram thought he could hear these words amidst them:—

"The world and Satan are o'ercome,
Before thee gleams eternal light.
Warrior, who hast won the strife,
Save from darkest shades of night,
Him before whose aged eyes,
All my terrors soon shall rise.'

The knight well knew that his father was meant, and he urged on his noble steed, who now obeyed his master willingly and gladly, and the faithful dog also again ran beside him fearlessly. Death had disappeared, but in front of Sintram there floated a bright morning cloud, which continued visible after the sun had risen in the clear winter sky to cheer and warm the earth.

CHAPTER XXVIII.

"He is dead! the horrors of that fearful night of storm and tempest have killed him!" Thus said, about this time, some of Biorn's retainers, who had not been able to bring him back to his senses since the morning of the day before; they had made a couch of wolf and bear skins for him in the great hall, in the midst of the armour which still lay scattered around. One of the esquires said with a low sigh: "The Lord have mercy on his poor wild soul."

Just then the warder blew his horn from his tower, and a trooper came into the room with a look of surprise. "A knight is coming towards here," said he; "a wonderful knight. I could have taken him for our lord Sintram—but a bright, bright morning-cloud floats so close before him, and throws over him such clear light, that one could fancy red flowers were showered down upon him. Besides, his horse has a reddish wreath of flowers on his head, which was never a custom of the son of our dead lord."

"It was exactly such a one," replied another, "that I wove for him yesterday. He was not pleased with it at first, but afterwards he let it remain."

"But why did you do that?"

"It seemed to me as if I heard a voice singing again and again in my ear: 'Victory! victory! the noblest victory! The knight rides forth to victory!' And then I saw a branch of our oldest oak tree stretched towards me, which had kept on almost all its red and yellow leaves in spite of the snow. So I did according to what I had heard sung; and I plucked some of the leaves, and wove a triumphal wreath for the noble warhorse. At the same time Skovmark,—you know that the faithful beast had always a great dislike to Biorn, and therefore had gone to the stable with the horse,—Skovmark jumped upon me, fawning and seeming pleased, as if he wanted to thank me for my work; and such noble animals understand well about good prognostics."

They heard the sound of Sintram's spurs on the stone steps and Skovmark's joyous bark. At that instant the supposed corpse of old Biorn sat up,—looked around with rolling, staring eyes,—and asked of the terrified retainers in a hollow voice: "Who comes there, ye people? who comes there? I know it is my son. But who comes with him? On the answer to that hangs the decision of my fate. For see, good people, Gotthard and Rudlieb have prayed much for me: yet if the Little Master comes with him, I am lost in spite of them!"

"You are not lost, my beloved father!" Sintram's kind voice was heard to say, as he softly opened the door, and the bright red morning-cloud floated in with him.

Biorn joined his hands, cast a look of thankfulness up to Heaven, and said, smiling: "Yes, praised be God! it is the right companion! It is sweet gentle Death!" And then he made a sign to his son to approach, saying: "Come here, my deliverer; come blessed of the Lord, that I may relate to you all that has passed within me."

As Sintram now sat close by his father's couch, all who were in the room perceived a remarkable and striking change. For old Biorn, whose whole countenance, and not his eyes alone, had been wont to have a fiery aspect,—was now quite pale, almost like white marble: while, on the other hand, the cheeks of the once deadly-pale Sintram glowed with a bright bloom like that of early youth. It was caused by the morning-cloud which still shone upon him, and the presence of which in the room was rather felt than seen; but it produced a gentle thrill in every heart.

"See, my son," began the old man, softly and mildly, "I have lain for a long time in a death-like sleep, and have known nothing of what was going on around me; but within,—ah! within, I have had but too entire consciousness! I thought that my soul would be destroyed by the eternal anguish; and yet again I felt with much greater horror, that my soul was undying like that anguish. Beloved son, your cheeks that glowed so brightly are beginning to grow pale at my words. I refrain from more. But let me relate to you something more cheering: far, far away, I could see a bright, lofty church, where Gotthard and Rudlieb Lenz were kneeling and praying for me. Gotthard had grown very old, and looked like one of our mountains covered with snow, on which the evening sun is shining; and Rudlieb was also an elderly man, but very vigorous and very strong; and they both, with all their strength and vigour, were calling upon God to aid me, their enemy. Then I heard a voice like that of an angel, saying: 'His son does the most for him! He must this night wrestle with Death and with the Fallen One! His victory will be victory,—and his defeat will be defeat, for the old man as well as for himself.' Thereupon I awoke; and I knew that all depended upon whom you would bring with you. You have conquered. Next to God, the praise be to you!"

"Gotthard and Rudlieb have helped much," replied Sintram; "and, beloved father, so have the fervent prayers of the chaplain of Drontheim. I felt, in the midst of temptation and deadly fear, how the heaven-directed prayers of good men floated round me and aided me."

"I am most willing to believe that, my noble son, and every thing you say to me," answered the old man: and at the same moment the chaplain also coming in, Biorn stretched out his hand towards him with a smile of peace and joy. And now all seemed to be surrounded with a bright circle of unity and blessedness. "But see," said old Biorn, "how the faithful Skovmark jumps upon me now, and tries to caress me. It is not long since he used always to howl with terror when he saw me."

"My dear lord," said the chaplain, "there is a spirit dwelling in good beasts, although they are unconscious of it."

As the day wore on, the stillness in the hall increased. The last hour of the aged knight was drawing near, but he met it calmly and fearlessly. The chaplain and Sintram prayed beside his couch. The retainers knelt devoutly around. At length the dying man said: "Is that the vesper-bell in Verena's cloister?" and Sintram made a sign to express his undoubting belief that it was, while warm tears fell on the colourless cheeks of his father. A gleam shone in the old man's eyes,—the morning-cloud stood close over him, and then the gleam, the morning-cloud, and life with them departed from him.

CHAPTER XXIX.

A FEW days afterwards Sintram stood in the parlour of the convent, and waited with a beating heart for his mother to appear. He had seen her for the last time, when, a slumbering child, he had been awoke by her tender, farewell kisses, and then had fallen asleep again to wonder in his dreams what his mother had wanted with him, and to seek her in vain the next morning in the castle and in the garden. The chaplain was now at his side, rejoicing in the chastened rapture of the knight, whose fierce spirit had been overcome, on whose cheeks a soft reflection of that solemn morning-cloud yet lingered.

The inner doors opened.—In her white veil, stately and noble, the lady Verena came forward, and with a heavenly smile she beckoned her son to approach the grating. There could be no thought here of any passionate outbreak, whether of sorrow or of joy.* The holy peace which had its abode within these walls, would have found its way to a heart less tried and less purified than that which beats in Sintram's bosom. Shedding some placid tears, the son knelt before his mother, kissed her flowing garments through the grating, and felt as if he were in Paradise,—where every wish and every care is hushed. "Beloved mother," said he, "let me become a recluse like you. Then I will betake myself to the cloister yonder; and perhaps I might one day be deemed worthy to be your confessor, if illness or the weakness of old age should keep the good chaplain within the castle of Drontheim."

"That would be a sweet, quietly-happy life, my good child,"

* "In whose sweet presence sorrow dares not lower,
Nor expectation rise,
Too high for earth."
Christian Year.

replied the lady Verena; "but such is not your vocation You must continue to be a bold, powerful knight, and you must spend the long life which is almost always granted to us, children of the north, in succouring the weak, in keeping down the lawless, and in yet another more bright and honourable employment which I now rather dimly foresee, than clearly know."

"God's will be done!" said the knight, and he rose up full of self-devotion and firmness.

"That is my good son," said the lady Verena. "Ah! how many sweet calm joys spring up for us! See, already is our longing desire of meeting again satisfied, and you will never more be so entirely estranged from me. Every week on this day you will come back to me, and you will relate what glorious deeds you have done, and take back with you my advice and my blessing."

"Am I not once more a good and happy child!" cried Sintram joyously; "only that the merciful God has given me in addition the strength of a man in body and spirit. Oh! how blessed is that son to whom it is allowed to gladden his mother's heart with the blossoms and the fruit of his life!"

Thus he left the quiet cloister's shade, joyful in spirit and richly laden with blessings, to enter on his noble career. He was not content with going about wherever there might be a rightful cause to defend, or evil to be averted; the gates of the now hospitable castle stood always open also to receive and shelter every stranger,—and old Rolf, who was almost grown young again at sight of his lord's excellence, was established as seneschal. The winter of Sintram's life set in bright and glorious, and it was only at times that he would sigh within himself and say: "Ah! Montfauçon, ah! Gabrielle, if I could dare to hope that you have quite forgiven me!"

CHAPTER XXX.

THE spring had come in its brightness to that northern land, when one morning Sintram turned his horse homewards after a successful encounter with one of the most formidable disturbers of the peace of his neighbourhood. His horsemen rode after him, singing as they went. As they drew near the castle they heard the sound of joyous notes wound on the horn. "Some welcome visitor must have arrived," said the knight, and he spurred his horse to a quicker pace over the dewy meadow. While still at some distance, they descried old Rolf busily engaged in preparing a table for the morning meal, under the trees in front of the castle gates. From all the turrets and battlements floated banners and flags in the fresh morning breeze, esquires were running to and fro in their gayest apparel. As soon as the good Rolf saw his master, he clapped his hands joyfully over his gray head, and hastened into the castle. Immediately the wide gates were thrown open, and Sintram, as he entered, was met by Rolf, whose eyes were filled with tears of joy as he pointed towards three noble forms that were following him.

Two men of high stature,—one in extreme old age, the other gray-headed, and both remarkably alike,—were leading between them a fair young boy, in a page's dress of blue velvet, richly embroidered with gold. The two old men wore the dark velvet dress of German burghers, and had massive gold chains and large shining medals hanging round their necks.

Sintram had never before seen his honoured guests, and yet he felt as if they were well known and valued friends. The very aged man reminded him of his dying father's words about the snow-covered mountains lighted up by the evening sun; and then he remembered, he could scarcely tell how, that he had heard Folko say that one of the highest mountains of that sort in his southern land was called the St. Gotthard. And at the same time he knew that the old but yet vigorous man on the other side was named Rudlieb. But the boy who stood between them,—ah! Sintram's humility dared scarcely form a hope as to who he might be, however much his features, so noble and soft, called up two highly honoured images before his mind.

Then the aged Gotthard Lenz, the prince of old men, advanced with a solemn step, and said: "This is the noble boy Engeltram of Montfauçon, the only son of the great baron, and his father and mother send him to you Sir Sintram, knowing well your holy and glorious knightly career, that you may bring him up to all the honourable and valiant deeds of this northern land, and may make of him a Christian knight, like yourself."

Sintram threw himself from his horse. Engeltram of Montfauçon held the stirrup gracefully for him, checking the retainers, who pressed forward, with these words: "I am the noblest born esquire of this knight, and the service nearest to his person belongs to me."

Sintram knelt on the turf to offer a silent prayer, then lifting up the image of Folko and Gabrielle in his arms, towards the rising sun, he cried: "With the help of God, my Engeltram, you will become glorious as that sun, and your course will be like his!"

And Rolf said, as he wept for joy, "Lord, now lettest Thou Thy servant depart in peace."

Gotthard Lenz and Rudlieb were pressed to Sintram's heart; the chaplain of Drontheim, who just then came from Verena's cloister, to bring a joyful greeting to her brave son, stretched out his hands to bless them all.

END OF SINTRAM.

www.ingramcontent.com/pod-product-compliance
Lightning Source LLC
LaVergne TN
LVHW010252110826
845151LV00004B/1453
* 9 7 8 1 4 2 5 5 2 2 8 6 5 *